We Three: Search For Source

The Ipswich Chronicles

Julie L. Kusma

Praise for We Three: Search for Source

A beautifully woven tale of three teenage sisters, growing into themselves and each other while at the same time, coming to terms with their burgeoning mystical, magical powers. Set against a backdrop of past, present and future events, author Julie Kusma weaves yet another highly engaging and transfixing tale which is utterly believable. It is a literary journey which is one to savor.

Derek R. King

Derek R. King is an award-winning poet and author, as well as and musician. He lives in Scotland, where he enjoys the great outdoors, long walks in the hills, the seas and oceans, art, and photography. His other published work:

Poetry Collections
In Sun & Shade (Nature Poetry)
More Red Roses (Love Poetry)
Urban (City-Nature Poetry)
The Elegy (Dark Poetry)
Twelve Red Roses in Verse (Love Poetry)
Natyre Boy (Nature Poetry)
Noir [Or, When the Night Comes] (Gothic Poetry)
NonFiction
The Life and Times of Clyde Kennard
(Biographical-American Civil Rights)

Follow this Author
http://DerekRKing.uk
https://twitter.com/DerekRKing2
https://tiktok.com/@derekrking2

"There are two great schools of thought in the world—materialistic and spiritualistic. With one, MATTER is all in all, the ultimate substratum; mind is merely the result of organized matter; everything is translated into terms of force, motion and the like. With the other, SPIRIT or mind is the ultimate substance-God: matter is the visible expressionof this invisible and eternal Consciousness."

Henry Ridgely Evans

The Spirit World Unmasked, 1902

Each day brings us closer
to our destiny. Every day we
must strive to become
more prepared.

Chapter One

As her finger hovered above the return key, apprehension crept over Penelope Hale. She had opened her mother's email a million times and never found anything new. Today, a sensation that something was wrong felt too strong for her to ignore. She snatched the clump of coppery-red hair dangling in front of her eye, tucked it back behind her ear, and forced herself to click the button.

A sigh of relief passed through her lips. Only old messages filled the email box, yet the anxiety remained and piqued her curiosity. A notification flashed—new mail. Her eyes fixated on the subject line: I MUST SEE MY DAUGHTERS. Like hell, she told herself. Her greatest fear was realized in this one short sentence. She debated whether to read the electronic message sent from her and her sister's father or whether she should hit delete.

Nausea twisted her stomach, and a sourness rose in her throat. She swallowed hard and mentally pushed all memories of that man back down into the pit of her bowels where they belonged. Penelope stared at the subject line. She couldn't resist. Despite, or maybe because of her anger, she opened it.

Her father wrote that he wanted to visit them before their graduation. Her heart raced even faster. His message stated that he would be in Boston on the fifth. Penelope couldn't breathe. That was today's date.

A bolt of awareness struck her as she realized she and her sisters planned to be in the same city in a matter of hours. Like a moan emanating from her soul, a long, slow exhale escaped her. She wanted no part of this man because he had wanted no part of them. She wouldn't let him ruin her sisters' lives like he destroyed their mother's. Not today. Not ever. Penelope swore she wouldn't let him back in. Not ever.

In haste, Penelope responded to her father, posing as her mother. She told him there were no circumstances in which she would ever allow the girls to meet with him. She added that if he had wanted a relationship with his daughters, he shouldn't have abandoned them. Penelope slammed the laptop closed, and the loud clap snapped her attention back to her current life. She trusted he would believe the email was from her mother, and she prayed her sisters would forgive her. At least, she hoped they would if they ever found out. A few minutes later, she returned to the master bedroom and checked on her mother one more time.

"Penny, let's go," Katrina hollered upstairs, then slipped her macramé purse over her right shoulder. Her long honey-blonde braid caught underneath the strap. "Ugh, I hate that," she said as she pulled her hair free.

"Do we have to go, Kat?" Samantha asked. "I'd rather stay home."

"Sam, we graduate in three weeks," Kat rebuked. "Plenty of time to sit in your room then, especially since you haven't decided on a college or even lined up a summer job."

"Why do you treat me like this?" Sam glared at Kat.

"Like what?" Penelope chimed in as she bounded down the stairs as if the email situation had never happened. Penelope had already tucked the message away neatly in the back of her mind.

"Mean," Sam said, "why does she have to be so mean?"

"You *are* kind of bossy, Kat." Penelope offered Katrina a sarcastic smile.

"Are you kidding me, Penny?" Kat said.

"Yeah, I am." Penny picked up her cell and slipped it inside her denim jacket's pocket. "You're the sweetest one of us. Sam just believes *everyone* is out to get her, and now, she thinks that 'everyone' is you."

Sam rolled her eyes. "Is Mom alright?" For a second, genuine concern washed over Sam's face.

"She's fine. I fed her breakfast and put the pink floral nightgown on her," Penny said.

"Oh, she loves the flowery ones." Kat smiled.

"How can you tell?" Sam spoke with bitterness; the three of them could almost taste her tone. "She never talks anymore." Sam's chestnut-brown eyes turned as dark as her black hair.

3

Penny and Kat glanced at each other. What Sam had said was true. Not a single word left their mother's lips for almost a year, and they missed her immensely. But the three of them agreed that having her like this was better than not having her at all.

"Come on," Penny said. She waved for her two sisters to head out their front door. "If we don't get a move on, we'll miss the charter buses."

"Where are we supposed to meet again?"

"Gawd, Kat. Can't you retain any information? The library. Our whole senior class is probably already there," Sam said.

"Who's mean now?" Kat's eyebrows raised as she sneered at Sam.

As the three sisters stepped outside, they each whispered in unison, *keep our mom safe*. Penny closed their house door and locked the deadbolt. She joined her sisters on the walkway.

"Why am I in charge of the house?" Penny swung the house key in front of herself.

"Because you're the oldest," Kat reminded Penny.

"By nine minutes." Penny shoved the keychain into her pocket.

"Well, you are the responsible one. I guess those nine minutes make you wiser than Sam and me."

"She's only six minutes older than me," Sam added, and somehow, she believed that fact gave her a bit of authority over Kat.

"Now you guys *want* me in charge? Penny asked. "That's rich. You both remember that the next time I ask you to do chores around the house."

"We do plenty. Don't we, Sam?"

Kat and Sam continued to banter, but their words faded from Penny's ears. As the three girls rounded the corner of North East Street and North Main, Penny felt a strange pull on her attention, like a door had opened, sucking her toward it.

Now that they were on Main, she knew the library was only a few more blocks ahead, but the closer they got to their intended destination, the more she wanted to turn around. The sensation was one of being out of control yet remaining composed because the truth was, Penny wanted to go back and continue west where the road turned into High Street. She didn't understand why, but she needed to go.

Ditching school was something Penny never did, but the pull was strong. She felt drawn: lured, like she was being reeled in by something. Penny also understood the impression's intensity wouldn't cease until she complied. In fact, the pressure would continue to mount within her, and she had learned it was best not to resist.

She grabbed Kat's hand and leaped out onto North Main Street. She dragged her sister across the two lanes as she returned to the last intersection.

"Penny? What are you doing?" Kat slipped her hand free and looked over her shoulder for Sam. "What if a car was coming?"

Penny didn't answer.

Sam moved around to Kat's other side and caught up with Penny.

"What?" Sam glanced back at Kat. "I didn't want to go on the stupid senior field trip anyway."

Kat stopped protesting. There wasn't any point. When Penny got her mind fixed on something, no one could prevent her from doing it. Besides, there would be a reason. Penny always had a perfect and rational answer. Neither Sam nor Kat had ever won an argument with her. So, they both acquiesced and followed their sister on the wild chase.

Penny cut the corner between North Main and High Street and led her sisters through several private backyards. Finally, they emerged directly across from the Meeting House. Kat and Sam thought they were done, but Penny turned left. She ran all the way to the front gate of the Old Gaol Museum, where she finally stopped.

"The Gaol Museum?" Kat asked. "It looks perfectly creepy."

"Le geôle. The jail. It's the original jail," Penny said, catching her breath.

The three girls stared at the old timber-framed structure. White paint peeled across the aged slat boards, creating random patterns. The ruffled, weather-worn shake shingles struggled to hold their place on the building's sides.

Kat's eyes suddenly welled with tears. "The actual jail where the witches were held during the trials?"

"But I thought the jail was on Green Street?" Sam pointed behind them in the opposite direction.

"*That* jail was built in 1828, long after the witch trials," Penny said.

"I would ask how you know all this, but you're Penny," Kat said, "what don't you know?"

"Well, for one thing, I don't recall if the museum is actually open. And secondly, I don't understand what, but something calls to me from inside." Penny lifted the latch on the rusted gate. She expected the metal to crumble with her touch. It didn't. The hinges squeaked as the cast-iron gate swung into the property's front lawn. "Come on," she said.

Penny stepped to Sam's left and maneuvered Kat to Sam's right. The girls knew what would happen next; they would go inside the museum, whether it was open for business or not.

"Do we always have to be in birth order?" Sam said with a sigh. Ever since the girls could remember, they lined up in birth order, held hands, and stepped over all sorts of thresholds together.

"Just do it, Sam," Kat said as she reached for Sam's hand.

Sam took their hands, and the three were posed to enter.

"We're about to go into a dilapidated museum instead of hanging out with our friends in Boston," Kat said, even though the point was obvious. As she suspected, her words didn't matter. Penny fixated on the three of them entering the primitive building. "Let's just do this," Kat said. Nothing would happen. Nothing ever did. Penny would say she didn't understand, and they would return to normal activities. They'd still make the trip with their class if they were lucky. At least, Kat hoped they would.

She turned the knob on the entry door. Although she had trusted the place was secured, the door fell open and revealed a shadowy, eerie space. Kat drew a deep breath and raised her left foot a few inches off the ground. This signaled the rest of her trio that she was ready to enter the building hand-in-hand.

"First, shiny and new," Penny chanted.

"Then dark as night," Sam added.

"Before we're allowed to see the light," Kat said, which finished the triplet's sentences.

The girls huddled together at the top step; each extended their left foot before they entered the building in unison. A blast of cold air rushed over them as they squeezed through the door across the threshold, and their left toes touched the other side. A pale-blue radiant substance formed, sending shivers down each of their spines as they passed through some type of ethereal matter.

Chapter Two

"Everything you can see in the whole world obeys me..."
The World of the Witches

"**W**hat the hell was that?" Sam shook the chill from her flesh.

"You felt that?"

"Yeah, we felt that," Kat answered for both her and Sam. "Gross, it was like walking through watery Jell-O." Kat brushed her arm to remove any residue and realized she wasn't wearing her jeans and t-shirt anymore. She eyed her two sisters, realizing their attire had also changed. All three noticed they wore long dark dresses, and their bare feet stood on a cold earthen floor.

"Um, guys? We've got a bigger problem."

"WHERE ARE WE?" The triplets spoke together.

The three girls glanced around and took in the surroundings; some were comfortable and familiar, yet unfamiliar too. They experienced a sense of Deja vu. The place they walked into was old but not primitive like the one they stood in front of a few minutes ago, yet it occupied the same space. This building wasn't the current-day museum the girls expected to find. All the artifact cases were gone, and all the exhibit placards were absent. The interior was an open space with a noticeable odor of wet clay daubed around the wattle between a damp timber frame. Here, the air hung with the greenness of fresh thatch, not the dry-rot smell the museum exuded. This room, slightly larger than their home's living room, was divided by a lone wall of iron bars. A darkness hung in this space, absent of modern lighting.

"We're in the jail," Penny turned, tripping on the hem of her skirt as she dashed to the cell's door. "I didn't expect to walk into the actual jail."

"I don't understand," Sam said. "Where are all the historical artifacts? And where did this horrible clothing come from?" She asked, slightly raising her skirt off the floor.

"We must have walked through a time portal." Penny gripped the bars of the cell's door with both hands and violently shook them. She hoped the movement would force the stayers open.

"The cell is locked! We're stuck in this cell?" Kat was in a near panic. "Okay, okay," she said, as she paced within the confined space, "we'll wait until..."

"Until what, Kat?" Sam cried with desperation. "We're not in the museum anymore."

"Yeah, I know, and we've got to get out of this cell so we can walk back through the portal." Kat's voice shook with each word.

"What if the portal isn't there anymore?" Sam asked.

"Then, I guess we are stuck in here like Kat said." Penny didn't understand what happened to them either, but she wasn't ready to let them know—not yet.

"Well, the good news is we're in jail, so maybe we did something horrible, and if we're lucky, the sentence will be death," Kat said. She added a smile, which, under their bleak condition, was fake. "Does anyone else think the air in here is excessively hot?" Kat tugged at the white cotton shift.

A pounding from outside drew Kat's attention to the only window in the cell. She raced over and peered between the metal bars. She pressed her face against the cool iron, squinted, and tried maneuvering herself into a position to see out. "Some guy is hammering a few buildings down. Maybe I can yell at him." She pressed her face harder against the bars. "Hey, I see the Meeting House. We're still in Ipswich." Kat raised herself on the tip of her toes and smashed her face harder against the bars. "He's holding something furry. Oh, Jesus! He nailed a damn animal's head to the outside of that door." Kat closed her eyes and blocked out the gruesome scene.

"Wolves are vicious animals and rampant. We are safe from these beasts while imprisoned here," Penny said.

Kat spun around, and as she turned to face both sisters, Penny's demeanor changed.

"Sisters, calm yourselves," Penny continued in a stern, mature voice, sounding much older than the voice her sisters had grown accustomed to. "They can proveth not their accusations." Penny smoothed the front of her gray linsey-woolsey dress before she tucked a fallen lock of her copper hair back under her white cotton cap.

"Why are you talking like that?" Kat asked.

Sam rubbed her neck where her dress' stiff collar scraped at her skin. "What should we do?" Sam looked over at Kat, whose blonde hair splayed wildly from under her cap. Then, Sam spotted Penny's slight change in appearance.

Kat still appeared young, except for the visible lines etched around her eyes, now exposed by a stream of light that shone through the barred window. A mark that life here had been much harder than their modern lives.

"We should stop asking where we are. I think *when* is a better question," Kat said, her voice still her own. "Do you both feel like there is, um, like a whole other person inside this body with you?"

"Do not speak of the damnable, Sister," the new Penny said. "We borrow trouble, which I do not intend to own. Speak not of possession if you wish us free."

"What's the matter with her?" Kat whispered in Sam's ear while her eyes remained fixed on Penny.

Sam raised the book in her hands to her chest.

Kat swore Sam was about to weep, yet her sister didn't shed a single tear. Kat had a strange sense that although they were still themselves, somehow, they had stepped into their past incarnations. "Guys," Kat said, "you need to remember who you really are. Penny? Look at me." Her sister did not turn around. "Penny?" Kat was stern as she walked over and grabbed her sister's arm to force her attention.

"Sister, have you gone completely mad? My name is Prudence," Penny said.

"Of course it is," Kat said in agreement. The new name seemed more suitable than the one she had known her by their entire life. She played along. "Okay, so Prudence, why are we in jail, and what's your plan to secure our release?"

"Sisters, listen." Sam lifted the leather-bound book into the air. Her voice fluctuated in tone between her real self and this woman trapped inside the cell. "I hold a diary. My diary. I just wrote this," she said before she read the entry out loud. "Second day of May in the year of our Lord 1692."

"Sixteen-ninety-two?" Kat screeched.

"There's more, Kat," Sam said.

"You're still Sam." Kat embraced the moment she realized her sister called her by her twenty-first-century name.

"Yeah, but I don't think I was a minute ago. I was lost like Penny." Sam gazed over at her older sister, and the twinge of sympathy that crept in hardened. Sam raised the book near her face and scanned the page for the part she wanted to read. "She wrote a bunch of stuff about their lives and about feeling kind of foggy. I think she was aware I was in her body with her." Sam stopped and glanced up at Kat's widening eyes. Sam had found the line she wanted to read. "We three are the Sisters of Ipswich and stand accused of witchcraft."

"What?" Kat asked. "Witches?" She now knew Penny had been right. They walked through some sort of time travel portal and entered the same place but three hundred or more years earlier. They were now in the seventeenth century, during the Massachusetts Witch Hunts. She tried to recall exactly how the witches died. "We've got to get out of here," Kat said as visions of drowning, hanging, and burning swirled around in her head. *Witches*. Kat's mind began to reel. That would explain a lot, like how they always entered new and strange places, the silly chant they always said, and their fascination with metaphysics and the occult. "We're witches!" Kat said with excited disbelief.

"Bite thy tongues, ladies."

The sisters turned to find an ordinary-looking man on the other side of the cell. He seemed to recognize Sam.

"Hush, Sister," Prudence-Penny said. "We are surely set for the gallows as it is. No need to seal our fate with confessions."

Prudence leaned forward and gestured with her eyes, moving between Kat and then toward the man. "Beguile him, sister, if we are to be freed."

Sam rushed between her sisters and pressed herself against the cell's door. "It's Robert, isn't it?" the seventeenth-

16

century Sam asked. Her chest welled with each breath—warmth spread through her, causing a pale redness in her cheeks. "Do they seek to burn us?" Sam asked him as she gazed into his eyes.

"Aye, they do, and soon," Robert replied.

Kat stared at the pair as their eyes swooned and conveyed a deep conversation without the use of words. "You two know each other?" Kat asked. The Sam she knew was too coldhearted, bitter, and even resentful to fall in love. She shook her head in doubt. "It doesn't matter who the hell you are. Can you help us?"

"Sisters, it is the gentleman that passed through town last week. The one who sought lodging," the past-incarnation of Sam said.

"That I did, and I swore I would not forget you." Robert laid his hands over Sam's as she clasped the bars. "I promised I would come back for you, didn't I?" He smiled at her, then added, "Passage has been secured on the only ship at port, and she's about to sail. I can get us aboard, but ye must stowaway." Robert kissed Sam's hand and turned to search for the cell's key.

"Robert?" Sam cried.

"Ye be fine, lass; I'm hunting for the key." Robert scanned the dim room for a hook or nail that might hold the ring of keys. Then, he disappeared out the back.

Sam dropped to her knees and wept into her cupped hands.

"What shall we do, Sisters?" Prudence asked. "Shall we escape with this lad like poor old Henry Spencer?" Prudence added, "Of course, he wound up branded with a 'B' on the forehead. Poor soul. Do you think we've earned a 'W'?"

"They're not going to brand us—they're going to execute us at Pingrey's Plain." Kat didn't know what was worse, being trapped *in* the seventeenth century—or trapped *with* her seventeenth-century sisters. "Listen," Kat said after detecting the clank of keys.

"Only if you get caught, ladies; only if you get caught," a different man, a fair-skinned man, said. He approached their cell and fiddled with a set of keys that hung from a large iron ring.

The three turned their gaze to this new, unusual man. He had an otherworldly presence. His complexion and hair were so pallid; both appeared to be sculpted out of a pure white stone. Sam jumped up, no longer crying, and demanded he told her what had become of Robert.

"Be you the Keeper?" Prudence asked him.

"Calm yourselves. I am not," he said. He inserted the key into the keyhole and turned the key hard to the right. The lock clicked open. "Make haste." He pulled the cell door out of their way, so they could easily slip by. "The man you called Robert awaits you, ladies, on the ship, but you haven't much time," he warned.

Prudence exited the cell first. As she passed the man, he noticed something he hadn't anticipated. A dual energy emanated from the first woman, and his awareness of it took him by surprise. His mind sped through his memories of his lifelong studies. He was certain only another set of triplets from the same lineage could take possession of these three powerful witches. Yet, he didn't understand how. Witches have never had the gift of Time Walking. But somehow, another trio of witches had stepped into their past incarnations. His eyes shot open. *His* Time Walking portal. They must have stepped through *his* portal before it closed.

The dual energy became stronger as the second sister exited the cell. As Sam passed the iron door, some kind of visceral urge flooded his body and mind. He seized her hand and pulled her close to his side. His other hand pressed against her lower back, securing her in this position, and his hot breath rolled along her neck. Submissively, she leaned in. He wanted to kiss her, and she would have let him.

"What are you doing?" Kat said, witnessing the whole drama. Kat seized Sam's hand from the stranger's and drug her away from his clasps.

"It's not what you think," he suddenly explained.

"What I'm thinking, sir, if that's even an appropriate title for you," Penny said and grabbed Sam's other hand, "is you've made lewd advances toward my younger sister."

"This is a matter for another time and place," he said and gestured toward the jail's entrance. "Ladies, you must leave now."

The three accused women scurried to the door in haste. The man raised his left hand, pointed toward the jail's entrance, and drew a circle midair, and whispered, "Open a gateway to the Earthen timeline. Allow me to pass and safely arrive. Open a gateway to another time." A circle of ethereal pale-blue matter formed as an orb in the center of the door.

He watched the ball of shimmery blue light grow from this center spot, encompassing the entire entry and several feet beyond. The three women passed through, seemingly unnoticed, and headed toward the docks. The other three moved forward and disappeared into thin air. He only hoped that the tracking spell he whispered into Sam's ear as she exited the cell had generated an energy cord strong enough to allow him to follow these three witches to their current time. The man walked forward, and as he stepped into the portal, he said, "With gratitude."

The portal closed behind him.

Chapter Three

The Order of the Nine Illuminations, 2763 A.D.

D eep within the rock-hewn catacombs, under the remnants of a massive church built more than a thousand years earlier, several figures walked in single-file through the narrow tunnels. Two-hundred miles of passageways comprised the underground ossuary. The last time a man's footsteps touched this sacred ground was a millennium ago to intern the last poor soul's bones.

They trekked through the passages until they reached their destination. The three wielding torches placed them in the iron brackets mounted inside the vacant tomb. The flames' reflection illuminated the space and danced on the damp Lutetian limestone walls. These people were twenty-five meters below the Earth's surface and grateful for the shelter the isolation provided.

Ronan stepped forward and took the first stone seat. His fellow members followed and filled the eight remaining spots around the circular slab table, completing the circle. The Order of the Nine Illuminations, a secret organization, held the collective goal of restoring the high status of magic. At this point, they found themselves desperate to save any form of the Art.

In Ronan's current life, everything magical had disappeared except for his group, who practiced the Arts and kept the Sacred Words safe. Mankind had fallen into *The Great Sleep*. Slowly, like a drop that eventually empties the vat, the awareness of magic faded. Humans existed unconscious of their real identity. Completely unaware of the ancient god within and of their power to create. The Order recognized the importance and kept this mystic knowledge alive. At least, Ronan hoped they all did.

Ronan stood. "I call the Order of Nine Illuminations into session." He drew a line through the air straight down from top to bottom. He followed with another from ten o'clock to four and one from two to eight. Finally, he added one from left to right. His gestures formed an invisible asterisk-like symbol in the dusky ether before him—a representation of the sun.

The members stood, and under the torches glow, their colored hooded-cloaks became visible around their faces. "Hail, the Order of the Nine Illuminations." Each of them repeated before they retook their seats.

"The recent deluge of surface rainfall continues to threaten the vaults where we hold our sacred manuscripts. Although we have painstakingly moved every scroll, several are saturated and need transcribing." Ronan rubbed his forehead.

"Of what purpose is that now?" The youngest member on Ronan's left said. Jacob was an initiate. He wore white to symbolize the innocence of developing magical skills.

"Of every importance. If we too forget – if we are remiss – no hope remains," Ronan said.

"We hold little hope now. Forgetfulness swells in our world." Bruno sat on Ronan's right. He was the Order's expert on Practical Magic and claimed the ginger-brown robe as a symbol of the earthen stability and the protection this provided.

"You misunderstand, Brother. Without this, humanity has no chance, for without magic, all hope disappears." Ronan understood the necessity of this carrot that dangled in front of mankind. It pushed each individual forward. But, their world became so dim that even The Illuminations struggled to keep their faith.

"I am transcribing the scrolls." The elderly man in purple sat across from Ronan. He was Abraham, the oldest member of their group, and the decades spent underground had left his voice coarse and gravelly.

"Good man, Brother Abraham." Ronan smiled at the frail man.

"But I see no purpose," Abraham added, "my job has no end. I cannot complete the transcriptions. Not all of them. There are too many. It is my bones you eight shall carry to the crypt soon enough, not a stack of books."

Ronan had thought this very thing over the past several months. It was only a matter of time before Abraham drew his final breath. No one who lived on the surface remained suitable for initiation into the Order.

"We may not be able to awaken enough souls within our lifetimes..." Scarlet said, pulling the crimson hood back from her head and exposing her platinum hair. She offered a compassionate smile to the aged man. "But we can ensure the Order's secret knowledge remains intact and hidden away while we await a time when it can safely be rediscovered by the masses once again."

"Without any awareness of magic," Ronan said, "man cannot search for truth. He is doomed to fall into utter darkness."

"It is unprecedented," Matthew, their specialist in Enoch Angel Magic, said. "There have always been those like us, who kept the Words alive— hid meaning in art, or," he pointed a finger to cryptic scrolls, "or buried in allegories. We few always stir the desire for Light. But now..."

The Order fell silent as each contemplated their predicament.

"If an awareness of magic is required to move the tide," Ronan argued, "we must go back to those points and rewrite them. We must tip critical mass our way and right the wrongs which drove magic into obscurity.

"Are you suggesting that we Time Walk?" Abraham glared with skepticism.

"No. I suggest that *I* Time Walk."

Mumbling among the members echoed in the chamber, and the sound amplified like twenty or more spoke.

"Ronan, you have the greatest power of all of us." Abraham's irritation grew. "But you hold no abilities to undo that which has been done or to do that which had not been done."

"True, Brother, but I can divert a thing's path, hide it, or move it... with my brethren's aid, of course. I may not have the power to erase the past, but Time Walking allows the greater power to redirect and transmute," Ronan said. He stood and raised his hand, a signal the council meeting had adjourned.

"What do you intend to do?" Bruno asked.

"Go back into time; back to the perilous moments...the points when magic became marginalized and made out as an evil thing." Ronan stepped toward the vault's opening.

"Points? Like when?" Edward, the Astrologer's voice, rose over the clamor of voices around him.

Ronan stopped at the tomb's entry and turned to face his associates." I don't know, Brother," Ronan said. He shook his head before he glanced back up." You're the experts on history. What points do you suggest?"

"The witch trials of the seventeenth century, perhaps?" Edward suggested.

"No," the Illusionist Alexander chimed in, "before then. You must go farther back. To times and events which lead to the possibility of witch trials in man's mind."

Ronan gazed at Abraham, the organization's authority on history. "Give me the place where I can return and change the effect of our current, horrendous state of affairs."

"The year 1466 in the province of Guipuzcoa," Abraham said without hesitation." You can intercept the petition that is on its way to king Henry IV of Castile. The local, for lack of a better word, the mayor sent word to the king and demanded the witches be wiped out. Worse, he requested permission to execute all the accused without any of them granted the right to appeal."

"The province of Guipuzcoa?" Brianna, Scarlet's younger sister, asked. "You refer to the Basque County witch trial?" She was an expert on Natural Magic, particularly Alchemy.

"Yes," Abraham answered her, "Those trials, the mass executions, were some of the most brutal experienced by man. If Ronan can interrupt this, perhaps he can change events and change history. If Ronan is right, the meaning derived from this time period forward might forever be changed."

"I find this a dangerous proposition," Bruno said.

The old man Abraham sublimated the concerns by offering a warning as advice. "Ronan, you must remember magic is real to those 15th-century souls." He stared directly into Ronan's eyes. "And dark magic holds a greater foothold on those men than the reverence for the Divine ever could. Superstition is rampant."

Scarlet gave a devilish grin Matthew's way. She was the Order's Demonologist and specialized in all forms of Dark Magic. Matthew pulled his rose-colored hood over his pale head before he bowed and prayed.

"And, remember to immediately glamour your appearance." Alexander quickly wrote down a simple spell for Ronan to use. "You must fit in."

Bruno leaned toward Ronan. "I've prepared a protection amulet for you."

Ronan took the golden pendant. Carved into the stone was a female's face with a wild mane that licked like flames as it surrounded her. He peered up and met eyes with Bruno.

"The solar goddess Eki," Bruno said. "They believed her to be the protector of man and the enemy of all evil. With this amulet, you are safe."

"And what did they believe to be evil?" Ronan asked.

Scarlet glided forward. "Gaueko, the shapeshifter, Gizotso werewolves, or Herensuge, the dragon."

"Is that all?" Ronan's sarcasm filled the room.

Scarlet displayed a huge grin in his direction. "No, you'll find a chimeric embodiment of evil. Her name is Etsai."

Ronan shook his head. Scarlet wasn't playing. What she said was true. He had read the same stories. He slipped the amulet's chain over his head. "So shall it be."

"So shall it be," affirmed the other eight.

Chapter Four

"Superstitions aren't easily destroyed. First, fear had to be turned into mockery among the masses, and that is precisely what led to the decline of witchcraft."

The World of Witches

After several days in the province of Guipuzcoa, Ronan returned to the tombs, where his fellow Illumination members informed him that his actions had indeed affected history.

"Great," Ronan said, "I was unable to intercept the letter, but I used Brother Alexander's spell to create an illusion over the contents. The king must have read this magical message." Ronan undid the jeweled neck clasp on his crow-black cloak. "What do we know?" He asked and placed the Eki amulet on the table.

"The content of the books changed." Brianna waited for his reaction.

Ronan silently stared at his fellow adepts. Their faces troubled him as he tried to conceive what had happened.

"The Trinity witches are no more." Scarlet's expression made it hard to tell if she was sympathetic or somehow pleased.

"That's impossible." Ronan sat at the stone table and waived for the youngest adept to fetch him water. "Something else occurred in the timeline to cause this. Where's Abraham?"

Jacob scurried to collect the old man who painstakingly copied the ancient texts in a separate vault. "Ronan has returned and requests to see what you've transcribed about the Trinity Witches. Do you have anything?"

"Why, yes. Yes, I do." Abraham rifled through the scrolls of recently finished writings. He grabbed the scroll tagged with the king's name and followed his colleague out and to the main tomb.

Ronan hurried to greet the old man at the table. "What is the variation to the sacred text our brothers speak of?"

"Earlier today, I transcribed the parchment of Henry V of Castile. In fact, the recipient of the letter you traveled back in time to intercept," he breathlessly explained.

"Yes, yes, get on with it." The signs of impatience colored over Ronan's usual steadfast demeanor.

"I recorded..." the old man paused as he struggled to catch his breath before he continued, "I recorded the beheading of the Trinity Witches near the end of his rein."

34

"Impossible. How can this be? The Trinity Witches have always existed. They were never hunted, not ever. They are far too strong for anyone ever to attempt such a feat." Ronan stood, then paced along the tomb's outer wall as he contemplated the inevitable chain of events that must have transpired.

"The king's sorcerer must have uncovered the spell and dissolved the illusion," Abraham added.

Ronan stopped pacing.

"King Henry declared that only the Trinity Witches' power could create such an enchantment as the high magic cast over that letter."

"But were they killed? Were the Trinity Witches executed?" Ronan begged.

"The King ordered the arrest of the three Supreme Witches, and the scroll records the beheading of two of them and subsequent burning of their bodies."

"Two?"

"The third witch, the middle one, was never found."

"Quick, the record of the Supreme Sublime. Do you know where it is, man?" Ronan pleaded with Abraham.

"I know the vicinity." Abraham collected the King's scroll and, as quickly as possible, headed back to his appointed tomb, where he worked as the group's scribe.

Ronan and the other seven members followed Abraham to his chamber and waited as the frantic old man searched for the requested material.

"Where is it?" Rona demanded.

"Give him a minute to find it," Brianna said, encouraging his patience.

Abraham scratched his forehead. "I haven't transcribed it yet, but it must be... there, behind that basket." He raised his hand to indicate the section where he believed the sought-after parchments lay.

The scroll lay barely visible on the cool limestone floor behind the square-bottomed, round-mouthed, woven container. A motif of green snakes appeared to slither near the uppermost edge of the basket, making Ronan hesitate. He reached into the dark space between the basket and the stone wall.

"My god, what have I done?" Ronan released one end of the scroll. The once six feet long parchment unrolled and exposed its new length. Now, only twelve or so inches in length.

"What happened to the scroll?" Jacob gawked at the minuscule record.

"Brother, *I* have happened to it." Ronan relinquished the scroll to the elder.

Abraham explained, "King Henry declared the Trinity Witches hunted down and all traces of their lineage be brought to an untimely end. This scroll is an account of the Trinity Witches through time, starting in Basque and following their lineage for the next ten generations."

"Ten generations? There were fifty — or more the last time we consulted this scroll." Ronan couldn't believe the change that had occurred.

"There is a detailed account of the captures and executions of each generation of triplets. But as with Basque, only two were ever captured. And always the oldest and the youngest. For ten generations, always the same," Abraham confirmed as he read from the scroll.

"What happened after ten generations?" Ronan asked, puzzled.

"The last three were captured together and all executed. This cruel act ended the bloodline of the most Supreme Sublime Trinity Witches." Abraham's head tilted down. "We have failed our vast mission."

"Where?" Ronan gripped Abraham's upper arms. "Where, man, where did this happen?!" Ronan shook him, insisting on an answer. "Where did the last capture transpire?"

"Ipswich, Massachusetts, 1692." The old man's voice quavered, shocked by being handled in such a manner. Abraham rubbed his arms where Ronan's hands had violently grabbed him. "The three witches were captured, and in a fortnight, they hung from the gallows before their lifeless bodies were burnt, dismembered, and finally cast into the sea."

"Then I must go there and set them free before this transpires."

"Ronan," Abraham said sternly, "you cannot change what has already been done."

"You keep telling me that, but apparently, I can."

"You're changing the details...not the result," Abraham said. He sat on his stool, relinquishing himself to his daily task of transcribing. He glanced up, "Magic is still in the same peril."

"How so?" Ronan asked.

"We're still here, trying to save it."

***

Ronan withdrew from the old man's tomb. This time, he would open another portal to Ipswich, where he planned to release the witches— prepared to do whatever it took. Ronan thought he could hypnotize the local magistrate and the whole damn town, one by one, if he had to. He would make all of them believe there was no such thing as witches.

The other seven Illumination members stood in the background as Bruno approached him. He walked to Ronan's side and held a necklace out in front of himself. It was a locket made from malachite and surrounded by tiny amethyst stones suspended from a thick, golden chain that matched the gold mount.

As Ronan bent down to receive the amulet, Bruno said, "Brianna transmuted the gold. I selected the stones. Matthew engraved Uriel's sigil. And Jacob blessed it."

"Now the goddess seals the magic within with a kiss," Brianna said and waved for Scarlet to join her.

Ronan straightened upright, and the two female members of the Order both kissed the amulet. But, as Scarlet turned to rejoin the others, Brianna raised herself up on the tip of her toes and pressed her pale lips against Ronan's cheek. This kiss she offered to him alone.

Ronan's eyebrows furrowed. He wasn't quite sure what to make of her actions.

"Oh, and Ronan," Edward said, "I cast an astrological chart on this endeavor. You should be safe, but I must warn you something quite unexpected is likely to occur."

Ronan nodded that he understood. The seven of them witnessed him open another portal and disappear through the opalescent ether of suspended time. Yet, none of them comprehended that the twenty-first-century incarnations of the Trinity Witches walked toward the same jail, which in their time was a museum, and that they walked through the jail's entrance at the exact moment Ronan opened his portal and Time Walked into the same location in 1692.

***

Ronan stepped through the ethereal matter like it was an ordinary door and emerged inside the jail. The Trinity Witches were in the lone cell as expected. One, who sat on the wooden bench positioned against the back wall, wrote in a type of journal or diary. The red-headed witch cupped her face with both of her hands. And the blonde witch? She traced a circle with her toe on the cell's dirt floor while she mumbled melodic rhymes.

The three hadn't noticed his presence and this pleased Ronan. He needed a moment to figure out what he would say. Should he tell them the truth or give them as little information as possible? He was unsure, but he decided to announce himself, planning on improvising after he observed their reactions.

The hairs on the back of his neck stood. The portal. The energy from his portal increased, and for a second, he thought he caught a glimpse of three teenage girls passing through the gateway he had created. Ronan hid behind the door.

He watched the three captured witches' behavior suddenly shift. Their dialect and mannerisms no longer aligned completely with the seventeenth-century culture. The three women were, in fact, surprised by their clothing and predicament. The blonde one seemed in a near panic. Yet, the red-headed witch accepted the seventeenth-century demeanor without reservation. He heard the panicky one blurt out they must be witches seconds before someone's footsteps announced their approach from the jail's back entrance. This rendered the women silent.

As Ronan peered from behind a door, he witnessed a man clutch the dark-haired witch's hands as she gripped the cell's iron bars. The other two witches appeared enthralled with the drama which unfolded in their cell. No longer as objective as he would have liked to remain, Ronan struggled to control his own emotions.

He listened to the brawny man tell the witches he had arranged their safe passage as stowaways on a docked ship. The man said he needed to find the keys to free them, and

Ronan took that as his opportunity to rid himself of this unwanted interference.

Ronan heard the man, the one the witches called Robert, tell the witches he must hunt for the cell's key. So, Ronan dashed out and around the wooden building. He readied himself outside. Just as anticipated, this man walked outside of the jail. While Robert searched the building for a nail or hook that the keys may have been kept, Ronan seized his opportunity. It was his only chance to release the witches and change their destiny and the destiny of magic.

Ronan lunged at the man and maneuvered himself into a better position. He wrapped his right arm tightly around Robert's neck, squeezing and choking off the man's supply of oxygen. Robert desperately grappled for Ronan's arms, frantic to free himself. His boots slipped in the dry earth as he kicked, struggling for his life. Ronan only abandoned his tight hold when he felt the man's body fall limp. He lowered Robert to the ground, knowing he only had a few minutes before Robert regained consciousness and could think clearly again. Ronan would have to move quickly to release the witches in this window of time.

He entered the jail.

"They're not planning on branding us. They're executing us," the blonde witch said to her sisters.

"Only if you get caught, ladies. Only if you get caught." Ronan said as he approached their cell.

The dark-haired witch sprung up from where she knelt and demanded he tell her what he had done with

Robert. Ronan didn't answer her question. Instead, he told her to calm down as he inserted the key into the old iron lock. "The man you called Robert waits for you on the ship. Little time remains," Ronan warned.

The red-headed witch exited the cell first, and Ronan sensed an electrostatic charge as she passed. He couldn't imagine what could create such intensity except when encountering a possessed soul. Two entities with the same form generated a massive amplitude of energy. Certainly, no others could possess them but another set of triplets. Of course, they would have to be witches of the same lineage to accomplish this. Still, witches, not even the powerful Trinity Witches, had ever been gifted the ability to Time Walk.

Ronan's eyes widened with his realization that he had done it. It was his Time Walking portal the modern witches had passed through before he closed his gateway. His mind reeled. He had to follow these new witches to their timeline. The dual energy he felt became stronger as the dark-haired witch exited the cell. He had to know who they were.

As the dark-haired one passed the iron door, some kind of visceral urge flooded Ronan's body and mind. He seized her hand, pulled her close to his side, and secured her place against his body while he whispered a tracking spell into her ear. He sensed her submit to his grasp, and a soft groan escaped his lips.

"What are you doing?" The blonde witch seized the hand of the sister from his grasp

"It's not what you think." Ronan realized how his actions must have appeared. But his words didn't stop the first witch from admonishing him with her eyes as she passed. "This is a matter for another time and place, ladies." Ronan urged them forward as he gestured toward their escape. "You must leave now." He kept his eyes on the three witches as he raised his left hand, drew the symbol of the sun in the air, and harnessed his power. He pointed at the jail's entrance and drew a counterclockwise circle as he said, "Open a gateway to the Earthen timeline. Allow me to pass and safely arrive. Open this as a gateway to another time."

A tiny circle of ethereal pale-blue matter formed as an orb in the center of the doorway. Ronan witnessed the ball of shimmery blue light grow from this center spot until large enough to encompass the entire entry and several feet beyond.

The witches each passed through without notice. The three seventeenth-century witches headed to their right and toward the town's docks. Then he witnessed the other three emerge, like ghostly images, separated from the physical forms of the other three. Their spectral bodies moved forward and disappeared in the time portal. Now, he could follow his tracking spell's energy cord back to their timeline. Ronan entered the doorway and offered his gratitude to magic before the portal closed behind him.

Chapter Five

Ipswich, Massachusetts- Present Day

K at still held one of Sam's hands as she pushed her forward and closer to Penny. Penny immediately took hold of Sam's free hand. If the magical portal had disappeared, Kat feared they would be trapped in that awful place and trapped in the seventeenth century.

Together, the three stepped, left foot first, through the threshold of the old jail. Each prayed to themselves that they would return safely to the Old Gaol Museum in the twenty-first century. The sisters stepped out through the museum's entrance and found themselves on the top step where their bizarre journey had begun earlier that same morning. Collectively, they sighed as relief washed over them. They were back.

"What the heck just happened?" Kat asked. "I mean, are we three really witches?"

"It doesn't make sense." Penny rubbed her forehead in an attempt to pacify her emerging headache. "If everything is energy, and all things exist simultaneously..." she continued to rattle off random bits of truths as she questioned her understanding of all the metaphysical research she had done over the past few years. "No, I don't believe in witches."

"What are you talking about, Penny? I don't remember much of what happened, but you were in 1692 with me. With Sam." Kat spun around, afraid she had lost track of her other sister. "Sam?" She shouted.

Sam still stood at the curb, and Kat followed her sister's gaze to the other side of the street. A person stared back. A man. Someone they didn't recognize.

He waited there and observed them as he rolled what appeared to be a coin across his knuckles.

"Who is that?" Kat asked.

"I don't know," Sam whispered back as she scrutinized the stranger.

"Well, he creeps me out," Kat said. She continued to study the odd individual.

"Kat?" Penny asked, "Do you sense anything now?"

"Yes. Like, we better figure this all out—fast." Kat picked up her pace and walked next to Penny. "Sam? Come on."

Sam ran to catch up with her sisters, who had reached the corner, but before joining her rightful place between them, she glanced back over her shoulder.

He was gone.

***

The girls raced toward the library, past the road where their high school was, and swung into The Jackal's Brew coffee shop to hide for a moment. Penny headed for a table in the back while Sam joined Kat in ordering their usual iced coffees. Penny took hers with a splash of cream. Sam's was black, of course, and Kat's choice depended upon the day and her mood. She always checked the menu board in case she wanted the flavor of the day. After everything that went down, she was too freaked out to think straight. She found herself glazed over as she attempted to read the chalked words. Sam rolled her eyes at Kat and told the girl behind the counter her sister would take the same thing she had just ordered. A few minutes later, with drinks in hand, they slid into the back booth with Penny.

"Who was that weird guy, Sam?" Kat asked.

"I told you. I've never seen him before," Sam replied.

"He seems like someone we met before. Does he go to our school?" Kat asked.

"For the millionth time, Kat, I don't know."

Kat made a slight growl as her frustration seeped between her lips. "Penny? Did you see the guy outside the jail when we stepped back through?"

"No," Penny said. "Why?"

"She has no reason. Just being Kat. So, do you think we're in trouble because we missed the field trip?" Sam asked. "That would be my luck."

"I took care of it." Penny rubbed her thumb across the shop's logo on her cup. She liked where the image's steam rose in the shape of three shadowy jackals from a coffee cup.

"Took care of what?" Kat came out of her fog and sipped her drink. "Yuck. This is black coffee. Gross."

"You'll be fine," Sam replied. She found a bit of pleasure in her sister's discomfort.

"Quiet," Penny scolded. "Kat, go put some cream and sugar in your drink or flavored syrups. Whatever you have to do so you can drink it. Do it and hurry back here."

Kat scooted on the bench to the edge of the table before standing. She grabbed her cup. "I think we are witches," Kat said and walked away.

"What did you do, Penny?" Sam asked.

Penny stared down at her cup. "I don't understand why, but last week I typed a note to excuse us from school. I didn't say we were sick. I said Mom was."

"Well, you're not wrong," Sam said. "Wow, I didn't believe you had it in you to skip school or to lie."

"I didn't write it because I wanted to lie." Penny squirmed as she readjusted her position on the bench. "I somehow knew to type the note and hang on to it until it was needed."

Kat sat back down, but this time she slid in next to Penny. "What did who lie about?"

"Penny wrote a letter last week explaining we would miss school today." Sam raised her eyebrows.

"Cool," Kat replied. "I told you. We're witches."

"Penny, you have to admit it would explain a lot, like our obsessive interest in the occult," Sam said.

"Plenty of people study the occult and metaphysical subjects," Penny said. "They're not all witches."

"You do believe. You said they're not all witches. So, that means you think some of them are witches. Like us." Kat was proud of her argument. She took a long drink through her straw before she took it and swirled the whipped cream into her heavily syrup-laden, self-made coffee concoction.

49

"Okay, I'm not going to say impossible," Penny answered. "Clearly, some people think they are witches. I believe what most people consider magic is science. We simply don't understand how it works yet."

Kat looked at Sam and mouthed 'witches' as she pointed at herself, then circled her index finger to include her sisters in her comment.

Sam smiled and nodded in agreement.

"So, what do you think we should do next, sis?" Kat asked Penny.

"Research. We need to do a lot more investigating." Penny shoved her wadded-up napkin into her empty cup. "Let's check on Mom first; then, I want to dig up our family tree."

"We should go back and see if the portal is still there. I mean, is it the place, or did we do it somehow?" Sam said.

"I'm not sure about that," Penny replied, "I think we should consider ourselves lucky. We made it out of there once. Let's not tempt fate."

"I thought you didn't believe in any of that; what did you call it? Oh, yeah, silliness like destiny and fate."

"Um," Kat said. She nudged Penny to gain her attention. "That guy Sam and I told you about— he just walked in."

Penny and Sam whipped around and looked. The three of them glared at the man they saw earlier stroll toward their table. Somehow, under the shop's fluorescent lighting, his skin seemed translucent, and his veins left blueish trails along his neck and across his temples.

"What do we do?" Kat asked.

"We leave." Penny slid toward Kat and forced her sister to stand. "Let's go. Don't make eye contact. Walk right past him."

They started toward the coffee shop's door hand-in-hand. And, as their path met with the stranger's, all three of the girl's skin crawled with goosebumps when he stopped. His body blocked the only open aisle. The girls, forced to split apart, moved around him. Penny and Kat moved to his left and squeezed by. Sam went around his right; her arms hugged tightly to her chest. She refused to give in and forced him to twist his upper body and make room for her to pass. Sam did the one thing Penny urged them not to do— she glanced up. His watery gray eyes locked with hers. Sam only broke away when she walked past him and was unable to turn her head around any further. When she reached the shop's door, the triplets looked back in bewilderment at the man who stood in the center of the coffee shop. He peered back at them. His eyebrows were so fair they were only visible when the light glistened on them. Everything about his appearance was washed out, creating a ghastly and stunning appearance—a living alabaster sculpture. Cold shivers ran down Sam's spine. Was he a ghost from her past or one from her future? All she understood was that she found him beautiful, and that was something she would never let any of them know.

***

Back at their house, the girls huddled at their front door. Kat stood guard with her back toward her sisters, hoping they hadn't been followed. "Hurry, Penny. We've got to get inside before that guy sees which house is ours," Kat urged.

Penny tried to shove their house key into the lock, but her hands uncontrollably shook under the pressure. "I'm trying."

Sam lost her patience and snatched the key from Penny. She slid it into the keyhole and opened their home's front door. "Come on." When they all were inside, she shut the door with such force the pictures on both sides rattled, threatening to fall to the floor.

Kat ran to the front window and peeked through the meager space she created when she pulled the curtains slightly away from the wall. "I don't see him. I don't think he followed us."

"I want to know who the hell he thinks he is to stalk us," Sam said with a hostile tone.

"It's a coincidence. The Jackal's Brew is the only coffee shop within miles," Penny said, still sounding undecided.

"Really? Some weird guy happens to be outside the jail, and then miraculously, he decides to get a coffee exactly when we do?" Sam retorted.

Penny hung her jacket on the tree stand hook, ignoring her sister. "I'll check on Mom. You two argue about who he is." Penny climbed the stairs and hoped her mother was asleep. She wanted to look up the women from the jail on her ancestry program. From the top step, Penny heard Kat tell Sam she was off to meditate, and Sam replied she would make herself an herbal tea. Everything was back to normal.

In their kitchen, Sam filled the tea kettle with cold tap water and placed the water-filled kettle on the stove. She turned the stove top dial to high, then remembered her handwritten journal where she recorded the properties and uses of herbs. Flipping through the pages, unable to find what she wanted, she stopped and closed the book. "Okay," she said aloud, "show me the seed. Make clear the recipe for what I need." Instinctively, she picked the book up and, in a swift movement, opened it and read what was written on that particular page. "You've got to be kidding me." With excitement, she gathered a sprig of mint from the container on the window's sill to increase her psychic powers. Lavender from the drying rack mounted on the wall for clarity. And for divination, a dandelion flower from inside a glass jar on her mother's spice rack.

Sam placed the dried ingredients in a granite mortar and crushed and ground them together with the pestle until the pieces were tiny enough for the hot water to extract all their properties yet big enough to remain securely inside the screen of her cone-shaped infuser.

The kettle's whistle startled Sam out of her deep and thoughtful creativity. She added the herbal tea to the infuser, carefully keeping it loose to allow the water to flow freely, and hooked the end of the handle over her cup's rim. As the steam floated up into the air, Sam leaned over her cup and inhaled the beautiful, delicious aroma. She added a drop of fresh honey before she cozied up in her favorite yellow and pink floral chair in their sunroom on the backside of their house.

Penny hollered for her sisters from the top of the stairs, "Sam? Kat?" Penny took the steps two at a time. "You're not going to believe this." She raced to their dining room.

From opposite directions, Kat and Sam entered the dining room just as Penny dropped a stack of papers on the table. They each glanced back and forth at each other, then Penny and Sam both busted out, "We're witches!"

"Totally called that," Kat sputtered. "Glad you two are finally on the same page as me."

"Guys," Sam said, "I made a tea, and when I drank some, it helped me understand that we are hereditary witches."

"Why don't we already know this?" Kat asked.

"Mom has been out of it for so long, even if she knows, she was never in a condition to tell us," Penny reminded her sisters.

"Okay, but if we are witches, where are our powers? Shouldn't we have powers?"

"Maybe we get them when we turn eighteen or something," Kat suggested.

"I suppose," Penny said, "that would make sense."

"Well, our birthdays are soon, so I guess we'll know then," Sam said.

"What else did you find, Penny?" Kat gestured toward the papers.

"Oh, this is pretty cool." Penny picked up the papers and shared what her ancestral research had uncovered. "I started researching our family tree a couple of months ago, but I only had mom and her mother on there. I remembered the software program kept prompting me each time a new relative was found, but I ignored them because mom's an only child, right?"

"Yeah," Sam and Kat replied. They both leaned in with anticipation of Penny's findings.

"But I also assumed Mom's mother was an only child because I don't remember ever hearing anything about her having aunts."

"And?"

"I decided *not* to ignore the hints. I decided to let the tree grow itself if I accepted all the ancestors the program suggested." Penny picked up the stack of papers. "Mom has two aunts. Her mother is the middle sister in a set of triplets."

"What? Our grandmother is a triplet like us?" Kat dropped down on one of the dining room chairs.

"Okay, so what? Wouldn't being triplets be a genetic thing?" Sam asked.

"Yes, fraternal twins or triplets can be hereditary, but not like this." Penny laid one paper on the table. "Here we are." Penny pointed to the last row of triplets on the page with their names assigned to the colored squares. Above them, Penny pointed to their mom's name, Renee Glouster-Hale. "And here." She moved her finger to the next row, "this is who the program linked to us as our grandmother. And here, look, her two sisters."

"Sylvia Howe, our grandmother Lyndia Howe-Glouster, and Louisa Howe," Sam read.

"Okay," Kat said, "So we have great-aunts we've never met."

"Great-aunts who abandoned their own sister," Sam chided.

"There's more," Penny said. She spread the rest of the papers out in the order she had printed them. "Every generation, only one of the triplets has children, and she always gives birth to another set of triplets."

Both Kat and Sam walked closer to see for themselves.

"How many generations back?" Kat asked.

Penny counted the generations on the printed tree. "Like thirty-seven, so far."

"And every time, the pattern is identical?"

"Yes," Penny said, "so far, I've traced our lineage back to the year 1249 to a woman named Pressina, whose husband died the same year her triplets were born. And, every time, it's the middle triplet who gives birth to the next set of triplets."

"Woo, Sam," Kat teased, "You're the lucky one this time."

"Shut up, Kat. I'm not having kids. I don't even like them." Sam's lip curled up on one side.

"Well, I think you did like that guy in the jail." A memory flashed in Kat's mind. "Hey, the guy who followed us, he's the same person that set us free. I remember his face now."

The girls stared at each other as the images of the two men simultaneously formed in their minds.

Sam grabbed the papers. "Where are they?"

"The women from jail?" Penny asked, a little confused.

"Yes."

Penny took the printed tree and riffled through the now unorganized pages. "Here." She handed a page back to Sam. "Prudence, Cherilyn, and Kathryn. Born 1674. Their mother was Felicity, born 1623."

Sam knew the moment Penny said the name Cherilyn it was true. She had been with this woman; shared her body. Cherilyn was her previous incarnation. "When did they die?" Sam released the paper, and it floated softly to the floor.

It felt like an eternity had passed before Kat picked the paper up and read what year those triplets had died. She prayed the date was anything other than 1692, and she prayed they hadn't caused their deaths if time walking had interfered. Kat read the paper, "Cherilyn lived until 1733. She gave birth to triplets in 1693. The middle daughter she named Joliet."

"And her sisters?"

Penny took the paper from Kat, whose eyes filled with tears. "Both of Cherilyn's sisters were hung for witchcraft in 1692." Tears trickled down her cheeks.

"Did we do that to them? Is it our fault the two of them died?" Sam was visibly shaken too.

"I'm not sure," Penny answered.

"What if the white-haired, weird guy was there to kill us, I mean them? Maybe Cherilyn escaped and made her way to the ship," Sam said.

"Or perhaps he's our great-great-great-grandfather," Kat said.

"Here from the seventeenth century to finish the job?" Sam taunted.

"Why not? If one can travel back through time as we did, I suppose traveling forward is an option, too," Penny said as she tried to work the concept out in her head. "Oh, and he would be our thirteenth great grandfather if he is indeed the one Cherilyn conceived a child with."

"Why don't you think I... I mean, she had a child with Robert?" Sam asked.

"Just a hunch," Kat replied.

"Well, smarty, what did you learn while you were meditating?" Sam asked.

"Nothing," Kat admitted, "I was trying to get to the Akashic Records, but I haven't figured out how to go directly to them." Kat thought about all the information she had read over the years, about meditating and how to access the records. None of the techniques worked for her. She had only ever reached the Great Hall and stood outside the doors of the Akashic Library. It was extraordinary to her that one could go to a place with their mind and witness every event, perceive every thought, hear every word, and feel every emotion that had ever transpired. All are logged in a nonphysical locale like the cloud technology used today. Kat took a pouch from her pocket and pulled out a three-inch long, tapered stone suspended from a chain. She held it up and let the sunlight illuminate the pale rosy, shimmery color. It slowly twirled as it unwound. "I can ask my pendulum."

"Ask it what? If we are to blame for our ancestors' deaths?" Sam snapped.

"I'm just trying to help, Sam." Kat dropped the delicate pink Rose Quartz pendulum back into its pouch and watched its silver chain gently coil around it.

"I know you are, and I'm sorry," Sam said the words, but they were devoid of emotion. She didn't feel sorry, not really. Why did she have to be the middle triplet? One thing she knew for sure was that she would never fall in love. She would never marry. And she definitely would never have a baby, let alone three. Ever.

"You okay," Sam?" Penny asked.

"Why the middle triplet? Does anyone know that?" Sam asked.

"No," Penny replied, adding, "but I have read that it was a pagan belief that a child takes the mother's powers. I think that's why, and perhaps with the Trinity Witch line, it couldn't be risked. If all three sisters bore children, all powers would weaken."

"That kind of makes sense," Kat said. "Think about it. The bond between a mother and her child is powerful."

"Well," Sam replied, "if and when I finally figure out my powers, I won't need to think about it. I'm not sharing them with anyone." She stared at her sisters. "We need more information about what's actually going on. We should go back to the jail, not to time travel, but to get my diary."

"Yeah," Kat said. She jumped up, "Her diary. I bet we can find out what happened to them, too."

"The museum is closed. It's after five o'clock," Penny said, "plus, I have to make Mom her tea and feed her dinner."

"Being able to use witchy powers would be awesome, especially now," Sam said.

"Can't we just teleport ourselves there or twitch our noses and make the diary come to us or something?" Kat suggested.

"Maybe we can ride our brooms," Sam mocked back.

"That's on television, not how it happens in real life," Penny said. "We'll have to nab the diary the old-fashioned way."

"By breaking and entering?" Kat raised her shoulders and looked at her sisters questioningly.

"Okay, here's the plan," Sam said. "I'll make Mom's tea and dinner. Penny will feed her and get her ready for the night. Kat, you find some tools we can use to break in the old joint."

"We're not breaking in, and we're not stealing the diary," Penny scolded. She already felt guilty that they had entered the building once without permission.

Sam recognized Penny's expression. "Okay, we'll read the diary there, but unless you found a magic spell to unlock doors..."

"Fine." Penny marched up the stairs, "We will go back tonight and break in if we have to, but first, see if you can figure out how to make a spell or get some herbs to protect our house and Mom while we're gone."

Before the girls could begin their tasks, they heard a knock at their front door.

"TOO LATE," the triplets said together.

Chapter Six

"You must live magic; not believing, but knowing it to be so."
The First Book of Natural Magic

T he girls stared at each other like proverbial deer frozen in an isolated car's headlights— not a single part of them moved. They were shocked. No one came to their home, not since they were little kids. Not since their mother became incapable of carrying on a conversation, let alone entertaining guests. Their heartbeats seemed to pause, and their breath became imperceptible. The knock occurred again, only louder, more urgent this time.

"What do we do?" Kat whispered.

"I guess we answer it," Penny replied.

The girls still didn't move.

"For god's sake." Sam pushed past her sisters and stomped toward the door. She swung the door open.

The strange, blanched man, seen twice already that day, stood outside their door.

"What do you want?" Sam demanded. Suddenly, she realized how vulnerable she was with their door held wide open. Reckless. Something Kat would do, but not her. She couldn't make her body cooperate and close the door. Instead, Sam glared at their stalker as the hairs on her arms rose with her shiver.

Penny stepped forward and waved for Kat to join the barricade she made with her body, positioning herself next to Sam. "Why are you following us? Are we supposed to know you?"

"You think I'm stalking you?" the peculiar man said. "My name is Ronan."

"Well, you were waiting outside the museum, and then you walked into the coffee shop. We saw you," Sam said with venom.

"And I saw you in the..." Kat said.

"Shh," Penny interrupted, "Don't say anything. I don't know if we can trust him."

"Well, how did you girls end up in the closed museum?" Ronan asked, unsure if they were aware of what had truly transpired.

"None of your business," Penny said.

"Why are you here?" Sam asked. "What do you want from us?"

"I'm here to help you," Ronan calmly answered. Then uncertainty over their reception of him crept in. "You need me," he blurted.

"Help us? Need you? The only thing we need is a restraining order, you freak." Sam's shock had worn off, and she regained her command. She pushed the door hard, planning to slam it in the guy's face, but he stopped it with his hand.

"I'm afraid you *do* need my help," he said before the door slammed shut with a sharp bang.

Sam turned around and looked at her sisters, "Why would we need him?"

"He's not telling us the real reason he's here, but I don't think he intends to harm us," Penny said. Her voice was absent of the usual confidence that came with her perception of someone's true motives.

"How long do you think he was out there?" Kat asked.

"Good question," Penny said.

"Do you think he heard us talking?" Kat asked.

He better not have been listening to us," Sam said. Something about him genuinely got her worked up. She didn't understand what, but he was fingernails on her chalkboard.

"I don't know what that was about, but we should have questioned him until we found out." Penny was unable to sort her intuition and pinpoint what she sensed. "Come on, let's get on with what we need to do and return to the museum as quickly as possible."

"Okay," Sam said, "but I'm taking my pepper spray."

***

As Penny secured their front door, the tinkle and clank of the bells caught her attention. "What the heck is that? Did you put bells on every handle?"

"They're Witch Bells, and yes, I did place them on the inside of every exterior door," Sam proudly said.

"Do they protect the house from bad stuff?" Kat asked.

"Yes. I looked some stuff up online, and they're supposed to scare off evil. But I also want the bells to warn us if tall, pale, and eerie decides to pop in uninvited later," Sam said.

"He knocked, Sam," Kat said in his defense.

"Well, I agree with Sam. I don't think we should trust him quite yet," Penny said.

Sam tossed a handful of fresh leaves across the entryway. Next, she crumbled a dried plant and sprinkled it on top of the greenery.

"What is all this?" Kat asked.

"The green stuff is vervain to prevent evil spirits from entering. The dried-up brown stuff is mandrake. That one's a doozy. It's used in exorcisms but also increases the potency of other plants. That's why I'm using it."

"We should put some in mom's room," Penny said.

"I put a stem of angelica next to her bed while you put your shoes on," Sam said. "Angelica is a powerful protector, plus the name is cool. Definitely one of my favorites."

"You really thought ahead. Thanks, Sam." Penny smiled at her sister.

"Sure," she replied. "Now, put this in your pocket." Sam tossed an orangey-brown object at Penny and then one to Kat.

"Gross," Kat yelled as she put her hand up to block it and let the root drop to the ground, "it looks like a mini baby hand."

"What is this, Sam?" Penny scrutinized the piece of organic matter, which resembled a small, mummified thing.

Sam bent down and picked up the piece Kat flung away from herself. "This one is salep root, but the common name is lucky hand root." Sam scrutinized the tiny dried tuber that laid in her palm. "It does look like a tiny hand, doesn't it?" Sam offered the item back to Kat. "It comes from an orchid and offers protection from all harm." She tugged a white gauze pouch out from her jean pocket. "See, here's mine."

"It can't hurt, Kat," Penny reassured. "Just put it in your pocket."

Kat thought the root was unnerving, but she nodded in agreement. They could use all the help they could get.

"Oh," Sam insisted, "we have to say a spell to empower the plants at the door. We have to give them a direction, an intention."

"Any ideas, Kat?" Penny asked.

"Well, all the spells usually sound like a song or something. Oh, and they rhyme."

"Great."

"Hang on." Kat flipped her pocket-sized notepad to a clean page and scribbled some words down. Then she moved into position on Sam's right. Penny instinctively moved to Sam's left. Together, they faced their front door and read aloud, "We three consecrate thee. Protect thy house by day and night. Send evil off in desperate flight. So it is done."

The girls headed down their front walkway. But Sam stayed a few steps behind and opened the gold, heart-shaped locket of her mom's, which she always wore around her neck. She sprinkled a bit of mandrake inside, and as she snapped the locket closed, she whispered *praesidio*: the Latin word for protect. Then, finally, she caught up with her sisters. When the three reached the sidewalk, Penny looked back at their home.

"She's okay," Sam said to Penny.

"I know," she replied.

***

Penny, Sam, and Kat strode toward the Old Gaol Museum at a steady pace. Each traffic light along their ten-block path favored their course by acquiescing as they reached each intersection and offered the right of way. They didn't stop even once along their route until the museum came into view.

"What the hell?" Sam asked. "This is unbelievable."

Believe it." Penny said as she saw what Sam had done. She marched forward toward the entrance with both sisters closely behind. The triplets didn't stop until mere inches from Ronan's face.

"Seriously?" Sam asked him.

"What took you three so long?" Ronan playfully taunted. He tucked a small leather journal into his cloak, pulled out a coin, and coolly maneuvered it across his knuckles.

"I'm not asking how you knew we planned to come here. I already know. You eavesdropped." Penny's face reddened to equal her frustration.

"But why are you here?" Kat finished Penny's sentiment.

"I told you." Ronan slipped his coin into his pant pocket and extracted a short, crooked stick from his jacket. "You need me." Ronan held the wooden implement in the direction of the museum's entrance, aiming at the lock.

"What are you doing?" Sam spat.

"Unlocking the door," Ronan answered.

"With a stick?"

"It's a wand. More specifically, an Acacia Koa wand," Ronan explained as he drew an invisible triangle and added an inverted triangle in the same space.

"A magic wand?" Kat asked.

"Yes," Ronan answered. He smiled softly at Kat. "I suppose I would be called a wizard, and this is my magical wand." Then, with a quick whip and a stab at the air,

Ronan's wand undid the lock, and the museum's old door squeaked open.

"A wizard?" Sam asked, snorting as she laughed.

He pushed the door open and gestured for the three to enter. "Yes, a wizard, and had you not slammed the door in my face earlier, we could have been properly introduced."

Penny entered the museum first and purposefully broke their tradition of entering together. The chance of another portal activation was a risk she was unwilling to take. Sam eagerly followed her oldest sister. As Sam passed through the held door, Ronan whispered they needed to stop meeting this way. Kat tailed in last and smiled at Ronan.

"I'm Katrina Hale, but everyone calls me Kat."

"My pleasure, Miss Hale." Ronan bowed in front of her, and she giggled.

"The taller one near the back with red hair is our oldest sister Penny. Her real name is Penelope. And the mean one," Kat said, as she pointed at Sam, "is Samantha or Sam." Kat glanced down at her feet. She wiggled her toes inside her shoes.

"I find it interesting that you are sisters because you don't resemble each other. One red head, one black-haired, and you..." Ronan paused, tempted to touch her hair. "You're blonde."

"Yeah, I know. Weird, right?" Kat said.

"Yes and no. Weird for the general population, I suppose. But you three aren't part of the general population, are you?" Ronan slid his wand back inside his jacket.

"We're triplets," Kat added.

"Triplets?" Ronan replied. He pretended to be surprised.

"Did you have to learn magic, or have you always been a wizard?" Kat asked.

"He's not a wizard, Kat." Sam inserted herself between Ronan and Kat. "More like an amateur magician. Probably a con artist. I'm sure he picked the lock before we got here."

Kat gave Ronan a sympathetic look as she stepped away and left Ronan with Sam. Kat tried to avoid Sam's wrath at all costs. Besides, she wanted to do some of her own investigating. Kat touched the wall where the iron bars had once been. She could sense the wall's age; they were built sometime in the early seventeenth century after the new stone jail was built, and this place became a private home—the Isaac Lord House. Kat stood in the place where she and her sisters stood imprisoned that same day. She ran her hand along the various pieces of furniture and gleaned that the items belonged to the Lord family's private collection, left at the museum's disposal for their displays.

She exited the former cell and strolled over to Penny. "Do you detect the same energy you did this morning?"

Penny glanced at Kat. "No."

"Me either," Kat said. "Did you know this was the home of Isaac Lord?"

"Um, yeah." Penny searched her memories. "Why?"

73

"I just remembered that I guess." Kat pondered how and why this popped into her mind.

"I'm sure I told you at some point," Penny replied.

"Yeah." Kat picked up an old rusted key off the hook on the wall next to the building's backdoor. She stared at the key, mesmerized by its crackled surface, and wondered if it was the same key that unlocked the cell and freed them. No sooner had the thought run through her mind did a floodgate of memories rush into her. Not her memories, but another woman's memories— the woman she had possessed earlier while trapped in the seventeenth century—Kathryn's. She had been Kathryn Gutt, and her sisters where Prudence and Cherilyn. Their mother's name was Felicity Gutt, and she had given her maiden name to her daughters after her lover abandoned her upon learning she was with child.

Kat's mind raced as vivid details played in her head. She recalled the jail where they were kept. They were dragged against their will from their home. When the constable from Salem had gone door to door, demanding the names of any persons suspected of the practice of witchcraft, a neighbor accused the three. The witch-hunt was at its height, and the town they had faithfully served and loved had turned on them. Kat fell against the wall. She saw the key slip in the lock and a man who looked like Ronan holding the cell's door open. The women ran toward the jail's entrance. They hoped for freedom and turned to the right toward the docks. Their bare feet pounded against the dirt and rocks, scraping the skin of her soles. Cherilyn ran toward Robert. The three were almost free until someone's hands grabbed her from behind.

She fell to the ground hard. Her arms twisted behind her as a rope entwined both of her wrists. She writhed and kicked at her captor, but the man was too strong. There would be no escape for her this time. Penelope's screams pierced her ears, and she witnessed her sister receive the same unfortunate fate as her. Then she turned to see if Cherilyn had made it to Robert. She had, but her sister railed against Robert's hold. She screamed as she tried to break free, her voice silenced by his hand held against her mouth. Her words were trapped inside.

Kat was grateful one of them made it, and she felt blessed Cherilyn wouldn't be alone. If Robert hadn't held her, she knew without a doubt that Cherilyn would have screeched their names and, in doing so, directed the evilness of the hunt her way. Kat gasped at these revelations and slid to the floor of the museum.

"What happened, Kat?" Penny pulled her sister back to her feet.

Shaken, Kat shook her head, still foggy by her vision. She looked at the key and threw it from her hand. "That key," Kat stammered, "when I picked it up, our fate unfolded before me."

"You had a premonition of you and your sisters?" Ronan asked as he and Sam joined Penny at Kat's side.

"No, not of our fate. The women in the jail." Kat wept.

"Psychometry?" Penny asked.

"It appears so," Ronan said. "And you three were unaware of this gift?"

"Yeah," Penny said. "We were unaware that we were even witches until about ten hours ago."

"An amazing gift. The ability to discern information from objects is outstanding." Ronan placed his hand across his mouth in deep thought.

"We shouldn't have left them," Kat announced. "They died because we deserted them. We just left them there to burn in the town's square."

"They didn't all die," Penny stated, "if they had died, we couldn't be here. The Grandfather Paradox."

"What are you talking about, Penny?" Sam asked.

"If all three of them had died in Ipswich as witches, we couldn't be here. They are our ancestors. We wouldn't exist and therefore would not be alive to go back in time."

"I understand that, and I know you said our family tree showed Cherilyn had one daughter. She's our ancestor," Kat said, "but what about her sisters? We could have saved them. Maybe they wanted marriage and children too."

"Impossible." Ronan retrieved his coin from his pocket. "Not the part about potentially saving them, but about the other two sisters and children. It's not how this works."

"How what works?" Sam glared at Ronan.

"How being a Trinity Witch works," Ronan said. He tossed the coin into the air and caught it before instinctively rolling it across his knuckles.

"A Trinity Witch?" Penny asked.

"You girls are the current generation, the incarnation of the Trinity Witches." Ronan waited for their reaction. He remained uncertain if they would become empowered by this or remain resistant.

"I never heard of the Trinity Witches," Sam countered. Maybe all this information would be a bit more interesting, she thought, if she wasn't the middle sister and expected to carry on their family's legacy.

"I have." Penny's eyebrows furrowed as she tried to recall exactly where. "I think I read about them in Dr. de Laurence's A Precise History of Magic. The title is much longer, but I think I read about the Supreme…"

"The Supreme Sublime?" Ronan finished her sentence.

"Yes," Penny said, puzzled that he knew this too.

Ronan moved to a larger open space that allowed him to pace again.

Penny put her arm around Kat. "Listen, if it makes you feel any better, the witches weren't really burned. Burning at the stake is a myth, at least in America. They would likely have been hung from a tree, and their bodies dropped into the ocean."

An image of a woman's body cut from where it hung from a tree and dropped to the ground like a hundred-pound bag of potatoes filled Kat's mind. The poor dead woman's body was kicked and pushed over the edge, where it bounced off the rocks along the stony cliff as gravity plummeted her battered remains into the salty water. "That really doesn't help," Kat replied.

Penny added, "The Ipswich jail only housed Salem's overflow of the accused." She combed her hair behind her ears with her fingers. "In fact, only twenty individuals were executed. Actually, one died from a torture procedure. They piled rocks on top of the body until either the accused confessed or died."

"Well, two of us were two of them. Do you want to know what really happened? Then help me find my diary. That's why we're here, isn't it?" Sam said.

"Your diary, yes, that might prove quite useful," Ronan recalled Sam's past life and that she had held a handmade journal.

"You're still here?" Sam glared at him. "And stop playing with that coin. It's annoying."

His eyebrows furrowed, and he glanced at Kat, his only ally. Kat mouthed, "I told you she's mean."

An abrupt crash of glass broke in shards and rained down on the floor.

"Sam?" Penny and Kat said together.

"What?" Sam snapped, "I found my diary." Sam reached into the artifact case, pushed aside the logs of marriages, christenings, and deaths recorded by the town, and tugged her diary out from under them.

The museum's alarm suddenly squealed.

Penny covered her ears and yelled that they had to leave before the police arrived. Ronan grabbed Kat's arm, and they headed for the front entrance. Kat spun toward Sam and told her to come on, but Sam just flipped through the pages of her diary.

"Let's go, Sam," Penny ordered.

Sam shoved the dairy into her shirt. She tucked the hem into her pants to secure the book in place. Penny and Sam followed Ronan and Kat.

Ronan stopped as he reached the door. Chills ran through his body, a warning sign not experienced in a long time.

Penny cried out, "NO. That way isn't safe."

"You can sense that?" Ronan asked.

"Yes, something is out there," she said. Penny's whole body quivered with chills.
The alarms continued to blare.

"We've got to get out of here. Follow me." Ronan remembered the back exit he had used in their past life. First, he had to lead them to safety; then, he would figure out the evil presence he and Penny had felt.

Penny and Sam hesitated, uncertain of Ronan's intent.

"Come on," Kat pleaded. "We can trust him; besides, we don't have a choice now."
Kat was right. Ronan was their only hope. They needed him to get out of there. So the four of them ran out the back door

and escaped the alarm of the building. They ducked behind an alley garage. The blinking red and blue lights flashed in the dark.

"We can't go to our house," Kat said. "The police can see us if we go in that direction."

"My house is just down this block. If we cut through the alley, we'll come out right by my root cellar," Ronan encouraged." We can hide there."

"This just keeps getting better and better." Sam ran behind Ronan and Kat. She looked over at Penny." Don't you think this whole day has been a little coincidental? And now, we're following some strange albino-looking guy to his cellar."

"I admit I don't relish following him to his home." Penny ignored her inner sense that another untruth had just been told them by their new friend, "But, we've got to get off the street."

"Oh, we'll be off the street, alright. After he chops us into a million pieces in his basement and throws our body parts out with tomorrow's trash."

Penny wondered if the evil she had sensed as they escaped the museum might have been her perception through Ronan's veil of deceit. What if it were *he* that was the evil? What if he was lured to some secluded place to do horrible things?

"Over here." Ronan darted into a backyard just out of the street lamp's glow.

Kat readily joined him. "Come on, you two," Kat said in a whispery yell.

Penny and Sam glanced at each other as Ronan held open the door to the underground cellar attached to a house draped in utter darkness.

Chapter Seven

The Order of the Nine Illuminations, 2763 A.D.

E dward, the Order's astrologer, and soothsayer, rushed through the catacomb halls until he reached his private chamber. His hands trembled as he wiped the dust from the ancient chest and exposed the lock. Edward pulled the dark braided cord from around his neck and drew out the key tucked under his fern-green robe. He opened the box and dug through his most revered divination tools contained within.

Edward located the sought item; he removed the black velvet pouch from the container. He pulled the gold drawstrings revealing several gemstones. Edward poured the rocks out on top of his cot. Twelve beautiful stones shimmered under the torches flame. He nudged each stone away from the others. Their energy needed separate space. The stones represented the nine areas of life, plus a stone for the sun, one for the moon, and lastly, one which signified magic itself. They comprised his collection of ancient lithomancy stones.

He couldn't remember the last time he had used this divination tool. Edward held each stone and meditated on its frequency. First, he picked the piece of light honey-colored transparent Citrine, the Golden Ray Stone, and held the specimen in his hand. *The power to create and the power to destroy,* he whispered to the stone. He placed the sun's stone in the pouch and took the moon's stone in his hand. *The unseen.* He carefully released the piece of translucent olive-colored Moldavite into the pouch. Next, Nuummite, the Sorcerer's Stone, was selected. He held the opaque blackish stone. *Magical influences be shown.* This was added with the other two stones, and he gave them a moment alone. He added the nine stones for the areas of life: Pyrite, the Stone of Potential denoted the sector of success; Lapis Lazuli, the Stone of Knowledge; Malachite, the stone of celestial influences which cleared one's path; Shungite, the Great Purifier for health; Peridot, the Manifestation Stone for the wealth and abundance sector; Obsidian, the balancer of ego and determinate of fame or infamy; Emerald, for creativity and communication; a Ruby, the Stone of Venus for divine love. Edward gazed at the last lone crystal. He held the hunk of clear crystal quartz to his lips and whispered, *enhance the powers of each of these stones, let the fate of man be revealed.* He slid the crystal into the bag, pulled the golden cords tautly, and raced back to Abraham.

The formidable yet old mystic lay prostrate across a stone slab, only comforted by a worn patchwork of fabric meagerly stuffed with straw. This was his mattress. Edward had asked the old man why he refused one of the cots like they slept on. Abraham always answered the same; comfort comes from the mind, not the bones. At his side knelt Jacob the Initiate, whose forehead rested on Abraham's arm. At the end of the slab, Brianna sat and rubbed oil upon Abraham's bony, alabaster feet.

As Edward entered the tomb, Alexander gazed up at him with sadness in his eyes." He grows weaker."

"Shall we see what this means?" Edward held his sacred pouch out and moved toward the place where Abraham lay.

"Yes," Scarlet purred, "does death approach us?"

Edward stopped. He wanted to turn around and tell Scarlet how inappropriate her comment was, but he moved forward, still focused on his task. Matthew stepped toward Jacob and stood at the head of Abraham's bed. Bruno moved to flank the bed's foot. As Edward reached Abraham's side, Brianna tenderly released the old man's foot and scooted to the end. This allowed room for Edward to perform his divination.

"With Ronan's indefinite absence and demise which looms over Abraham, we must seek a new leader." The words rolled off Scarlet's tongue like a song.

"Scarlet!" Matthew's harsh glares and words scolded her.

"What? Did I get it backward? Is it Ronan's looming demise and Abraham's indefinite absence?" Scarlet taunted.

"You do understand; you're only a member of this Order because no one else has your gift?" Matthew spat.

Scarlet felt the lick of his words sting her soul. Her eyes eclipsed into total blackness. In contrast to her ivory skin, a ghoulish contrast was created." You want me to leave? That makes you happy, Matty?" She glanced at her sister Brianna, but Brianna looked down when Scarlet's eye met hers. Typical, Scarlet thought. She exited Abraham's tomb but hid outside the entrance. She desperately wanted to learn if the old man was indeed dying.

Edward raised his hands, indicating he was ready to begin. He knelt and drew a deep breath in, and slowly exhaled. Alexander approached Edward's side and handed him a piece of limestone. Edward reached for the piece of chalky stone without looking up, and with his left hand, he drew a large circle on the stone floor. He mumbled his incantation and sanctified the space inside the unending line. Edward rolled the pouch gently between his palms, which mixed the stones.

He formulated his question. "Is Abraham's time here on Earth short or long to last?" He poured the stones from the bag upon the old man's chest where they would align with Abraham's energy. Edward drew back. He was surprised by their placement. He glanced up at Abraham and hoped the old mystic's eyes had remained closed.

Abraham faintly smiled. "Go on," he coughed, "read the stones."

Edward gathered the stones and cast them into the sacred circle. "Don't move," he cautioned. The stones, finally, came to rest.

Jacob rocked, staring down at the rock which nearly touched his foot.

Edward closed his eyes as he divined the interpretation of each precarious placement. He took the limestone chalk and connected the stones. A small, inverted triangle was created around three stones, and the crystal quartz was contained in the center. Next, he drew a larger, upright triangle that housed the inverted triangle. That accounted for seven of the stones. He searched for the others. The Shungite rested in front of himself. Good, he thought, this stone provided confirmation that negative energy did not influence the stones. The Obsidian had taken its place at Jacob's feet, and the piece of Pyrite landed off to the right. Both still remained in the circle.

"The other two stones?" Edward counted the pieces he saw. "Locate the other two."

Jacob didn't move because Edward held one hand out in a gesture for his stillness.

Brianna slid to her knees and searched under Abraham's raised stone bed. Alexander scanned the floor's surface. She pointed under Abraham. "There! The dark charcoal one." She gazed at the stone, whose appearance changed from dark to reddish and back to a blueish-black.

"Nuummite," Edward said, "the Sorcerer's Stone."

"It fell outside of the sacred space," Brianna said questioningly as she dreaded the ominous sign.

"Yes. Now, where is the..." Edward was interrupted by Scarlet's reentry into the tomb.

"Moldavite?" Scarlet raised her palm to display the flat, transparent, and dark olive-green piece of stone.

"Edward jumped up. "The Moldavite went to you?" he asked the demonologist.

"Yes." Scarlet plucked the stone out of her palm with her other hand and sauntered toward Edward. "Is that a problem?" She dropped the stone in his outstretched hand.

"It is my moon," Edward stated. "It represents the unseen."

"So?" Brianna wondered how the stone had moved such a distance without notice.

"So, there is something we are not seeing. Something about your sister," Edward explained.

"Sounds like an inquisition is about to start right here," Scarlet said. "Where's good old Ronan when we need him?" Her sultry voice dripped with wantonness. "The only unseen things around me are my daemons. I'm happy to summon one or two if you want to see for yourself."

"Scarlet!" Matthew implored.

Jacob, unable to contain his own uncertainties, blurted out, "What about this one? The one at my feet?"

"Edward, please. Give us the reading," Bruno pleaded.

"Yes, the inverted triangle is male, and in this case, it represents man. Citrine, Malachite, and Ruby hold the three points. The interpretation is one of celestial influence, acting in accord with divine love, to bring about—to bring about destruction."

Everyone gasped, though each of them secretly feared those words were destined.

"The upright triangle is feminine. Peridot, Lapis Lazuli, and Emerald hold the points; Abundance of knowledge communicated herein as the creator swallows the manifestation of the man we have known as Abraham returns to Source. The time for his transition draws near. The Quartz crystal, lying in the center, quickens and amplifies the nearby stones."

The tomb fell silent as each member pondered the implications of Abraham's foretold death.

Jacob jumped to his feet. "This one?" Jacob plead. "What about this one?" His toes nervously danced as if the stone contained enormous heat.

"Obsidian, Jacob." Edward pointed at the stone. "The one at your feet portends a fate for you which either brings fame or infamy. I suppose this depends on your ego."

"The boy has no ego," Matthew said. "Are you sure there is no other meaning?"

Bruno, the Order's gemologist, stepped away from the foot of Abraham's bed and studied the stones for himself. "My specialty is not divination, but the meaning the stones hold, as told by Edward, is accurate." He nodded respectfully at Edward.

"Infamy? I cannot believe Jacob would do a dishonorable thing. Not ever," Brianna said.

"The last stone? Fool's gold, is it not?" Alexander asked, "What of it?"

"Pyrite is the protector of the physical form." Edward walked over to the circle's right and joined Bruno and Alexander. "Again, with the position far removed from the cluster of stones, the meaning is like reading a tarot card in reverse position. Here the stone no longer heals. It no longer aids in manifesting the organic matter we see as his body."

"Then it's final. Abraham dies, Jacob takes over, and his ego blooms to match Machiavelli's." Scarlet almost sounded pleased. She stepped through the stone's circle and knelt at Abraham's side. Their eyes met, and Abraham reached out. He shook as he placed his hand on her cheek. She immediately cupped his hand with her own.

"Pretiosam," Abraham uttered. "We are each a light that the Divine can only bare to be apart from for so long. My Earthly flame grows dim but now shines brighter than ever in Heaven."

Scarlet raised the old man's hand, and his purple sleeve slipped, exposing his bone-white skin. She kissed the back of his hand and watched his eyes draw away from her gaze as he fell seemingly into deep thought. She stood and revolved around to face her fellow members. Scarlet sensed their faith wavering.

"Is he dead?" Brianna wiped her sniffling nose.

"He's asleep. Let us leave him to his rest." Scarlet exited the tomb and headed for the meeting chamber.

"What is pretiosam?" Brianna whispered to Bruno as they walked to the tomb's doorway.

"It's Latin," Bruno replied. "It means precious one."

"How noble of him. I suppose God must love the Devil in the same strange way. After all, he created him," Edward posed after he overheard Brianna and Bruno's conversation.

"If you believe in that old way of thinking," Alexander joined in, "seems to me that might be the greatest illusion of all."

***

Scarlet dashed down the corridor. The speed at which she ran parted her crimson robe, exposed her slim milky-white legs, and threatened to reveal the secret sigil at the top of her left thigh. If she got to the conclave quickly, she would have the privacy needed to conjure. She pulled her sash tighter to hold her garment in place, but honestly, she would have preferred to let it drop to the ground. She became most empowered when she was naked.

She entered the dim space and lowered herself to her knees in the center of the room. Scarlet traced her middle finger clockwise through the dusty grit layered on the limestone floor and produced a circle. "I conjure thee," she said as she completed the circle. She drew the daemon Morail's seal as she said his name aloud. The symbol consisted of a smaller circle with a line drawn from left to right that extended beyond this circle's edge. She drew a line straight down upon this extended horizontal line and made a prone cross to which a half circle bound a smaller cross that touched the small circle. She added a half circle within the shape on top of the horizontal line. Then at the midpoint, a tiny circle was placed and appeared like a drop from its end. To the left, on the outside, a shape was drawn like a child might draw a bat, except it was upside down, with a cross contained within. Finally, three crosses were added across the design's top, and three inverted crosses hung from the bottom half. "Make visible to me what I desire to see." She held both hands upward and opened in a gesture of receptivity.

The daemon Morail always appeared invisible, but she knew he had acquiesced to her request as soon as the dirt and sand within the circle began to swirl around. It pushed upward and formed a tornado-like dusty silhouette of the gigantic beast. "I command thee, Morail lifter of the immense and weighty veil, make visible to me the human Ronan Magus."

From the center of the seal, the summonsed spirit stood still. Without warning, the dusty form zoomed across the circle. Dust and sand plummeted to the floor at the circle's edge, bound by the circle's spell-cast shape. As the earthen matter fell, a wind gusted through the boundary straight for Scarlet. Her hood flew backward off her head as the wind rushed toward her. Her hair billowed in the current. She squinted her eyes and tightened her lips as she held her breath. The strength of the air's stream turned her head ever so slightly to her left. Her robe blew open and uncovered her sigil. Involuntarily, her hand clasped over it to conceal the inked design of a circle with a dot flanked by mirror images of two crescent moons. Around the center dot, encased by the circle, were the ancient triskelion triple spirals. Scarlet bore the seal upon her thigh of the most ancient goddess—the Creatrix Asherah.

Angered that the daemon might have exposed her secret sigil to the members of her order, she opened her eyes and glared at the invisible daemon she sensed. When her eyes met his, a vision flashed in her mind. Ronan stood in an ancient library. Beside him was a young blonde girl. The vision swiped drastically right and panned the library—A red-haired girl held an ancient manuscript like the one's Abraham transcribed. The vision panned left and showed a black-haired girl. Three females. A blonde. A red head. And one with raven-black hair. Ronan was with the Trinity Witches. Scarlet instantly intuited the black-haired one was the middle witch.

Scarlet hurried to her feet and swiped her foot to obscure the sacred cast circle. "Go in peace to the places where you dwell. Go in peace until beckoned with my spell". She knew the others would follow her because she had planted the seeds of doubt deep within their thoughts. Now, it was a matter of time.

Brianna ran into the tomb. "Do you know something about Ronan? Do you know why he hasn't returned?"

For a second, Scarlet feared that somehow, Brianna sensed what she had done and what she had seen. That would be impossible. Only she was consort to the daemon spirits. "Of course not. Ronan would never contact me," Scarlet responded.

Edward, Matthew, Bruno, and Alexander entered the tomb together.

"Have any of you heard from Ronan?" Brianna begged as desperation hung in her voice.

The four men looked at each other. They denied with a shake of their heads that they had not been in contact with Ronan.

"I'm sure he is fine, Brianna," Edward said. "But this uncertainty you express concerns me."

"Yes, Brothers. I think I'm experiencing the same doubt and wonder if Ronan's return is insured. I question whether the Order can survive without him and Abraham." Bruno rubbed the back of his neck.

"Abraham's condition unsettles me," Alexander admitted. Although he had always believed that the Order's strength came from Ronan, the situation seemed to indicate something more disparaging. The truth was that Abraham held them together. Abraham bound them to each other by his virtue, faith, and his promise of a better life— one of salvation. Minus Abraham, the flock would inevitably find itself lost.

"Perhaps we are beginning to succumb to The Great Sleep ourselves," Bruno suggested.

"We have remained untouched by that plague of ignorance. Why would we be susceptible now?" Edward asked.

"The time line," Scarlet said, "with more alterations to history, who knows where we find ourselves moment-by-moment." Her thoughts returned to her vision of Ronan with the witches.

"We can't allow ourselves to forget. This is our one task—our sole purpose for being," Matthew urged.

"We won't let ourselves forget," Brianna said. She understood it was against the Order's, well, Ronan's code, but she felt they had no other choice. "We must practice magic," Brianna said, "every day, we must practice so we don't forget."

"Fantastic idea, sis. My necromancy skills could be honed. What a perfect idea. You never know when we'll need to ask a dead person a question or two." Scarlet grinned; with her insinuation, she could talk with Abraham that way soon.

"We only use magic when necessary. Magic is not a plaything for our entertainment," Matthew scolded. "We study the sacred texts. Nothing more."

"To be fair, Matthew, magic was relegated to illusions and sleight of hand. In fact, secret knowledge lays hidden even in ordinary playing cards," Alexander corrected.

"You know what I mean, Alexander. When done every day and without purpose, magic becomes an act without meaning—a mindless ritual, and we become no better than those asleep." Matthew moved toward the tomb's entry.

"You can remain on your high horse if you believe that serves the Order best, but for me, I'm doing whatever it takes to keep my powers." Scarlet glared at the back of Matthew's rosy velvet robe. The color of compassion. What a joke, she thought.

"What is it that you suggest? We kidnap surface dwellers?" Edward asked in jest.

Matthew ignored him and continued across the room.

"Oh, I hadn't thought of that. What a wicked idea." Scarlet said. "I was thinking we should do away with our vow of celibacy and make our own initiates, but your idea would be faster. Not as much fun, but certainly faster." Scarlet glided across the floor intentionally toward Matthew. He would find her encroachment in his proximity disturbing. After all, he was still a man.

"We do none of this. The Order is fine. We simply get word to Ronan of Abraham's condition," Edward said.

"Fine," Scarlet said, "I will send a messenger to Ronan."

"No, I will summons Gabriel for the task." Matthew dropped to his knees and prayed for the aid of his angel.

"Your servants are no better than mine. Perhaps, they're worse," Scarlet spit. "Maybe I'm wrong, but I thought some of your angels disobeyed God. Didn't they sleep with human women?"

Chapter Eight

Ipswich, Massachusetts- Present Day

Ronan held the door open that led to his home's underground space and waited for the three girls to step down into his cellar together. A cool waft of air greeted them as the door creaked closed behind them. The musky odor of old books, their pages, the ink, the binding, and the glue all melded together and settled in the air with a particular scent only aged manuscripts could create.

"A library?" Penny asked. She marveled at the rows of books that surrounded them.

Ronan circled the room. He paused at each bronze, cast sconces placed evenly around the room, and turned every switch to the *on* position. The lights, one-by-one, threw a warm glow through the amber-colored cylinder mica shades and created a charming and cozy mood. "Yes," Ronan replied, "this is my study."

"In a dilapidated old house, you've got this amazing space in its cellar?" Sam questioned. She approached the bookcase nearest her and ran her fingers along the wooden shelf.

"I wouldn't say dilapidated. In need of repair, yes, but dilapidated? I started my restoration in this section first." Ronan sat at his massive mahogany desk, reached across the inlaid black leather top, and flipped the double-shaded lamp on. "All of this is very real," he said. He took a journal out of the drawer. "Look around," he added, curious about what books they would be drawn to. He opened his book and logged what had transpired so far.

"Clearly, the place is real. We're standing in it." Sam eyed Ronan. Something was off, but she hadn't figured out what. She glanced at Penny, who was enthralled by the number of antique books housed in the same place. Sam looked for Kat and found her sister had settled crossed-legged in an enormous brown leather club chair in the corner.

"Is this a copy of *The Discoverie of Witchcraft?*" Penny asked. Her finger hooked the top edge of the binding and tipped the book slightly down. She pulled the manuscript off the shelf and opened the cover. She immediately turned to the publication page. "1584?"

Sam wandered around the library and looked for the staircase leading into his home.

"You hold an original copy. Maybe the only original copy still in this world." A sadness tinted his words.

Penny read the seal on the brown leather binding. *The Society of Writers to the Signet.* "Original? This must be worth thousands of dollars." She placed the book back in its spot and lightly ran her fingers along the spines next to the rare manuscript.

"Seventy-six thousand last time I inquired," Ronan stated.

"The Hammer of Witches," Penny said as she read the title of another extraordinary find.

"*Malleus Maleficarum*, or Hexenhammer in German," Ronan said. "Please, pull it down and take a look. Published in 1487. Quite remarkable, isn't it?"

Penny continued her exploration. "*Invectives Against the Sect of Waldensians*," Penny read out loud. "I've never heard of this one. What is it?"

"A precursor to the Hammer of Witches. Published in 1460, originally in Latin. That one is in medieval French, published in 1465. Take it down. One of the first illustrations of the infamous witch riding a broomstick."

Penny examined the faded title. Her fingers moved to the discolored hue on the corners of the worn leather. She didn't take the manuscript down; instead, she continued her scan. Her hand stopped before she touched a blackish, leathery-like bound book with curled edges. She turned and glared at Ronan. The sourness rising in her throat became harder to stop from coming all the way up.

Sam and Kat hurried to Penny's side. They sensed their sister's fear. Kat immediately focused on the black-bound spine. She reached her hand out, prepared to touch it.

"DON'T!" Penny remembered Kat's newly discovered gift of psychometry. "Don't touch it." She didn't want Kat to experience what she had learned through her claircognizance.

Kat froze as she stared at the ancient book. Then, without warning the others, she thrust her hand forward and contacted the spine. She stumbled backward. "It's— human skin," Kat uttered.

"I'm sorry, Kat," Penny said, "I told you not to."

Sam turned toward Ronan." Who the hell are you?" she demanded.

"I told you. I'm a wizard, and I'm here to help you."

"Help us? You mean help yourself to us. What? Are you planning on binding more books after you skin us?" Sam stepped backward, stood in front of her two sisters, and stretched her arms out to her sides in a protective gesture. "I won't let you hurt them!"

Ronan stood. "I wouldn't hurt you." He moved closer to them.

Sam's arms instinctively pressed back on her two sisters. Penny leaned in a whispered to her that Ronan did speak the truth. Sam glanced over her shoulder at her oldest sister and winced.

"Maybe you are being truthful, but you haven't told us everything. I may not have the gift of clear sight like Penny, but I can tell that much," Sam pointed out.

"You're right," Ronan began, "I'm not from here. I didn't even know about you three until..."

"Until you helped us escape the jail in 1692," Kat revealed that they knew it had been him who had unlocked their cell.

Ronan cut his eyes from one glaring sister to the other. The time had come to reveal a bit more. "It *was* me in the jail."

"But how?" Kat asked, "Did you come through with us?"

"You three crossed through my time portal."

The three girls looked at each other.

"Kind of freaky, really," Ronan explained, "you must have passed through at the exact moment, well before my portal closed."

"Why were you time traveling to 1692?" Penny asked, uncertain why the knowledge of these events eluded her.

"During my travels, I learned of the Trinity Witches and their incarceration in the Ipswich jail. I couldn't let them be executed for witchcraft."

"But we were executed," Sam spat.

"No," Ronan corrected, "they were." He pointed to her sisters." You escaped—that incarnation of you. She gave birth to the next generation that would birth the next set of Trinity Witches."

"So, if all three had died, you feared magic might have ended in the seventeenth century?" Penny pondered the possible outcome.

"Precisely. It was fortuitous to have witnessed your presence in those three women's bodies in the jail."

"About that," Kat asked, "why were we trapped within their bodies, and you were there as yourself?"

"Time travel is a bit tricky. I have learned from experience not to enter a time period in the exact location an incarnation of myself might be present. When that happens, the traveling soul enters the existing soul's corporeal form, and they share the space until one personality overpowers the other and takes dominance."

"Yeah, I noticed that about Penny and Sam," Kat agreed.

"I came and went. I wasn't totally lost like Penny," Sam reminded Kat.

"Why didn't I get overpowered? I mean, I was still just me," Kat asked.

"I'm not sure," Ronan said. "I suppose because that incarnation of you and this one must be very similar."

"I did feel the same." Kat agreed with his explanation.

"So, what's with all these books?" Penny asked.

"This is my private collection of books with any reference to magic or the occult," Ronan said.

"But you would have had to travel all over the world to get these original manuscripts," Penny said.

"And pay millions to get them," Kat added.

"Or, like I said," Sam concluded, "he's a con artist and stole them all. Isn't that right, Merlin?" Sam smirked at Ronan, wishing he played with his stupid coin right then, so she could make a dig about that, too.

"I have done no such thing." Ronan walked to the closest shelf and gazed at the books housed in that section. "These manuscripts, and a few others I keep at another location, are all that is left of magic in the world. They are facsimiles, but no one would be able to tell. The real ones are kept in a very sacred place."

Sam chuckled. "Forgeries? I told you; he's a con artist."

"He's serious, Sam." Penny knew through her claircognizance that Ronan had told the truth.

"And that manuscript..." Ronan gestured toward the black leather-bound book that began the whole uproar— "it was a common practice in the seventeenth century and eighteenth century to use human skin for the book binding. The practice is referred to as anthropodermic bibliopegy, and I agree, the whole thing is disturbing."

"There's more," Penny urged Ronan to continue his confession.

"I don't have any more information about the practice," Ronan replied.

"Not that," Penny corrected, "you said you must help us, and you have secured our way out of the jail, helped us break back into the museum, and returned us to safety here in your library after Sam stole her diary from the museum. And now, there is more help required? How?"

"I suppose, helping you figure out who you really are," Ronan said.

"Why?" Kat asked.

"Yeah, why do you care?" Sam added.

"Because," Ronan paused to formulate his thoughts, "I need your help in return."

"There it is," Sam announced." Always an ulterior motive, isn't there? You guys figure this out. I'll wait over there." Sam walked over to the desk and sat on the opposite side from where Ronan had sat earlier. She pulled her diary out from her inside her shirt, where she had tucked it for safe keeping when they fled the museum.

Kat joined her, and Ronan followed closely behind her. "Well, read it to us. We might as well hear what happened to them," Kat said. "Penny, come over here. Sam's about to read from her diary."

"Okay, be right there." But Penny continued to scan the titles of Ronan's masterful, creepy collection.

Sam opened the cover and read the page displayed.

I once followed my sister to the water's edge and hid within the bunches of switch grass. From there, I observed Kathryn work her magic by the brook. At first, she appeared mesmerized by the babbling water as she stared at the ripples; until the moment she decided to control it. I watched as the liquid obeyed her. It turned in upon itself in a spiral motion that matched the movement of her delicate finger. The water might have spun on forever had she not smiled upon it, at which point, the water opened itself up to her and created a smooth disk-

like scrying glass at its center. This is how she
prophesied. My sister holds the gift of hydromancy.
I wonder if I took her there now, could she see our
fate? Truth be told, I suppose we already knew our
fate.

Sam paused. She needed to allow some time, some
space between her past incarnation. She compassionately
relived the emotions she had encountered back then before
she continued:

If I close my eyes, flashes of our lives come to me.
Some memories are so sweet and tender, yet others
are too painful ever to fade. I should start, I
suppose, with the here and now as I sit bare of foot,
dirty, and in desperate need of a pint. No, ale won't
suffice. This predicament requires whiskey. We
three are accused of witchcraft. Nonsense, and to be
truthful, we did dabble with different spells when we
were young—turned toads to stone—made birds
float mid-air. Silliness. Child's games. Even as we
grew to be of age, and we three became versed in
brewing healing potions and were able to create
philters and the such, I swear, we three practiced no
darkness. We hold no communion with the Devil or
his like. Sure, we had made amulets and talismans,
but kill chickens by staring, make cows bleed at their

will in their milk, or cause the pastor's daughter to writhe and convulse? We had no hand. Ever.

We would have been shrewd to heed the words spoken to us by those much wiser, but alas, we had not. We practiced our craft in the open, and for the better part of our lives, we enjoyed liberty among our neighbors. They called on us for bodily cures, to mend their broken hearts, and for restoration of their barren wombs. Witchcraft? I say not. Why we three are nothing more than cunning folk, learned of herbs and the natural ways of the elements. No harm can be assigned to us. Even the toads I turned back from stone as a child. But to hold true knowledge; to understand the nature of truths; of God, this is a powerful thing. We embraced this blessing, while the average man, the man who claims belief in God, it is him that festers with fear and hatred; and allows jealousy into his heart, and his soul hath blackened with such diseased thoughts. Providence hath not brought this upon us; nay, it is the minister himself, driven by his own darkness, who wishes dead upon us. If an evil abounds in Ipswich, I say it is this.

Sam glanced up and saw that she had her sisters' and Ronan's full attention.

"Come on, Sam. Keep reading," Kat urged.

*I fear the unlovely truth is; I hath ushered our
situation through my unabashed attraction for
Robert. The young man, barely acquainted with our
small town, shared our home and, as the custom,
bundled with me. This is not peculiar in itself, and
many find that they have received a bundle of joy
some nine months later. But my joyful seed had been
planted months earlier, a secret I bore alone. Yet,
the next morning, as Robert and I strolled through
town, my seed sprouted forth and pushed my belly
out. This drew the attention of more than one.
Rumors abounded that I had conceived and grown
full term within yet a night. This apparent
abomination, along with my sisters' and my
inherited mysterious qualities, created within our
town a terrible delusion of witchcraft.*

Sam stopped. "I was—she was pregnant, but not by
Robert. Who was her baby's father?" Sam hadn't felt the life
within the woman's belly while she briefly shared the same
corporeal form with her. Still, it was a sobering realization of
what the three of them had learned because it was true. The
middle triplet bares the sole daughter who births the next set
of Trinity Witches. Sam's thoughts flew to her own mother,
the last sole daughter of a set of triplets. Her grandmother
Lyndia, like her, was destined to carry forth and birth a lone
daughter. Lyndia had given birth to her mother, Renee. "I

need a moment." Sam pushed the chair back and stood. Renee, their mother, was a single child and had given birth to the three of them.

"Okay," Kat posed a question to Ronan, "Let's say we are the Trinity Witches..."

"You are," Ronan interjected.

"We didn't understand that we were witches until today. We never learned how to be witches," Kat confessed.

"So, maybe you help us develop our powers?" Penny paused at the bookshelf near the partner's desk, where Ronan and Kat remained seated.

"I can teach you what I have learned, yes, but what I can't..." Ronan gestured to his extensive library, "you can learn here."

Kat jumped up and spun around. "I love it in here." She twirled over to Sam. "Don't you love it, Penny?"

Penny laughed. What she loved was Kat's playfulness. One thing was certain; they could always count on Kat to lighten the mood and bring joy back into their hearts.

"I do love it, well, all except that one disturbing book," Penny said. "Where do we start, and how do we become our full witchy selves?"

A book threw itself from the shelf and, with a thud, landed at Penny's feet. Kat, Sam, and Ronan each froze in place.

"Did that book just jump off the shelf?" Kat asked.

"Yes, it flew off the shelf straight at me." Penny bent down, grabbed the book, and noticed it had no title.

"Quick." Ronan rushed toward Penny. "Hold the book near your heart and bring it to the desk." Ronan cleared off the end of the desk covered with files and papers from earlier, forgotten work. "Now, place it, spine down, on the desk. When you are ready, let go and allow the pages to open. Close your eyes and allow your finger..." Ronan took her hand and steered her hand to the open book. "Allow your finger to scan these two pages until your hand seems to stop on its own."

Penny slowly glided her finger over the pages, allowing herself to relish the smoothness. She followed the page to the center, down into the crevice, and back up on the other side. She felt that the words were not printed text. "There." She stopped midway on the right-hand page. Her fingertip aimed at the word *possible* in a handwritten line. "All things are possible," she read.

"Your first lesson is Bibliomancy," Ronan exclaimed. "And brilliant. I've never witnessed the act myself, only studied how it should unfold."

Penny closed the book and caressed its earthen cover. "The raised symbol on the front," she said, tilting the book, allowing the lamp's light to define the shape. "This half-circle, or more like a mound, and three stalks grow from it. Each with a..." She tilted the book toward the light again, "with a bud or flower-like thing. In the center is, I guess, a stamen. No, that isn't right. The female reproductive part; the pistil emerges from it."

"Let me see." Ronan took the book from her hands.

"Hey," Penny protested.

"Do you know what this is?" Ronan didn't expect an answer. "Amazing. You asked where you should start to learn your powers, and voila, a book jumps off the shelf. But not just any book. The Trinity Witches Book of Shadows. Don't you get it? The three stalks are you three. From one comes three."

Penny grabbed the book from Ronan's hands and flipped through the parchment pages.

"Were you aware this book was here?" Sam asked Ronan.

"No, but a lot of things have changed recently, and... never mind." Ronan thought of the changes he had inadvertently made to history due to his Time Walking. "It's a personal joke," he muttered.

"This book is full of all kinds of information," Penny said. "It has a list of magical tools."

"Like what," Kat asked, completely intrigued. "What kind of tools do witches need?"

"An athame, a chalice, bell, crystals, stones, salt water, candles, feathers..." Penny read out loud. These items seemed quite ordinary to her. A knife and a bowl? Every kitchen has those. Crystals? Stones? So what, she thought. Candles? Something everyone has as well. "These are just common household items. How are these the tools of witchcraft?"

Ronan studied her. "I suppose everything is ordinary until we look closely and see the extraordinary, the Divine aspect contained within everything."

"Penny? Do you still not believe we are witches?" Kat asked. "That biblio-whatever was super cool, and this is our ancestor's book of shadows. Not some book by Abramelin the Mage or something obscure...."

As the last words left Kat's lips, a white feather tipped in black floated down from the ceiling and came to rest at Ronan's feet. His eyes cut to Kat. "Why did you say Abramelin the Mage?"

"I don't know. It just came out of my mouth," Kat confessed. She placed her hand over her lips as her eyes grew wide and pleading. "Why? What does it mean? I don't even know who that is. Is it a real person?"

"Abra-Melin the Mage was an instructor of sacred magic and a scribe of these sacred words," Ronan explained.

"Kat doesn't know who he is; in fact, I don't know anything about him either," Penny said. "Do you think the name is connected to the feather somehow?"

"Everything is connected. Everything means something." Ronan reached down to pick up the feather. "Like this feather." He held the plume before him, knowing in his heart it was an angel message sent by Matthew back home. "Enochian Angel Magic," he explained, "is a form of magic where angels are summoned to aid those working

God's will. A white feather with black connotes a change is coming, and I believe, because of Kat's words, the message of change is about my dear old friend and mentor Abraham."

"Is he like a father to you?" Kat asked.

"I suppose he is." Ronan softly smiled as he twirled the plume with his fingers. "Speaking of that, you girls have never said anything about your father."

"We have one, of course, but he left when we were little," Kat explained.

"Yeah, and we haven't ever heard from him. What a bastard," Sam said.

Penny turned away. Guilt welled. She hadn't told her sisters about the email she sent that morning. She hugged her ancestor's book close to her chest. Without warning, the memory of their third birthday replayed in her mind. Their father had gone to pick up the cake and balloons. She remembered her father waiting at the door for her mother. He kissed her forehead. Penny saw the smile on her mother's face as he turned away. She recalled the rich blackness of his hair right before he walked out the door. She couldn't recollect his face. Too much time had passed. But there was one thing she would never forget; he never returned. He never even called or tried to connect with them in any manner until today.

"Don't call our father a bastard, Sam. We don't even know him," Kat said.

"Exactly, and that makes him a bast..."

"Stop it! Both of you. Just stop it," Penny cried.

"You stop, Penny," Sam argued, "I'm sick and tired of you bossing us around."

"Listen," Ronan said, "to develop your craft, you cannot be at odds with each other. The Trinity Witches' power only works when the three of you work together. Go home and sort this out. I'm sure the streets are safe now. Besides, I need to check on my friend."

"May we keep the book?" Kat asked.

"Yes, of course. It is yours," he said. "Now, go home and rest."

The girls ambled up the cellar steps. Sam was all too ready to leave, and she pushed hard and thrust the wooden door open. The night air whipped her raven hair around her face. Penny and Kat were close behind her, bracing themselves against the forceful night air.

"Brrrrr." Kat lowered the cellar door back in place. "I wonder if he sleeps down there?"

"Why would he sleep down there?" Sam asked. "You sure are wrapped up in Ronan. By the way, did he tell us his last name?"

"I'm not *wrapped up* in him, Sam. I just meant because the rest of the house isn't renovated. That's all. And no, I don't recall his last name. Do you, Penny?"

"I'm sorry. What was the question? I was deep in thought about Mom." Penny's words lacked truthfulness. She had been considering whether or not she should tell them about the email from their father. But, if she did need to, she didn't know how she would.

"Does Ronan have a last name?" Sam impatiently asked.

"No. Well, of course, he does, but he didn't tell us," Penny answered.

"That's what I thought. Some weird guy shows up in our lives, and now you two can't stay away from him for ten minutes. Both your heads are lost in the clouds," Sam said.

"Sisters?" Penny said. "I need to tell you something."

Chapter Nine

"All charms must contain part of the person
for whom they are made."
The World of the Witches

"Y ou did what?" Sam pressed Penny to explain why she had lied to them about their father's attempt to reach them.

"You didn't have the right to speak for us, Penny." Kat's eyes watered as she mourned the lost opportunity to see her father after fifteen years finally.

"I'm sorry, but he hurt Mom so bad—and us, too, by leaving." Penny attempted to justify her actions. She looked down, and her hair fell forward, closing like curtains on a stage. With her face hidden, she stared at the floor. "It was hard for Mom to raise us on her own, even before she got sick." Penny glared at her sisters through the veil of her copper hair.

"I think you were more worried about how much he hurt you. You lied to us, your own sisters, and your actions didn't help the situation in any way. In fact, I'm not sure I can trust you anymore." Sam scowled at Penny.

"Why now?" Kat asked.

"Why not now? Penny always thinks of herself as in charge..." Sam's words were choked off by Kat.

"Not why did Penny lie to us, but why did our father reach out *now*?" Kat posed.

"I wondered that myself." Penny eyed her sisters a bit softer.

"I mean, it is kind of uncanny. The same day we discover we are witches, he pops into our lives." Kat waited for her sisters' replies.

"Do you think he wanted to lure us away from Mom?" Sam's expression turned to one of fear. "We've been away more today than we ever are."

"Oh god, do you think he did something to Mom?" Kat cried.

The three girls dashed down the street and across to the sidewalk. They ran as fast as they could until they arrived in front of their house. They didn't rest until they were inside.

"Come on," Penny called to Kat.

"Go," Sam said. "I can lock the door. And I'll check everything on this floor."

Penny and Kat nodded to each other and leaped up the flight of stairs. They took two steps at a time. At the top of the landing, they saw their mother's door was open. Penny looked over at Kat and froze. She always shut her mom's door and remembered that she had closed it that morning, specifically because Penny was always afraid her mom would wander out into the hallway and possibly fall down the steps. Guilt swept over her. Sam was right; they had been gone a long time today. Penny ran into her mother's room and found Kat already there, standing bedside. "Mom?"

"She's okay, Penny." Kat gently brushed her mother's hair away from her mother's eyes with her hand.

Penny let out a long exhale as she sat at the foot of her mother's bed. "Thank God. This whole day could have ended horribly. I can't even think about it. I don't know what I'd do if anything happened to mom." Penny reached out for her sister's hand. "Kat? For what it's worth, I'm sorry I didn't tell you guys. About Dad, I mean."

"I understand. You don't need to worry about me, but you need to make it right with Sam."

"Yeah, you're right. Hey, stay with Mom for a minute while I prepare her tea, and if I see Sam, I will talk with her too."

"Okay." Kat lifted her mother's shoulders and repositioned the pillows behind her tiny frame. "Mom, guess what happened to us today..."

***

Penny took the stairs more slowly this time. She hesitated because she believed Sam would become hostile almost immediately. At least, Penny feared she would. Why should Sam forgive her? Penny probably wouldn't forgive either of them had they been the ones who had done the same thing. Then again, isn't that what you do when you look after someone's interest? Sometimes keeping information is the best choice, especially when the information is hurtful and doesn't serve anyone's best interest.

By the time Penny reached the kitchen, where she found Sam, she had convinced herself her actions were necessary. Penny would apologize for lying, but she wouldn't apologize for the choice to protect her sisters. She entered their kitchen.

Sam glared at Penny as she approached the center island. "Is Mom okay?"

"Yeah, she's fine." Penny paused to gather her thoughts. She went to the pantry to retrieve her mother's favorite tea and took the unlabeled, plain metal tin from the shelf.

Sam cut through their uncomfortable silence. "You don't need to say anything, Penny. I get it."

"You do?"

"Yeah, I do, but that doesn't mean I forgive you. You were wrong."

"I know."

"No, I don't think you do."

"I should have told you about the email."

"Yes, but the part that makes the situation so wrong is that you took away Kat and I's right to choose whether we have a relationship with our father or not."

"He's not a good person, Sam." Penny grabbed a tea cup and turned the stove top on to boil some water.

"I comprehend that. I think he sucks, but Kat doesn't see it that way."

"She said she forgave me." Penny turned away from Sam's penetrating glare and aimed her eyes toward the ceiling, hoping to prevent her tears from pouring out. Kat was the sweetest of the three of them. Maybe she was just being kind when she said she understood. It didn't matter. Penny did what she did for a reason. "He's up to something. I'm not sure what, but I sensed his ill intent," Penny said indignantly.

"Okay, sure. We'll go with that." Sam turned away from Penny to gather some herbs.

The teakettle whistled with a puffy cloud of steam.

"I'm right, Sam. I don't want us to get hurt," Penny said. She poured the hot water over an infusing spoon that held the loose tea leaves inside.

"Too late," Sam replied. "Except, you're the one who hurt us, not dad."

Penny exited their kitchen without a word and carried the hot drink upstairs.

In her mother's room, Penny placed the pink floral China cup with its matching saucer on the nightstand. "Her hair looks great, Kat." Penny admired the braids Kat had managed to weave into their mother's shoulder-length, mousy-brown hair. Short, wiry, gray hairs poked out near her mother's ears and curled in on themselves. "You even changed her nightgown." Penny sat on the other side of the bed.

"Yes, she wanted the solid pink one," Kat said, pretending that her mother had voiced an opinion. "Time for your evening tea, Mom," Kat said. She draped a hand towel across her mother's chest like a small child's bib.

"Give me her tea, please." Penny found difficulty releasing her role as the primary caregiver.

"Okay," Kat said. The thought just registered that her mom had to be a witch too. So, what had happened? Why didn't her mom's mother or her mom's aunts heal her? Weren't they Trinity Witches too? "Night, Mom." Kat bounded out of her mother's bedroom. If she was quick, she would have time to log in and read the email for herself. All she needed was the hotel's name or the address of where their father was staying. A lump welled in her throat, but she pushed her emotions aside. Their father could tell her what had occurred if she found him.

Sam stood at the bottom of the stairs and hollered up at her sisters. "Penny? Kat? Get down here."

Kat sprang up from the desk, closed the laptop, and raced to the landing, nearly knocking Penny over as they collided in the hallway.

"What happened?" Penny asked.

Kat shrugged her shoulders. Together, they took the stairs side-by-side.

"Sam?" Kat called out.

"Sam?" Penny bellowed as they searched for their sister.

They found Sam in the kitchen holding a huge basket.

"What's wrong?" Penny asked.

"We are. We're what's wrong," Sam replied. "We can't be at odds with each other if we want to come into our powers."

"You scared us to death." Penny rolled her eyes. "So, now you're taking Ronan's advice?"

"Well, he's right," Sam said.

"What are you doing, Sam?" Kat asked.

"WE are making a Witch's Chain."

"What?" Kat sat down at their table.

"Well, a spell of sorts. It would normally bind a male suitor to an intended bride. Instead, we're adapting the spell to bind ourselves together." Sam laid the greenery on their wooden farmhouse table.

"Adapt the spell?" Kat never considered this as a possibility.

"We are already bound to each other. We're sisters. We're bound by blood." Penny didn't understand why this ritual was necessary for them.

"We are bound by blood, and now, by choice." Kat looked over at Sam.

Penny's lips tightened. She was sure that the last remark was intended specifically for her.

"Exactly," Sam agreed. "Blood binds each generation together, but in *this* incarnation, we shall choose to link ourselves as one in this life."

She snipped a piece of holly near the end, where the branch was soft and pliable. Then, twisting it around on itself, she created a loop from the twig.

"Take a piece of holly and bend it to make a link. Then take the juniper and do the same thing, but interlock it with the first loop. Oh, wait. We have to attach an acorn at the end of each link. Like this, I think." Sam held a needle made from reed and threaded a length of white cotton string through its eye. "I soaked the acorns for a bit, so they should..." she paused, struggling to pierce the acorn's shell. "There, that wasn't too bad," Sam added the acorn in its rightful place.

Kat giggled as she gathered some greenery and began her own link. "You said we could improvise, right? Maybe we could make a binding spell with duct tape." Kat giggled again.

Sam and Penny glanced at each other. "Stop being silly, Kat. This is serious. Oh shoot, we need mistletoe berries too." Sam's frustration with Kat showed.

"Oh, let me make the mistletoe berry links." Penny grabbed one of the three pieces of reed Sam had laid on the table. She threaded the needle, selected a berry, and held it between her thumb and index finger as she punctured the miniature poisonous fruit. She gained a slight sense of pleasure as the reed moved through the round, soft, white sphere. "Why are we using these berries?"

"Supposedly, the holly tree doesn't cast a shadow, which would symbolize nothing left in the dark. For us, it represents leaving nothing unsaid—no resentments for any of our past actions," Sam explained stoically.

"Or inaction?" Kat asked.

"Yes," Sam said. "And the mistletoe follows along that same path by killing diseased thoughts. I read that European countries use injections of mistletoe to treat cancer." Sam continued to make her links.

"I thought it was poisonous?" Kat said.

"To animals, but it can be toxic to humans too."

"And this?" Penny pointed to the juniper.

"Christmas juniper signifies the Goddess Asherah," Sam said. "The acorn is lucky, but it also is about the feminine and masculine aspects."

"Where'd you find all this stuff?" Kat asked as she looped springs of juniper in links for the chain and connected her finished piece to one of Penny's. Next, she did the same to one of Sam's. "How long does this chain thing need to be?"

"Thirty-six inches, so if we each make our pieces about a foot long when we hook them together, it should be perfect." Sam realized she actually enjoyed the three of them working on a project together. She even enjoyed simply being in the same room. That was new for her. Typically, they each went off separately to do their own part. When each was done, they would meet and put the three pieces together. "Most of this stuff grows in our backyard. Thinking about it now, it did seem weird to me that mom had all these jars and containers full of all this crazy stuff. As a kid, I guess I didn't think it was weird. Sometimes, I collected my own things and put them into jars. I guess that's why I like plants and cooking," Sam said.

"And spell making," Kat added.

They laughed.

"But the real answer is that Mom has to be a witch, too," Sam stated.

"Yes," Penny said, "she has to be a witch, doesn't she? So, how did this happen to her?"

"I wondered the same thing when I braided her hair," Kat said. "I wish we knew how to get her back. You know, get all of her back."

The three of them stared down at the pointy leaves of the holly branches and the pile of juniper branches strewn across the old wooden table.

"What do we do now?" Kat stood and held the full length of their evergreen chain.

"We cast our spell while wrapping the chain around a log, and then we burn it in the fireplace," Sam said.

"Did you write the spell yet?" Penny asked.

"Nope, I think we should do this one together. Another way to symbolize our bond." Sam reached across the table and opened the ancestral Book of Shadows. "Any ideas?"

"I think it should start with something like..." Kat thought of which words to use, "linked together, we form a chain..."

"Wait," Penny said. "Sam, where's the log?"

Sam lifted a modest-sized log from the bottom of her basket. "Beechwood, which is excellent for Binding Magic." She offered the piece of firewood to Penny.

Penny held one end of their Witch's Chain to one end of the log. "Okay, begin to cast the spell as I wrap the chain around the log."

Kat nodded, and Sam placed her thumb on the end of the chain where Penny held it so Penny could use both of her hands to wrap it. Then, Kat began the spell, "Linked together; we form a chain. Three minds become one. Three hearts become one. Three spirits are bound forever as one. Wrapped in this life, we three shall always be as one. The chain destroyed; this bond can never be undone."

The three repeated the spell until the Beech log was adorned with the last link.

"So it is," the three said in unison.

Penny carried the log into their living room, and Kat rushed ahead to open the fireplace screen. After Sam laid the log on the grate, Penny turned the gas key to the on position, held a match to the invisible billow of gas, and ignited a flame. They watched the log with its evergreen chain burn intensely as the blaze consumed the wood and greenery. Acorns popped as the fire grew hotter, and the mistletoe drupes bubbled, melting into nothingness.

"It is done," Sam said. She plopped on the sofa and rested her feet on the edge of their coffee table.

"As simple as all that?" Penny asked.

"If it's not, it ought to be," Kat chimed in as she sat next to Sam. "So, now what?"

"I guess we..." An unexpected knock at the front door interrupted Penny.

"Who's that?" Sam asked.

"Ronan," Penny replied before she reached the door.

Sam rolled her eyes. "You mean Ronan and his damn coin."

Chapter Ten

"Magic is neutral."

The First Book of Natural Magic

S am leaned over and whispered to Kat, "Don't you find Penny so annoying when she knows stuff like who's at the door before she opens it?"

Kat smiled and giggled under her breath. The camaraderie between the sisters had been revived by casting a spell together.

Penny pulled their front door open, and the Witch Bells Sam had hung on the doorknob jingled. Their new and very pale acquaintance waited outside.

"A cloak," Sam said as Ronan stepped inside their foyer. "How Dungeons and Dragons of you."

"Dungeons and what?" Ronan pulled his hood from his head and undid the metal clasp.

"Never mind. Just a game people play here on Earth," Sam jeered.

"Okay?" Ronan's confusion over Sam's comment was replaced with curiosity over the scent hanging in the air. "Are you burning Beechwood, holly, and," he sniffed again, "juniper?"

"Why yes," Sam said as she walked toward him.

Her actions made him nervous, uncertain of what she was capable of doing.

Abruptly, she bent down and pulled the gas valve key out from the flange set within the floorboards next to him. Sam smiled a wicked smile at him, then turned to walk away.

"Juniper and holly? Did you three perform a spell?" Ronan asked with a tinge of panic in his tone.

"Yes," Kat said. "Why? Aren't we supposed to do witchcraft?"

"There's an awful lot to know before one carelessly performs a cast," Ronan said. Then, before the girls could respond, he added, "Did you cast a sacred circle first? Did you consecrate the items you used? Did you..."

"Okay, okay," Sam butted in. "No, we didn't do any of those things first. We're witches, aren't we? We just did it," Sam said.

"But you don't do this. You didn't even believe this before today," Ronan replied.

"So, is something bad about to happen to us?" Kat asked, with a look of concern. "Did we break some rules or something?"

"There aren't any, Kat," Sam announced, "tell her I'm right, Ronan. Rules don't exist."

Her eyes reminded him of the catacombs and how Scarlet's always turned darker when she was purposely cruel. "There should be rules. Like integrity. Like harming none. Like..."

"Like we do everything your way," Sam interjected.

"I think you need to learn a bit more about how all this works before you cast spells. Actions have consequences."

"They do, Ronan." Penny agreed with his sentiment, "Understanding this concept was what our spell was about. The consequences of my actions earlier today. I kept something about our father from them, and the secret pried a wedge between us."

"Well, what kind of spell did you use?" he asked.

"A binding spell to connect us three by choice and not just by our blood link," Kat shared.

Ronan sat on the chair next to the fireplace. "I shouldn't have acted so judgmentally, and I apologize. Let's start over. Everything is energy, and it is the very nature of energy to transform."

Penny searched her memory for the thermodynamic principles she had studied. "Yes, energy cannot be created or destroyed," she said.

"Correct," Ronan replied. "Yet, it can be transformed, and this concept is at the heart of magic."

"Isn't that alchemy?" Penny asked. "Are you speaking of Hermetic Alchemy?"

"Yes and no," Ronan answered. "Energy is all there is. The principles of Alchemy define how to transform energy. Magic is the art and the act of transforming energy."

"What are the principles?" Kat asked.

"Let's talk about energy first. It's crucial you truly understand everything is energy. Not just intellectually grasping the concept. I need you to integrate this idea within your very being. Look at the air. Can you see tiny particles moving? Can you see the air—the ether moving?"

The girls stared at seemingly nothing. Each tried to catch a glimpse of the mobile particles of air.

"Air appears to be nothing, but it is mainly made up of the gases like oxygen, nitrogen, and carbon dioxide," Ronan explained.

"This is rapidly becoming more boring than science class to me. I know, Penny...not for you. You love learning," Sam teased. "Besides, what does air have to do with magic?"

"I'm trying, I guess very poorly, to demonstrate not everything can be seen, and just because we can't see it doesn't mean it's not real. In fact, the things which are unseen are more real than the things you are seeing."

"Why didn't you say that? I get that." Sam glanced at Kat and made a circle motion next to her head with her index finger as she mouthed the word *crazy*.

"Ladies, you can look up more about energy later if you want to fully understand."

Sam rolled her eyes. "Thanks, Professor Ronan."

"Seriously, how can energy be manipulated?" Penny asked.

"Manipulation is an easier concept to comprehend. Once you understand energy, it can be manipulated into a blast or formed into a ball through the use of one's physical body or mind. Both of these require the skill to harness energy first. Alchemy, on the other hand, is based on a set of universal principles. Mentalism: everything is the mind.

Correspondence: the macrocosm and the microcosm reflect one another. Vibration: everything is in a state of motion. Polarity: everything consists of both a negative and a positive pole. Rhythm: everything ebbs and flows. Cause and effect: every effect has a cause, and every cause has an effect. Finally, gender: everything is both female and male in its aspects."

"And these alchemic principles are?" Kat couldn't sort all this information out quite yet.

"These principles are the tools used to transform energy." Ronan jumped up, overly animated in the gestures with his hands, and explained further. "Yes, like jumping rope. I observed children on a playground once."

"That's creepy," Sam said.

"Two children stood four or five feet apart; each held the opposite ends of two ropes. They swirled the ropes in contrasting directions, which created a huge cylinder of space."

Sam's face scrunched to a peculiar expression. "I've never heard Double Dutch explained quite so weirdly."

Ronan was too engrossed in his concept to allow Sam to deter him. "Not only did the children have to find the control to generate the rhythmic movement, but they also had to maintain it. In this manner, Mentalism is at work as everything is a thought first. Second, the microcosm of the ropes' movement reflects the macrocosm of the thought in the invisible realm of ideas. Once the ropes began to move, holding the continuous motion became easier due to vibration's nature: to inertia. Finally, cause and effect are at play as the effect of the rope moving is a direct result of the thought—the cause."

"You forgot the female and male principle," Kat said.

"One might propose that the rope itself is female in its dormant state and then male once it is moving. Conversely, the rope is male because it is a manifested thing within the world and no longer an idea or possibility waiting for birth. The concept would be female."

"So, how is this an example of the principles of alchemy?" Penny asked.

"Well, I tried to demonstrate how these principles are always in action," Ronan said before adding, "now, if you wanted to join in as the jumper, you need to use these same principles to enter the cylinder of space inside the ropes."

"I get it," Penny announced. "If I wanted to jump inside those ropes as they moved, I would need to align my vibration with the ropes. I would have to study the rhythm in my mind. My body would begin to match the rhythm, preparing me to jump in. I would also need to study the negative and positive space generated by the movement. As the rhythm ebbed and flowed, I would jump in one of the negative spaces between the actual rope, and if I had aligned myself properly, I would become part of the swirl of the ropes and move with them. However, if I didn't calculate correctly, the effect of that cause would be to trip on the ropes and stop their action."

"Precisely!" Ronan exclaimed.

"So, what you're saying is Double Dutch is magic?" Sam said. She wanted to laugh so bad she couldn't stop her mouth from pulling into a humongous grin.

"It certainly appears magical to anyone who hasn't mastered it," Ronan said. "I was quite mesmerized by the scene when I first saw it."

Sam burst into laughter.

"Sam, stop it." Kat nudged her sister with her elbow. "He's trying to help us understand."

"I can see that Sam doesn't like me." Ronan comprehended he had no business getting attached to the three girls, but somehow Sam's behavior stung his heart.

"She does like you," Kat said, afraid Ronan's ego had been hurt.

"No, actually, I don't." Sam stood and left the living room.

"I'm sorry." Kat apologized because she knew her sister never would.

"Perhaps I'm not the right teacher for you three. But I feel responsible for your unexpected visit to the seventeenth century. And, for how you learned who you are." Ronan snatched his cloak from the coat tree near their front door.

"Please don't leave," Kat begged.

"Ronan," Penny said, "We want you to stay. Sam too. Even if she won't admit that now."

His posture softened with their words.

Kat took his cape and rehung it on the same hook. "Sam does like you."

"Ronan, would you like some tea?" Penny asked.

"No, but thank you. I never developed a taste for it," he said.

"You like coffee, right?" Kat asked. "Oh, or were you just following us?"

"I do like coffee, but I did follow you three there."

"To trace the effect back to its cause?" Kat said.

"Exactly." Ronan grinned as a bit of pride crept over him. She understood his lesson.

Since no one wanted tea, Penny sat across from Ronan, who had taken a seat next to Kat on their sofa.

"If you don't mind me asking," Ronan said, looking across at Penny, "what happened with your father?" He moved his coin from one hand to the other with a magician's sleight of hand.

Penny was taken back at first and cut her eyes to Kat, who offered a sheepish smile and a shrug of her shoulders as a reply. Penny decided to tell him. "He left our mother when we were three years old. We never heard from him our entire lives."

"Until today," Kat said.

"What did he want?" Ronan asked.

"To meet with us before our eighteenth birthdays," Penny answered.

"The really weird part is that he is in Boston, and we were supposed to go there before the whole follow Penny into the seventeenth-century thing happened," Kat said.

"It was Penny who led you?" Ronan asked.

"I can sense energies, I guess," Penny said. "The otherworldly and dark kinds."

"Like when we both knew something bad was outside the museum?" Ronan asked.

"Yes, and the pull from your time portal," Penny said.

We need to make a list of your powers. For all three of you," Ronan said.

Kat grabbed their Book of Shadows from behind the sofa pillow next to her. "What? I hid it when he knocked on the door."

"Good. You three must protect the book. That is your Book of Shadows now," Ronan said.

Penny listed her known skills out loud, "Well, I know a bit about our family tree; I study history and theology."

"No, your psychic skills," Kat corrected.

"Oh, I suppose I sense energies. Is there a name for that?" Penny asked Ronan.

"Yes. Clairsentience is the sensory perception outside of our physical realm."

"Sometimes I know things I never learned," Penny said.

"Claircognizance is a clear knowing," Ronan explained. His brows furrowed as he thought how remarkable it was that their abilities had naturally developed without knowing they were witches.

"Oh, you also can tell whenever anyone lies," Kat blurted out.

Penny smiled at Kat but would rather have kept the information to herself. "I can." She eyed Ronan.

"Amazing, that kind of goes hand-in-hand with your clairsentience and claircognizance. Socrates called this elenchus—the ability to obtain truth through a series of questions that test the credibility of a statement. However, to know that someone is lying. That's something quite different. An intuitive empath is aware of when someone lies and knows their intentions. Sometimes the lie told is to oneself. Can you read those types of lies?"

"Yes, I can." Penny studied Ronan's expression. "Well, in other people, not when I do it to myself. I also become aware of one's motives that underlie someone's actions and words."

The room was silent as Penny and Ronan stared at each other. If this were a stare-off, Penny would win. She always won with her sisters, but the thought entered her mind that perhaps Ronan could read her. "What are your gifts, Ronan?"

Kat turned a curious eye his way and waited for his answer, too.

"Well, for one, I can open portals and Time Walk," he said.

"Right," Penny replied, "we've experienced that one. Any others?"

"As I said before, I'm a wizard."

"Yes, the wand. I had almost forgotten about that. What else can you do with your wand?" Penny asked. She watched Kat's eyes grow wider and felt her own face grow warm.

"I am learned in some aspects of Greater Magic," Ronan said.

"Greater?" Sam spoke as she returned to their living room.

Ronan glanced over his shoulder, his eyes fixed on Sam as she strolled into the room. She held an apple and bit into the ripe fruit. He smiled. The irony of the symbolism wasn't lost on him. "Glad you came back." He held his coin in his closed palm and waited for Sam to choose a seat. She plopped down in the only remaining chair and causally draped her leg over its arm.

"There is both Greater and Lesser Magic. The first is the practice of harnessing and focusing one's energy for a specific purpose."

"Like to open a portal?" Penny asked.

"Yes."

Sam glared at Penny. She searched for any sense of what had transpired between them while she had been in the kitchen. She looked over at Kat, and a cold sternness enveloped her as she noticed how Kat smiled at Ronan. Sam thought her sister looked like an obedient little puppy who waited for a pat on the head. Sam wouldn't allow Kat to win this guy over. If anyone got the guy, it would be her. Well, she didn't really want him. She just didn't want Kat to have him.

"What's Lesser Magic?" Kat asked.

"Manipulation through psychological techniques, like using wiliness or scheming to get the results desired. Even using superstitions to sway a person's actions is lesser magic," he said. "But, practical magic falls here as well because it is the use of things already manifested, like herbs, gemstones, or other objects, to focus one's mind or influence another."

"So, Greater Magic is the use of one's own energy to get a desired result, and Lesser Magic is the use of other people or things to achieve your desired result?"

"You're right," Ronan answered, "but the latter is primarily psychological in its effect. Like a magician or illusionist. The magician manipulates the environment to create his illusion, but in order for the trick to work, the viewer must be directed to look at something else, so they won't observe the trick." He opened his palm to reveal the shiny coin. "And for Practical Magic techniques to work, the targeted person must believe the magic can impact them." Ronan waited for this tidbit of knowledge to sink in with the girls. "Now, there is also a Left-Hand path and a Right-Hand path. The Right focuses on the mind-body-spirit connection and employs traditional rituals and practices. The left path focuses on breaking tradition, the things we consider taboo. It is for this reason that the Right-Hand path is considered white magic, and the Left-Hand path is considered black magic, but that isn't necessarily true."

"So, there really isn't such a thing as black magic?" Sam removed her leg from the chair's arm and placed her foot on the floor. She scooted forward, eager to hear what he had to say.

"No, black magic is definitely real," Ronan said emphatically. "White magic is geared toward helping, improving, and uplifting. Its use is considered selfless. In Latin, the term would be *Beneficium*. Like potion making, candle magic, talismans, or amulet making. Even alchemy and Elemental Magic. But, Black Magic— *Maleficarum* in Latin, is the selfish pursuit of one's own gain with no regard to the effect upon others. It has evil intent and is practiced in curses, blood magic, and possessions."

"But," Sam challenged, "if the potion is poisonous, that white magic is no longer white, right?"

Kat looked up. If she had to scratch out another passage she had just transcribed in their book, she would scream.

"All the types of magic could be used either way, so I suppose the best explanation of black or white magic is in the practitioner's intent," Ronan answered with a tight smile.

"This has been fun." Sam stood." I'm making myself a hot drink. Ronan? Would you like tea, or are you unsure whether I'm a good or bad witch?"

"I don't drink tea, but thank you for offering." Ronan stared, puzzled by Sam's constant need to jab, poke, and prod at everyone's emotions, particularly his.

"Suit yourself. The tea our mom drinks is delicious, and she loves it. Happy to make you one." Sam walked off pleased at her own success. She had unsettled him.

"Can we go back to our witchy skills list, please?" Kat asked, still holding her finger between some previous pages where she had started their lists.

"Of course, Kat," Ronan said. "What are your gifts?"

"Let's do Sam. She the middle one, so she'd come after Penny," Kat said.

Penny thought for a moment, then said, "Sam is our herbalist and an excellent cook. She is also well-learned on the subject of gemstones."

"Does she have any of the clairs? I believe there are six different ones. Claircognizance is clear knowing. Clairvoyance is an inner vision of the non-physical.

Clairaudience is an inner hearing of non-local communication. Clairsentience is clear intuition. Clairgustance is receiving information via taste buds. And Clairolfaction is receiving information via scents."

"Um, no. Not that we know of," Kat answered after glancing at Penny for confirmation. "What kind of smells? That sounds like a super gross gift."

"It doesn't have to be. Let's say your grandfather, for example, did he smoke?" Ronan asked.

"We never met our grandfather. Men don't seem to stick around for long in our family tree," Penny said.

Ronan's mind immediately went to Sam. If all the men met her first, and she acted the way she did toward him, he could see why they didn't stick around. "Anyway, if he had smoked and you had been close, then maybe you would smell his pipe tobacco. A sign that he was still near."

"Oh." Kat felt stupid for thinking the odors would be nasty and offensive. "Well, I don't think Sam acquired any of those, but you should probably ask her yourself."

"Yeah," Ronan said, imagining how that conversation might go. "Let's skip on to your page."

"Sure." Kat wrote her name at the top of the page and underlined it. "I'm good at—well, I like anything occult. Oh, I can use pendulums. I tried scrying once. I saw the moon on my first try, but after that, I never saw anything else."

"You got information in the jail museum when you touched the iron bars," Penny said to remind her little sister.

"Psychometry," Ronan stated. "The ability to read a place or an object through touch. I find this fascinating. I mean, there are things everywhere and..."

"And my hands are always with me," Kat said, interrupting Ronan's comment. They both laughed.

"Listen, the day slipped away from us. I should go. I stopped by because I wanted to check on you three." Ronan stood. He dropped his coin into his pocket. "You three are just fine, so..." He stepped next to the coat-tree and reached for his coat. He swung his cloak around until it landed on his shoulders and clasped the buckle closed.

"Why *do* you wear a cape?" Kat asked. "Sam's right; you do appear kind of weird."

"I don't know, just something my family has always done. Remind me to tell you about them sometime."

"And the coin?"

"Oh, something I learned in another life." He offered her a melancholic smile.

Chapter Eleven

"There are very great powers hidden in man, but because of the effects of which one can make unfair and unimaginable things, this knowledge does not exist in any book.

The First Book of Natural Magic

S am walked around the corner and rejoined her sisters in their living room. Suddenly, she acted like it was just any other night. "So, where'd the all-washed-out creepy run off to?" But she already knew. Sam overheard their entire conversation from the dining room, where she hid, tucked out of their sight.

"He went to check on his friend," Kat answered.

"I'm surprised you didn't tag along, Kat. You practically hang on his every word." Sam leaned against the living room wall. She hoped Kat took her bait.

Kat gathered the Book of Shadows and her pen. "I'm not interested in Ronan the same way you are."

"And what *way* would that be, Kat?" Sam taunted.

"Like liking him." Kat squeezed the book to her chest. "I don't like him like a boyfriend. I just like him, and I think he's interesting, kind of quirky."

"Sounds like you've got it all figured out." Sam pointed to the Book of Shadows. "Don't you need to add my gifts to *our* list?"

Kat looked down at the book. "What makes you think I didn't add them?"

"Well, I left the room, and you couldn't ask me. So how could you have added them when you're unaware of what they are?"

"You listened to us? Why? To hear if Ronan would say anything about you?"

"I'm not interested in ghost boy." Sam turned around, ready to exit the room. She wanted back inside her domain. The kitchen was the place she felt the most at home.

"Hello, remember me? I can tell when you guys are lying." Penny couldn't help but interject.

"Who's lying?" Kat and Sam said in unison.

"I don't trust him," Sam blurted.

"Well, that much is true," Penny said.

Sam stormed out of the room. She wouldn't listen to her sisters defend Ronan.

"She does like him, doesn't she?" Kat asked with a huge grin across her face.

"She certainly protests a lot for not," Penny said.

"I mean, Ronan's not the typical bad boy type she goes after, but I still think she feels something for him. Remember that last guy she dated?"

"Something with an S?" Penny asked. "Shawn?"

"Yeah, Shawn." Kat snickered as Penny let out a long sigh and rolled her eyes.

"There is something about Ronan," Penny said.

"I hope they get together. Ooh, maybe he's her baby daddy. You know the kid she's meant to have. The one that carries on the Trinity line?"

"Now you're ahead of yourself. Sam's pretty adamant that she doesn't plan on motherhood. Ever."

"She has no choice. She has to carry on the legacy. Wait and see," Kat said.

"I don't know. Ronan, he does hold back. She's probably right not to trust him too much. After all, we had only just met him. We don't really know anything about him or his family. I guess that's the part Sam's attracted to. She is self-destructive." Penny thought about the bad boy comment and the fact that Ronan held information from them. But she couldn't write him off yet. For some reason, like he kept saying, she thought they really did need him. She prayed, not for the reason Kat believed.

***

Sam dug through the Hoosier cabinet in their kitchen. Somewhere, in the mess of crammed papers and recipes torn from magazines, a notebook hid in one of the drawers. She always planned on straightening this cabinet.

157

Now, she wished she had just done it on one of those long nights when Penny and Kat were out on dates or had gone to a movie together, and she stayed home bored. Penny deemed herself the organized sister. And Kat? She had all the energy. Sam understood her place was somewhere in between. So, why was it her responsibility to purge everything?

"Yes," she said out loud. She struggled to free the soft-bound notebook. A part of her was filled with gentle happiness. She enjoyed it when they weren't at odds with each other, but another part believed it couldn't last. She would always be at odds with them at some level.

Sam took the notebook and grabbed a marker and a pen. She sat down at their farmhouse table. She flipped the book open. All the yellowed pages remained blank. Perfect, Sam thought as she wrote a title on the first page. *Samantha Hale's Herbal Grimoire.* She smiled, delighted in her secret book she had made for herself.

With excitement, Sam got up and ran to the pantry. She grabbed jars and bags of old and new cuttings from their garden. Some labels were old, and the letters had become difficult to make out. But somehow, as soon as Sam unscrewed the jar's lid, she recognized the aroma of the lavender as it filled her senses. The delicate purple flowers had faded, leaving only a hint of the natural living color. But she instantly knew the plant and its uses. If witches had a color, hers was green. She was a Green Witch, a Garden Witch, and a Kitchen Witch all rolled into one. This was her special gift, and she loved having it as her own.

She placed the jar of dried lavender on the table and wrote it down on her first page. *Lavender*. Then she drew a line under the word. *Relaxes the body and clears the mind. Brings love and happiness into one's life.* Sam supposed most people thought love brings happiness. Not her belief, though. A sensation swirled around her. A longing for something centuries forgot. She scrutinized the next jar's faded, peeled label. *Red Rose*. She studied the dried petals and their rosy-brownish color. *Love, lust, peace,* and *happiness*. Did these jars have a theme? *Courage. Healing. Health*. She took the jar labeled *Patchouli*. Again, the label read *love* and *lust*. She rifled through the jars. *Cinnamon: love. Witch Hazel: broken heart mend. Love. Dragon's Blood: adds power to love spells. Cornflower: love. Juniper Berries: love.*

"Argh," Sam uttered out loud. "Why did Mom have all these plants?" She stood, having given up on her Grimoire for the night. As she turned, her hand grazed across the tabletop and knocked her book to the floor. It fell between the table leg and the chair's leg, and the book wedged itself into an open position. She reached down to grab it, and as fingers touched the pages, a list of herbs, barely visible on the aged paper, caught her eye. Sam lifted the book to the light. "How did I not notice this before?" The list had been written in pencil, and now, upon a yellowed page, the letters were nothing more than shadows of their former words. "P-O-I-S-O... POISONOUS HERBS?" Sam thought she should throw the book away, but maybe it would be good to know which herbs to stay away from. She sat back down and traced each word with her pen. *Belladonna. Foxglove. Angel's Trumpet. Lilly of the Valley.* She paused as she recalled that Lilly of the Valley grew along both sides of their house. *Wolfsbane. Mistletoe.* Of course, she thought, Mistletoe was all over one of the trees out back. *Daffodil.* Those grew in their front flower bed under the living room window. *Hemlock.* Sure. *Mandrake.*

Sam put the jars back inside the pantry and took her book. Part of her wanted to go outside and examine all the plants which grew in their yard. She was certain she would find all these others and more. But why had her mom grown these plants? Was it for both—love and poison? Ronan's face popped into her mind. His soft white skin made him look like a porcelain doll.

He was perfect. Unblemished. His pale gray eyes mesmerized her when she looked into them. Maybe she had been too tough on him. She didn't understand why she always acted like an ass around boys. Plus, she didn't even know him, so how could she dislike him? He deserved a second chance.

Sam tiptoed upstairs and checked on her sisters. Both were asleep. She peeked in on her mother. Also, asleep. Sam snuck into her own room and hid her Grimoire under her mattress. But before she left, she stopped. "Won't hurt," she said to her book. She wanted to cast a protection spell over her Grimoire, but she feared that it required the power of three. Her sisters wouldn't understand what she was about to do, so waking them up and asking for their help was out of the question. She didn't need them for her herbal magic. "Think. What can I use?" The word Bergamot flashed in her head. "Yes, for protection." She didn't believe she had Bergamot in the kitchen. "Argh." Why would she even think about that herb if she didn't have any?

The image of her top nightstand drawer zoomed through her mind. She ran over and pulled the drawer open." What?" Sam didn't see anything. Then, just as she prepared to close the drawer, a shimmer, a twinkle of light, drew her attention. On the far-right side, next to a deck of tarot cards and a pack of gum, a glass bottle of essential oil waited for her. She picked the container up and tried to remember where it came from. "Oh, sweet." She danced, happy to have found what she needed. "It's from the new age market last summer." She unscrewed the lid to expose the silver roller ball topper. Her index finger dragged across the ball, oil glossed over it, and released the citrus scent of Bergamot, the earthiness of vanilla, and a hint of musky myrrh. Several other oils were added to the blend. She felt sure, but these predominate three would certainly act as a protective barrier for her book.

Sam scooted her mattress over and exposed her hidden book. She tried to remove the top completely, but the roller ball holder was stuck. So, she rolled the ball over her finger and wiped the oil on the box spring's fabric, but only a meager amount spilled out. She turned the bottle upside down and rolled the oil directly on the fabric in a manner that created a wet circle of protective oil. "Watch my book for me, okay?" She pulled the mattress back in place and headed down the stairs. Carefully, she closed their front door; Sam began her trek to Ronan's place.

She hadn't figured out what she would say to him, but hopefully, when she did think of something, it would be clever. *What if he slams his door in my face?* She'd deserve it, she thought, but she wouldn't allow herself to think about that now. She needed to focus her thoughts and steadily make her way back to the museum. She wasn't exactly sure where Ronan's house was, but she remained confident that she could find it if she went to the jail first.

Sam turned down the side street next to the museum and crept down the alley till she was behind it. "Okay," she said, "first, we went forward." She followed the path they had taken when they fled the jail. "Then, when we got to the next street, we darted off to the right and ran through a couple of yards." She stared at a vacant lot. "It should be right here. It was here." She twisted around, attempting to glean a different perspective of the property. Sam stopped. She recognized the painted wooden siding on the house to the left. *Ronan's is on the other side.*

She raced behind the house she recognized until she saw his cellar door. Finally, she had found the correct place. This was where Ronan had taken them. It was the same door, only before she hadn't noticed how worn away the gray paint was. The paint peeled in small curls randomly across the doors' surface. She spotted the same latch and wrought iron strap hinges, which appeared like spears pointing to the center where the two doors met. This was Ronan's secret library cellar, but in their haste to get off the street, some other details seemed unimportant, and she didn't see them the way she saw them now. Sam glanced around. The patchy grass struggled to grow. Only small clumps managed to find life and made the soil seem diseased. She stepped closer to the doors, staring at the black latch, and for a moment, she almost believed that the blackish-purple leaves on the overgrown shrub to the cellar's left actually moved. It encroached upon the space, prepared to invade. She listened for Ronan, but there were no sounds from the underground room.

Hi Ronan, it's me, Sam. She said to herself. *Stupid. He knows who you are. Hi Ronan, I was in the neighborhood.* She thought she would throw up. *Just knock.* She did. No one answered. She knocked again. Nothing. *Just open it, Sam!* She reached down, clasped the latch's handle, and flung the door open. Complete darkness filled the space. Sam took her cell phone, turned on the flashlight, and treaded slowly down the stairs. There was nothing. The entire area was empty—an old and vacant cellar. No books. No Shelves. Only darkness surrounded the faint glow of her phone's light. The putrefied smell of an aged home's rotten wood and the scent of the dank soil under her feet were the only things that remained of Ronan's magnificent library.

Chapter Twelve

The Order of the Nine Illuminations, 2763 A.D.

"Ronan," Brianna cried as she ran to him and flung her arms around him in a tight embrace. "You've been gone forever."

Ronan grabbed Brianna's hands and broke the grasp of her hands behind his neck. He pushed her away. "Forever is a bit of an exaggeration." He looked over and locked eyes with Scarlet.

Scarlet leaned against the catacomb wall just outside the Order's meeting tomb. When Ronan passed by, she said, "You don't need to be mean to her, but I guess you learned that from your new friends." Scarlet shouldn't have said it; she shouldn't have let on that she spied on him. Now, he would know she summoned a demon to accomplish the feat, but she didn't care. Anger stirred within her being. It was a powerful thing, and she savored the sensation. She watched Brianna trail after Ronan like a puppy who followed its master. Pathetic, she thought. Still, Scarlet felt a need to protect her little sister. Brianna only had Natural Magic to fall back on. Scarlet had an entire legion of demons at her beck and call.

"Wait here, Brianna," Ronan said as they approached the Great Hall with its massive arched cathedral-like ceiling.

"But..." Brianna pleaded. She reached for his hand.

"I'm coming back. I just need a moment alone with Abraham." He turned away from her and left her.

Scarlet strolled down the hall, trailing Ronan toward Abraham's room. Of course, he headed to the old man. Abraham was Ronan's mentor, and even though Ronan was appointed the Order's leader years ago, Abraham had been the voice of reason which guided them all. Scarlet didn't want to miss the expression on Ronan's face when he learned Abraham's time in this world was about to end.

Ronan paused outside of the entrance to Abraham's tomb. Scarlet stopped too. She lingered at the end of the corridor and observed Ronan. He rested against the stone wall and eavesdropped. Scarlet knew this because it was what she would do.

She remembered that Jacob had remained at Abraham's side ever since Edward's divination uncovered the untimely news. How perfect, Scarlet purred to herself. Now Ronan can experience the devastation of not being the chosen recipient of another's love. She moved closer, no longer filled with a desire to hide from Ronan's sight. Ronan would wait outside Abraham's entrance until he heard what was said. He was afraid Jacob had replaced him. She could smell the clamminess upon his pallid skin.

Ronan listened as Abraham told Jacob that Ronan was his own worst enemy and that he allowed his ego and pride to direct his actions—not his higher self. He wondered if this were the truth. The slithery sound of feet, as they glided on the dusty limestone floor, snared his attention, shifting his expression from captivation to loathing as Scarlet's presence entered his view. His lips moved without, but words did not escape.

"What?" Scarlet teased, "Leave? I wouldn't dream of it. The best part of the show is about to begin." She thought she saw his lower lip tremble. He was in way over his head. Entangled in the witches' lives. Every move he now made merely tightened his noose. The only thing that would garner Scarlet more joy would be if the rope around his neck weren't figurative.

"Go, Scarlet," Ronan demanded.

"Who's there?" Jacob called out from Abraham's room. "Is that you, Ronan?"

Ronan's rigid form maneuvered into the entrance. "Yes," he said.

"Ronan?" Abraham asked in an almost jovial voice that seemed disembodied from his weak, frail frame.

Ronan pushed forward and knelt next to Jacob at Abraham's side. "I've returned," he said, bowing his head. "Matthew sent a feather, and within my heart, I understood your time draws near."

"Have you saved the witches?" Abraham begged. "The Trinity Witches are alive?"

"I released the three from the jail, but only the middle sister survived," Ronan said in a monotone voice. "There's more," Ronan added. At that moment, he feared Abraham was right. Ronan didn't understand his need to save the three young witches he had met. But a connection existed. He didn't comprehend it yet, but he was linked to Sam. "I learned of the witches' incarnation in the twenty-first century. They are untrained and naïve in the art of the craft. I believe I have an obligation to teach them."

"An obligation?" Abraham asked. His boney arm wiggled under the weight of his upper body as he attempted to sit upright. Jacob pulled his teacher up and propped the old man against the stone. "Your obligation is to the Order," Abraham spat.

"I realize I have a duty to lead the Order, but..." Ronan attempted to explain.

"No exceptions," Abraham muttered. Drool seeped from the corner of his mouth. "Your first and only priority is the Order." He struggled to catch his breath after a deep and violent cough. "You took a vow to protect the nine, to protect magic, to..." Abraham lurched forward in another fit of coughs.

"Beloved teacher," Ronan said as he lifted Abraham's gray hand to his mouth. He kissed his mentor's wrinkled knuckles. And as his lips pressed to the parched skin, Ronan thought of the weathered wood he found as a treasure hunter in his youth. His head raised but did not look into Abraham's eyes, "I am mysteriously bound to these women, and every cell in my being urges me to protect them. The Order can sustain itself until my return." Ronan released Abraham's hand. "I'm sorry, old friend, but I must return to them until they find their true path." He turned to leave and spotted Scarlet as she stood in the doorway.

"Bound to the witches? Are you sure you don't mean one of them?" Scarlet glared past Ronan's eyes and into his core. She hoped her words stung his soul.

"Get out of my way, Scarlet," Ronan said sharply as he neared the archway. He wanted his words to bite back.

"No time to waste," Scarlet said, untouched by Ronan's insensitivity. She sensed Brianna's approach. "Isn't that right, Ronan? You have a baby to make," Scarlet said a little louder than she needed to.

"Silence, Scarlet. You don't know what you're talking about," Ronan said. His eyes cut to Brianna, who had just entered the doorway, and now stood next to her sister. "I thought I told you to wait."

"You're not in charge here anymore, Ronan," Scarlet said. "Not any more than you've ever been."

"Abraham," Jacob begged, "what are we to do?" He dreaded the spread of tension through the catacombs and feared the others if they became aware.

Ronan pushed through the two women who blocked his path. "I don't know the duration until my return." He didn't make eye contact with Brianna or Scarlet. He wished he had said that he didn't know if he would return.

Abraham pitched forward, clamped his hands around Jacob's upper arms, and held him firmly. "You are the future, Jacob. It is up to you to save the Order now," Abraham said. His voice commanded a strength equivalent to the energy coalesced in his heart and charged his words with a magical charge, "Virtutem meam relinquo vobis [I leave you my power]. Sic fiat semper [so mote it be]." His hands moved down to Jacob's hands, and he squeezed them until his fingers nearly touched bone. "Say it, son."

Jacob resisted his teacher's clutch, but the old man held him with his death grip.

Brianna lunged forward, prepared to run to Abraham's and Jacob's sides, but Scarlet grabbed her.

"Say it, Jacob, before it's too late," Scarlet ordered. She knew Abraham planned to confer his magic on the boy. And, if she believed there was enough time, she would knock Jacob out of her way and seize the power for herself. "Jacob, his magic is lost forever if you don't take it," Scarlet pleaded.

With tears trailing down his face, Jacob replied, "Sic fiat."

A whirl of faint blue wind sparkled and swirled around his body, enveloping the old man. His hair rose in the air and wildly blew around his face. The pale tornado of magic circled above his chest. It hovered and wobbled before traveling down his arm and wrapping the frail old hand with the youthful one of Jacob.

Crisscrossing over and around, the spell bound their hands. For a moment, Jacob thought their hands had melded together, for he could no longer distinguish where his fingers ended and Abraham's began. Then, the magical blue band of wind broke from their hands and hovered above them, then rushed at Jacob. He closed his eyes and winced as the sparkly blue substance formed a long straight arrow-like line and pierced his chest.

Jacob fell back as Abraham's grasp loosened. He clutched his chest where the magic had entered. Without warning, he gasped for air, not realizing he had held his breath during the incident. Abraham had transferred his powers to Jacob. The magical wisdom raced through Jacob's blood and penetrated his being.

Abraham sat upon his bed, looking as alive as he ever had. He pronounced his final words—a prophecy. "The Order is seven. Yet one more must leave. A betrayal awaits before power is fully restored." His expression fell, and his words lost their zeal. His eyes became dull and lifeless. "Not to worry, boy," Abraham whispered, "The Order of Six Illuminations will be much easier to handle and will wield far greater power than the Nine ever could." Abraham expelled the last of his breath and reclined backward; soft like a feather, he floated toward a place of rest.

Jacob jumped up from the ground and ran to Abraham's body, where he lay on the cold stone slab. He hugged his limp body. "He's dead," Jacob cried.

Chapter Thirteen

"Spirit comes from God, and from the Spirit comes the soul,
and from the soul does animate and quicken all
other things in their order."
The First Book of Natural Magic

R onan quickened his pace as he moved down the ancient corridor. His only thoughts were on returning to the catacomb's sacred space where his portals were made. Jacob, Ronan was sure, would remain with Abraham long after the old man's breath ceased. But Scarlet? Ronan was less sure of what her next actions might be.

A clamor of sobs trailed behind him. Matthew and Edward raced into the hall, quickly followed by Bruno and Alexander, to discover the cause of the commotion.

"What happened?" Matthew asked.

"Abraham is gone," Ronan said stoically to his four friends.

"Gone? When?" Alexander asked.

"Just now," Ronan answered. "He passes to the other side as we speak."

"Did he take your hand, Brother?" Bruno urged. "Did he take your hand?"

Ronan stared straight into Bruno's eyes. "He did not."

"Impossible. Abraham wouldn't take his power to the grave." Bruno shook his head. "Never. He wouldn't do such a thing,"

"Abraham conferred all his magic to the boy," Ronan replied. He concealed even the slightest evidence of his emotions and the evoked hurt this action generated.

"Jacob?" Edward asked, perplexed by what he found to be a reckless choice. He waved for Alexander to go to Abraham's room and confirm this new information.

Ronan drew the piece of reddish-brown Acacia Koa from inside his cloak. There, in the catacombs, he didn't hide his wand's slithering curves or its split end shaped into a serpent's mouth. Ronan made the symbol of the sun before him and harnessed his powers. He spoke words of praise to the Sun, the Moon, and the Air. He pointed the serpent, prepared to strike with its magical bite.

"Are you leaving?" Edward inquired, though he had already guessed the answer to his question.

"I must return to the witches." Ronan had convinced himself no other choice remained. He drew his wand in a counter-clockwise circle and brought the faint shimmer of a blueness into the enclosed space.

"Whatever for?" Matthew asked.

"Ronan? You cannot leave. Not now." Bruno glanced at Matthew questioningly.

"The Order needs your leadership, Brother," Edward added.

Ronan turned to face his peers. "Jacob is in charge now," Ronan said.

"Jacob? He is but a boy. He is not prepared to lead us," Bruno said.

"Of course, he's leaving," Scarlet announced as she and her sister joined their fellow members.

Brianna rushed to Ronan's side. "Is this true?" She reached for his embrace. "Please, Ronan. Don't leave me," she begged.

Ronan raised his hand to hold off Brianna's advance. He didn't want her any nearer. "I understand." He glanced over at Scarlet and then back to Brianna. "You feel something. But it isn't love. You're infatuated. It often happens with leaders. Let me be clearer. I hold no such sentiments toward you."

"But I thought..."

"I have no feelings for you, Brianna." Ronan's eyes were vacant, and his voice stern.

Brianna took a step backward. Her expression dazed with disbelief.

"Ronan," Matthew cautioned, "there is no need for unkind words. We are all still in shock over the loss of Abraham. Put aside selfish endeavors. We must support each other as we attend to our funerary tasks."

"My actions are not selfish. I'm trying to save us," Ronan rebuked.

"You're trying to save your witch," Scarlet said, pleased for the opportunity to expose Ronan's real motive for returning.

Brianna twisted toward her sister. "His witch? What do you mean by his witch?"

"Shall I tell her, Ronan, or shall you?" Scarlet mocked.

"There is nothing to tell. Scarlet thrives on the chaos she likes to create."

"Okay, Ronan," Scarlet said, "we can play this your way. You leave. The boy is in charge. Of course, he has no idea what he is doing, but he will lead us. My question is to where? Where shall this boy lead us?"

Ronan stared at her. His heart pulled him back to the three witches, but his mind told him he was needed there. He shook off his doubt. "You seven will decide the Order's direction."

"And if it is no longer to save magic?" Matthew interjected.

"The mission has always been to save magic. You may not think it so, but I am trying." Ronan clasped Matthew's forearm. "I am trying to save magic. I must return."

"But why these witches?" Brianna pleaded. "Why must it be these three witches?"

Scarlet grinned with anticipation for the weak excuse Ronan was about to spew from his lips. "Yes, Ronan. Tell us why these three. Well, more specifically, why Sam?"

"How do you know that?" Ronan demanded. But he knew. Scarlet could only know their names if she had summoned a demon. A memory flashed in his mind. Outside the jail, he and Penny picked up evilness right before they fled to his library—a demon of Scarlet's.

"How? Scarlet, tell me how," Brianna insisted.

"A demon," Matthew said. Judgment draped his words.

Scarlet winked at Matthew. "The question isn't how I know. It's how much do I know?"
Ronan's face appeared to grow paler if such a state was possible. He stared at the ground and searched for his real intent. "I... I have a connection to the witches. I don't understand it, but I am connected to..."

"To Sam?" Brianna stared directly into Ronan's eyes.

"And she's the middle triplet," Scarlet added, glided nearer Ronan's partially opened portal. "The middle one gives birth to the next incarnation of Trinity Witches. Isn't that so, Ronan?"

"Ronan?" Matthew asked, "You mustn't return. If there is a connection between yourself and the witch, you must not interfere."

"Matthew is right, brother. You are not that incarnation. Whoever you were back then, you must not intervene," Edward said.

"Listen to our brothers, Ronan. You must abide. Abraham warned you of as much when you started this whole mess. Nothing changed for the better," Bruno said.

"Ah, but he can't help himself," Scarlet bantered back, "he's in love with the witch."

"In love? Is this why your feelings for me have changed?" Brianna questioned. "You're in love with a ghost from the past?

"She's as real as you and I, Brianna. And yes, there's a connection with her." He scrutinized what he had with Sam and countered, "But I wouldn't call it love." Ronan turned back to reignite the portal spell he had begun before this drama unfolded.

"But you wouldn't *not* call it love, right?" Brianna cried. "You wouldn't say to her that you have no feelings for her as you said to me, would you?"

"No, Brianna, I couldn't say those words to her." Ronan raised his wand to work his magic.

Brianna's lip trembled, and her mouth parted like she was about to say one more thing, but she found nothing remained that she wanted to tell him. Not anymore. She turned and ran past Matthew and Edward. How childish of her to believe he cared for her. How absolutely foolish she was to have held him in her heart. To have seen herself with him, and their life together, as man and wife. She heard the sounds of their children's voices fill the catacombs and fade away. She ran from the pain of his presence out of the sacred hall, sobbing uncontrollably.

Scarlet's eyes darkened into a deep charcoal hue. The heat of her anger toward Ronan penetrated the room, so much so she might possibly internally combust from her soul's surging flame.

She had exposed Ronan, yes, but it wasn't enough. She wanted to avenge her sister. Scarlet wanted revenge. "You'll regret this. You shouldn't have embarrassed my sister. Not in front of the others."

Ronan stepped forward into his portal.

Scarlet lunged after him. "You'll regret this, Ronan Magnus!" She paused at the shimmering edge of the ethereal substance and yelled into the abyss as the last part of him disappeared. "You'll pay for hurting my sister. Did you hear me, Ronan?" Scarlet screamed into the magic portal. "I'll make you pay!"

"Scarlet? Compose yourself." Edward grabbed her arm and pulled her back. For a moment, he feared she would jump in after Ronan.

She only resisted for a second. When her eyes met Edwards, the darkness dissipated as rapidly as her anger arose. She tugged her arm free of his clasp. A redness emerged on her colorless skin where his fingers had seized her with force.

"Now what?" Matthew stood with Edward and Bruno. They scrutinized Scarlet and waited for their brothers' advice.

Scarlet scowled back at them. She wasn't sure what they would do, and she didn't care. She would make her own plan to stop Ronan. Because more than she wanted revenge for Brianna, Scarlet wanted him to cease meddling with the timeline.

Abraham always sensed when she summoned a demon and forbade her from doing so. Now that Abraham was gone, she could practice her black magic freely. Scarlet chuckled to herself. She found it humorous that Matthew and all his angels never seemed to sense when her demons were present.

"I will track him down." Scarlet centered herself in front of Ronan's portal as it closed. She held her right hand to her mouth with the palm facing up and blew a smoky black substance into the last fragments of shimmering blue ether. She took one step back, away from the nearly vanished portal, and watched her spell take the shape of a transparent horned, hoofed demon. "And when I find him, I will make him pay."

Chapter Fourteen

B efore her sisters had a chance to wake up, Sam dressed and went down to the kitchen and seeped her mother's morning tea. She flipped the espresso machine on, prepared to make Penny and Kat lattes whenever they stumbled down the stairs and joined her. Sam took the loaf of cinnamon bread, purchased at the local bakery two days prior, and untwisted the wire tie which held the plastic bag closed. She removed a slice and closed the bag.

She hadn't figured out how to tell her sisters that Ronan's library didn't exist. Sam believed her sister Penny found Ronan to be an asset, someone they would need again in some future event. She, however, understood he was a liability. Especially if he and Kat ended up together. Her fingers squeezed the loaf and pushed all the trapped air to the tied end. She would never be rid of Ronan if he was with her little sister. The bag popped under the increased tightness of her grip.

"What the heck, Sam?" Kat shuffled into the kitchen, clad in her pajamas and her slippers. "Are you supposed to smash the bread like that?"

Sam looked down, unaware that she had pulverized the bread. "Oh, sorry." She tried to shake the loaf back to its previous shape.

Penny joined her sisters for breakfast. "We're under a lot of pressure. All this is new, and we can't anticipate what's coming next."

Penny was right. Stress existed because they would graduate the next week and had their mother to take care of. Then, they learned they were witches. And their father started his comeback-into-their-lives tour this week too. The entire situation overwhelmed all three of them.

"I think," Penny began, "we need to learn more about the Trinity Witches and our powers."

"Yeah, we should so go back to Ronan's library," Kat said.

That was Sam's opportunity to tell her sisters, and she took it. "One problem with your plan. Ronan's library—it isn't real."

"Not real?"

"What do you mean not real? We went inside. Together, we three stood inside his library and held several books. You sat in his chair, Sam," Kat screeched.

"I don't understand what possessed me, but last night, after you both went to bed, I left. I wanted to talk to Ronan." Sam glanced at Kat. She wanted to pick up on Kat's emotions—if Kat felt a tinge of jealousy. "When I got there and opened the cellar door—nothing remained but a rotten and decayed basement. I told you we shouldn't trust him."

"You went to the wrong house," Penny suggested.

"Yeah, you went to the wrong house. The night was dark when we ran from the cops and evaded the evilness Penny sensed. You got confused and probably picked a different house," Kat chimed in.

"No, I was at the same location. You don't believe me? Ask Ronan. He should arrive any second. That is if today plays out like yesterday."

"Why would he lie?" Kat posed.

"He's not who says he is. He's the evil energy. He's here to erase magic and not save anything. Ronan admits he's done a great job of screwing everything up." Sam took a bite of her slice of buttered cinnamon bread.

"Those were accidents, Sam." Kat defended Ronan.

"Were they?"

"Possibly." Penny tried to pick up on any untruths she gleaned regarding this new information. The only truth Penny snared was that the three of them had no idea what was going on. "Where's Mom's tea?"

"Oh, yeah. Hang on, let me..." Sam paused as she tapped the tea strainer spoon on the side of the China cup. "Here, I almost forgot I made this." Sam lifted the saucer.

The cup balanced itself and slipped in alignment with the raised ring. She handed the tea to Penny. "There's something else strange. I can't smell this tea."

"Really?" Penny raised the cup to her nose and inhaled. "It doesn't emit an aroma, does it?"

Kat leaned in toward her sisters. "Let me sniff. Yep, the tea is odorless. What kind of herbs are unscented?"

"I'm not sure."

***

Penny fed their mother her breakfast, dressed her, and saw that the last drop of her favorite tea was drunk. She opened her mother's curtains, and the morning sun brightened the room. She helped her mother walk to the chair next to the window.

"Do you want the window open, Mom?" Penny didn't expect an answer. She cracked the bottom sash. The sheers lifted away from the wall as a soft breeze blew through the opened window. Penny tucked a throw blanket over her mom's legs and kissed her. "We won't be gone like we were yesterday, Mom."

"Hey, Penny?" Sam said from behind her, drawing her sister's attention away from their mother. "I can't find anything about scentless herbs used for teas or otherwise."

"What's that?" Penny pointed to the book in Sam's hand.

"Oh, I thought it was a blank journal, and I started writing down stuff about herbs last night. Then I noticed some very faint writing on a few of the pages," Sam held out her personal grimoire for Penny to examine. "Look." She opened her book.

"It does appear blank from here," Penny said.

"Watch." Sam moved closer to Penny, who brushed their mother's hair.

Penny glanced up and caught the page content growing darker.

Sam stepped next to the chair where their mom was sitting. The pages took on the appearance of newness—the writing fresh and sharp like it was recently added.

Their mother stirred and let out a soft, whiny breath.

"Hang on," Sam said. She walked back toward the bedroom door. "The writing faded again. This is Mom's Herbal Grimoire!" Sam raced back to the chair. "Mom? Is this your book? I wrote on top of your stuff." Sam turned the pages. The entire book is full of information. "Sorry, Mom." Sam sat on the floor and leaned back on the chair that held her mother.

"Is it all herbs and plant stuff?" Penny pinned her mom's hair back from her face.

"Yeah. This page lists herbs by element. Uh? I never thought of them like that. Here's a whole section on air element herbs, earth herbs, water herbs, and fire herbs. Whoa, and a list of scared plants." Sam continued to read the list out loud. "Sage, sweet grass, yarrow, black spruce, red clover, and dandelion." She flipped the page. "Oh my god, Mom created a correspondence list of the ancient names with their modern names. I can interpret and create some super old spells. Eye of Newt is mustard seed!"

Kat joined them after the excitement in Sam's voice called to her. "What's up, guys?"

"Sam found Mom's Herbal Grimoire last night."

"Cool. Hey, this proves it. Mom is a witch," Kat announced.

"Bat's wing is holly. Who knew?" Sam chuckled to herself. She truly enjoyed the discovery of priceless information. "Chamomile is the Blood of Hestia."

"What else is in there?" Kat reached over to examine the book for herself.

"Hey, this is mine." Sam tightened her grip.

"She's my mom, too," Kat said.

"Knock it off, you two. Remember, we don't argue in front of Mom. Anyway, we shouldn't fight at all." Penny stretched her hand out. "May I please hold the book? I won't keep it."

Sam handed Penny the grimoire.

"Really?" Kat said.

Sam replied with a crooked smirk.

"There's more here than herbs— candle magic? I've never heard of it, have you guys?" Penny asked.

"No, but it makes sense. Witches and gypsies in the movies always light candles," Kat said.

"Don't be stupid, Kat," Sam said.

"Mom's list of candle omens covers three whole pages. Anything about the colors and when to use certain ones?" Penny said. "And some information about gemstones. A lot is based on the color of the stones."

"There's more to it than that, but each of the colors carry a unique vibrational quality," Sam stated, "and their power is reflective of the quality."

Penny handed the book back to Sam.

"Here, Kat. You can look." Sam passed the book to her little sister.

"Thanks, Sam." Kat was genuinely surprised. Maybe that Witch's Chain spell had done what it was supposed to, she thought as she opened the book to a random spot. "Alchemical Transmutation," Kat read. "What the heck is that?"

"Ronan talked about yesterday," Sam said. "Remember the whole jump rope thing?"

"He taught us the Seven Alchemic Universal Principles, not how to transmute energy." Penny corrected both of her sisters.

"Okay, so how is energy transmuted?" Sam asked.

"Looks like there are seven of those, too. Tincture-pulverizing of a solid into a powder; coagulation-the thickening of a substance; solvation-the reorganization and bond formations, distillation-making a concentration; sublimation-vapors solidify; calcination-heating to remove a volatile substance, and putrefaction- decomposition through decay." Kat closed the book and handed it back to Sam. "Here you go. All Greek to me."

"Why would Mom need this?" Sam asked her sisters.

"Sounds like your mother is an Alchemist." Ronan's words startled the girls as he leaned against the door frame.

"Jesus Christ," Sam spat. "How the hell did you get in our house?"

"Seriously, Ronan. I think I just peed myself. You scared us to death." Kat clutched her chest. "The Witch Bells didn't ring."

"Did you create a portal in our hallway?" Penny couldn't believe he was in their home and stepped in front of her mother's chair and formed a protective barrier. She made a mental note Sam needed to double the efforts on the protection spells on their home.

"No. I walked in your front door." He stepped into their mother's bedroom. "Don't look at me like that. It was unlocked. I didn't break into your house."

"Come on," Sam said, "we're disturbing Mom." She didn't like Ronan's presumptuousness. What made him think it was okay to walk into their house uninvited?

Kat bounced over to Ronan's side as they all left their mom's room. "How's your friend? Is he okay?"

"No. He died shortly after I arrived." Ronan's voice carried a bit of despondence that only another person who grieved would recognize.

"I'm sorry," Kat said.

"Yes, me too," Ronan replied.

Penny and Sam followed Kat and Ronan back downstairs. "Tell him," Penny whispered to Sam.

"You bet." Sam hoped the opportunity would arrive soon, or she'd have to blurt it out of nowhere. "You just stay close by and turn on your bullshit detector when he tries to explain."

Kat led Ronan into their living room. "You might want your coin for this one."

He eyed her curiously.

"A nervous habit, right?" Kat asked. "I get it. Sam can be intimidating, for sure."

He glanced over at the two other sisters. "What's on your ladies' agenda for the day?" Ronan sat in the living room chair on the left of the fireplace.

Sam paused as she stepped on the last step. His cloak hung on the coat rack in the foyer. She bit the side of her top lip. He felt too comfortable around here, she thought. Maybe now was a perfect time to blast him out of the water and out of their lives. Sam let Penny pass by her, and she waited until she settled in a seat. "So, Ronan?" Sam shrewdly asked. "Where'd you go when you left here last night?"

"God, Sam. A bit harsh aren't you," Kat said.

"She's fine," Ronan assured Kat. "I traveled back to my home. I told you where I was headed." He leaned forward, rested his elbows on his legs just above both knees and tapped his coin on his upper lip. "Something happen?"

Sam placed her hands on her hips. "Oh, nothing. I just went to your house last night."

Ronan straightened up and almost dropped his fidget coin. "You went to my house? Whatever for?"

191

"Why couldn't I go to your house? You just pop in and out of here like a damn jack-in-the-box. Oh yeah, now I remember why—because you don't have a house!" Sam glared right through him as she waited for his cockamamie response.

"Here's the confusion. I told you three I was going home—not to the house where I showed you my library... my home."

"That's the confusing part?" Penny asked.

"No," Sam said, as her eyes moved back and forth between her sisters, "we believe the confusion is with where the hell the library went?"

"You went inside?" Ronan asked.

"Hell, yeah, I went in, and guess what?" Sam asked.

"It was vacant." Ronan eyed Sam, wondering why she had sought him out last night.

"Exactly, so where does an entire library go?" Penny asked. "I was there. It wasn't an illusion. I picked up a book and read from it."

"I opened a portal, but not to another time. I opened a portal to another realm. My personal realm. I took you girls to my Memory Mansion, which is full of all the books I have read in my current lifetime. And some of the artifacts I have seen."

"But it was real." Kat shook her head.

"How is that even possible?" Penny asked.

"Magic, ladies. Magic," Ronan answered. "If you ever want to come into your own power, and I do mean come into it, you have to start believing."

"Just because you've figured out how to open portals and move in and out of time doesn't make you superior." Sam resented everything about him.

"Yeah, Sam, it kind of does," Kat smirked at the end of her comment.

"Well, I believe what I see," said Sam. "We were standing in a library. What did you do? Hypnosis? Mesmerism? What?"

"Ah, we come to the first stumbling block. You should never believe what you see. Believe so that you can see."

"What?" Kat asked.

"One more time, please," Penny asked.

"I believe that my mansion exists without a single doubt. You ladies still only believe what you see. It's sort of a Sympathetic Magic, which works because the receiver believes so firmly that another has the power and that they have none. Simple suggestion—you didn't have time to doubt I took you to a real place. Why would you? Of course, as each of you acknowledged what you thought was real, you affirmed to each other that it was real. Magic, ladies, is contagious."

"So, if we didn't believe we would see anything, we wouldn't have seen it?" Penny asked.

"Reality is 'real'ity. The Latin suffix 'ity' denotes having the quality or characteristics of. In this case, having the quality of being real. But not actually being real. Haven't you ever looked for something, like your keys, for example, and know without any doubt where you last left them, only to discover they aren't there? They aren't anywhere. Then one of your sisters walks right up and picks them up where you thought they should have been?"

"I get it. I usually misplace my keys when I'm in a hurry. So, my belief switched from knowing where the keys are to knowing I won't find them because I'm already running late." Penny pondered the implications of her line of thought. "This is incredible."

Ronan clapped. "You girls are quite bright. We just need to dust away some of the cobwebs that block your true vision. And I am learned in hypnotism and mesmerism, but I wouldn't do that. Well, not without your permission, of course." Ronan offered a faint smile to Sam.

"So, how do we go back to your library?" Kat asked.

"I don't know if you can. You would have to believe my mansion exists for me to take you there again. Was there something you wanted?"

"Yes, I want to know all of it. I want to read every book in there." Penny's voice trailed off as she became lost in her own thoughts.

"Kat, what's the matter with your mother?" Ronan asked.

Kat looked over at Sam, asking for permission with her eyes. Sam replied by walking away. "I'll be in the kitchen if you need me," she said.

"Our mom has early onset dementia," Kat told him, even though Sam disapproved.

"That must be awful," Ronan said, "and your father? Why isn't he here?"

"He left Mom when we were three. She was okay for several years. Then by the time we were ten, she had short-term memory loss. She was moody, too. Sometimes we didn't know what to expect when we got home from school." Kat relived some of her worst memories in her mind.

Penny finished their story. "She couldn't always find the right word. She always seemed confused and sometimes didn't know who we were."

"Your circumstance is tough, particularly being on your own. But, wait, you're the Trinity Witches. Your mother is the daughter of a middle sister of a set of triplets." Ronan searched his memory. He tried to recall if he had ever heard anything about this particular branch of their family.

"We have never met any of mom's family." Penny looked down.

"None of our father's either," Kat said.

"And there's no treatment? No cure?" Ronan asked.

"No, but there is something else we don't understand," Penny said. "If our mom is a witch, why did she let this happen? We never saw her make herbal remedies or anything remotely witchy."

"But Sam found her grimoire last night. She was a witch and studied herbs," Kat added.

"It is quite strange. But it makes sense now why you three didn't know you were witches. Your mother forgot who she was and forgot what she needed to teach you. Your grandmother and your mother's aunts' absence, I can't explain," Ronan said.

Sam carried in a cup of tea and rejoined the conversation, "Here, Penny," Sam said.

"Thanks, Sam." Penny headed for the stairs.

"What was that?" Ronan asked.

"Mom's favorite tea," Sam said.

"Yeah, the only good thing our father ever did," Kat said.

"What's that?" Ronan asked.

"He ships a package of Mom's favorite tea here every month since he left. So she drinks it every day," Sam said.

Kat snorted, "Yeah, three or four times a day. She loves it."

Chapter Fifteen

"Rise above mere mortal nature and awaken
to the immortal soul."
Julie Kusma, 2019

"**E**nough about *our* mom. We're ready to hear about your family." Sam turned to Ronan.

"Yes, I suppose your right." Ronan sighed as he determined where to start his story, and he guessed his story should start at the beginning. "I come from a time and place very different from yours. Where I come from, the world is desolate and in ruins." Ronan placed his pale fingers across his faded pink lips and closed his eyes. He held the last image of his home in his mind. "I live with my family in a series of catacombs under Paris, France."

"Paris?" Penny rejoined Ronan and her sisters in the living room. "No one lives in the catacombs."

Sam glanced at her sister. She recognized Penny had scanned his words for the truth factor but couldn't tell what her sister had determined. "You said a different time. How different?"

Ronan's eyes widened. "Extremely." He waited for the girls to comprehend what he implied before he continued, but the girls simply stared back. "Where I come from, magic is all but gone. Some of us sought to save as much art and manuscripts as possible. That's why *we* went underground. We needed to preserve the precious treasures and hide this from all those aligned with the mission of destroying civilization. Their goal was to wipe magic out of human history. I was only ten when I began to rummage through the rubble of our fallen city."

"It sounds like you're describing ancient civilizations and the fight for the control of power. Like the religious battle to minimize and condemn paganism. Artifacts were destroyed, all except for those hidden."

Ronan smiled and rolled his golden coin. "Yes, history repeats itself."

"Repeats?" Sam was puzzled.

"I'm from the future."

"From our future?"

"From everyone's future."

"And all the population lives underground?" Kat asked, finding fascination in Ronan's tale.

"No, the government built environmental enclosures—habitats of a sort, with growth chambers for farming, rather like the space experiments in your timeline. Theses environmental bubbles are climate controlled and offer artificial sunlight, but after centuries under these conditions, the human form reflected these environmental changes. No real substitute for the sun." Ronan displayed both hands near his face and created a frame for his own appearance as evidence.

"Everyone looks like you?" Kat asked, "I mean the pale skin, white hair, and light gray eyes like you?"

"Achromasia or albinism," Penny said. "Living inside the bubbles would interfere with melanin production. So it would take generations, centuries for this type of mutation to occur."

"Yes," Ronan confirmed, "it did take a long time." He stared down at his leather boots, and a memory of himself, as he climbed over hunks of collapsed building structures, drifted across his mind. "When I was twelve or thirteen, I found a cache of hidden metaphysical and occult manuscripts. I brought them back. I did this at night in the shroud of darkness. During the day, I studied these ancient texts, and one day I discovered how to harness and wield the power the books described was contained within. After several more years, I learned how to create portals and travel through time. I was convinced, with this skill, I could travel into the past and fix... change the events which slowly ate away and eliminated the practice of and the belief in magic. Not everyone in our group agreed. Our faction split and left only nine of us. We are the Order of the Nine Illuminations, and it is our sworn duty to restore magic."

"What year is it, Ronan? Because Paris is standing. No place lies in ruins except cities ancient to us today," Penny asked.

"The year is 2763."

"What?" Sam's mouth gaped open. "He said magic was gone where he was from, but are you saying, to be here, you are in your past, which is our present?"

"He is," Penny said. "But, why are you here...with us, specifically?"

Ronan sensed this was his opportunity to come totally clean with them. If he held anything back, they would never trust him. Never. But he didn't know if they were equipped to handle everything. Sometimes it was too much for him. "I told you I inadvertently altered the timeline, and my actions led to the Trinity Witches having been tried in Ipswich. I went back to free them because if they all died that day, the Trinity Witches wouldn't exist."

"You saw us separate from our past incarnations and knew we were unaware we were witches?" Kat asked.

"Yes. Now you can understand why I had to come here. Why I have to help you."

"Do you lack such self-awareness that it never occurred to you that you are the reason magic disappeared in the first place?" Sam asked.

Disbelief spread across Ronan's face.

"You, yourself, told us your actions altered history, and your meddling was responsible for the witch trials." Sam continued.

"But I went back to fix that." His voice insecure now.

"The Grandfather Paradox." Penny dropped down on the sofa next to Kat. "Magic wouldn't be gone if you never went back to fix it, and going back to fix it was the reason magic disappeared. This creates an endless loop."

"I believe the timeline...history can be changed." Ronan's enthusiasm brought him to his feet, and his confidence returned.

"You've more than demonstrated that," Sam smirked at him.

Ronan ignored Sam's insinuation and continued with greater passion. "I'm sorry. But I believe this can all be fixed."

"I just don't understand how a civilization goes from planning to inhabit other planets like Mars to the entire world turned into a wasteland and people living in bubbles," Penny asked in more of a statement than a question.

"One theory is that the government had it planned all along." Ronan had clearly thought this through. "First, you get the people to forget history. Then, you have to remove all evidence of other ways to live—of other beliefs. And the biggest obstacle that needs to be removed..."

"Is magic," Penny said, finishing Ronan's sentence.

"In my time, we live under what is called, *The Great Sleep*. Wisdom of the ancients, the magic of the ancients, the ways of respect and honor for life all forgotten."

"The same could be said of our time, too." Penny felt sympathy for his world.

"So, you know about the Trinity Witches from those manuscripts you saved?" Sam asked. "Is there some kind of prophecy or something?"

"Unfortunately, no. And if there ever was one, it doesn't exist anymore. Every time the timeline is altered in some way, the manuscripts reflect the alteration."

"You witnessed this?" Sam asked.

"I haven't, but my mentor Abraham did; he was the Order's scribe. He is the one that told me of this occurrence. He told me that the three witches had died in Ipswich. Then the books reflected only two deaths after I Time Walked and helped them; you escape."

"Does that happen to the books in your Memory Mansion?" Penny asked.

"I don't know. Why?"

"Because if they were saved the way you remember, the answers might be there." Penny contemplated the implications of what she said. "Wait." Penny paused and tried to conceal the hopefulness she felt. "There might even be a cure for our mother in your library."

"I don't think so. I'm sorry. Magic was eradicated hundreds of years ago in my timeline. Your world is actually more aware of magic than my world ever was. Only the nine of us..." Ronan's expression fell into a gloominess. "My friend Abraham is dead. There are only eight of us who even know what magic is. Each of us is educated in a particular branch of magic, but healing? I'm afraid nothing in my world is of any help for your mother."

"You could hypnotize her," Kat said. Their expressions rebuked her idea. "Why not? He said he studied hypnotism."

"Hypnotism is a form of Lesser Magic—the magic of man. For it to work, her mind must be in a suggestible frame. From what you have told me, she is confused and unaware of even her surroundings. She is not a suitable candidate. Again, I'm sorry."

"She's a witch too," Sam said, "and we could use her help. We must cure her."

The girls soon reflected Ronan's despair. They were witches, but they had no way to cure their mother. It was hopeless. Ronan was a powerful wizard from the future, but he offered nothing for her, either. Plus, it seemed he screwed more things up than he fixed.

The only hope, if one could call it that, was they would be gone before their world ended and everything dangled from the thin thread of magic held in the Order's eight fingers.

"There is something we can do," said Sam. "We can do what Ronan has attempted to do. We can go back in time and make magic strong again."

"Why do you think we would be able to do it? Ronan couldn't," Penny asked.

Sam's eyes brightened with a twinkle of hope. "Because Ronan didn't have the Trinity Witches to help him."

***

Ronan paced behind their sofa as he thought. "You really want to Time Walk?" he asked them.

"YES," the girls said in unison.

"It happened once...by accident, but that doesn't mean you can control it. So I think I should take one of you for a trial run..."

Penny interrupted him, "It won't work. I think our magic only works when the three of us do magic together. Kat and I tried to cast a spell last night, but it didn't work."

"You cast a spell without me?" Sam said, "What the heck?"

"Well, you left to go see Ronan without us. And you started your own secret grimoire." Kat's face showed her shock.

"It's Mom's grimoire," Sam said.

"You didn't know that when you found it and started writing in it," Kat snipped back.

"Ronan, you told us that the Trinity Witches' magic only works when *we three* are together and harmonious." Penny glanced between her sisters as she spoke.

"And we've proven that to be true."

"Yes, it seems that perhaps as solo witches, you can perform Lesser Magic, but all three of you are required to perform Greater Magic. So, work as a team. Until then, here's how it has to go. I open the portal. The three of you go back in time and walk around for a few minutes. Then, walk back through," Ronan explained, still pacing. "Oh, and you won't touch anything or talk to anyone." He stopped and turned to look the three girls in their eyes. "Agreed?"

"AGREED," they said together.

"Where are we going?" Kat asked, full of excitement.

Ronan stared at them for what seemed an eternity. "Brook Farm, 1841," Ronan said. He was pleased with his assigned location.

"A farm?" Kat asked. "At least we moved up a bit into the 19th century. I didn't care much for the seventeenth-century stuff." The image of the wolves' heads nailed outside the Meeting Hall filled her mind, and a shiver ran through her.

"It's not just a farm, Kat." Penny knew of the place. "Brook Farm was the idea of a man named George Ripley. He attempted to establish a utopic community in West Roxbury. It was a failure."

"So, you want us to go to the Farm and make it not fail?" Sam asked Ronan and wondered how they would manage that feat.

"No, I want to go and get a feel for Time Walking when you can do so without a misstep into previous incarnations of yourself. Your past selves should be nowhere around that place," Ronan said.

"So we step through your portal and into West Roxbury, Massachusetts, in the year 1841?" Kat asked.

"You do understand that West Roxbury is just south of Boston?" Sam asked.

"Dad?" Kat asked, excited to see any incarnation of him.

"You won't run into him. You're going back to 1841. Who knows *where* or *if* the man was even around or not?" Ronan assured the girls. "Just in case, I can open a port to my library. From there, you can Time Walk. If anyone walks through my portal uninvited, it will occur there and not here, where your mother could be harmed."

"Good idea, Ronan," Kat said.

It really didn't seem likely that the same thing would occur twice, but if it did, Ronan believed in his library, he could prepare for the unexpected. "Ready?" He asked.

"As we'll ever be," Penny said.

Ronan hurried to the first door he could find. Their front hall closet would do fine. His wand, nearly hidden completely by his arm until he pulled it out, swirled quickly, and morphed the door into a blue wiggle of a shimmer. "After you." He gestured with his arm an invitation to step through the portal to his private realm.

Sam waited for Ronan to step through, although her skeptical expression didn't disappear when he did. However, the creation of her own secret realm sounded delicious. She needed to figure out how to accomplish this amazing feat for herself.

"What about our appearance?" Kat asked.

"Say these words as you step through. *Though I cannot erase time nor space, I choose to reflect the place.*"

Ronan watched them memorize the glamour spell Alexander wrote for his own Time Walking excursions.

"You're not going with us?" Kat asked.

"I have to hold the portal open until you three learn to do this for yourselves." Ronan smiled pleasantly at the three, but the truth was, he couldn't go back. The risk was too high. He might meld with his own past life.

"We're ready, Ronan." Penny led her sisters to the spot where Ronan intended to open the portal. Sam took her place between Penny and Kat, and the three girls held hands as each stood with their left foot forward, posed to enter together.

Ronan drew his serpent wand and held it in his left hand. He pulled the snake through the air and created the symbol of the sun, which should have been invisible, but energy poured forth and left a mark. This glow resembled an asterisk, and it hung in the air like the afterlight of a lit sparkler's movement on the backdrop of the night. The snake moved counterclockwise, circling the mystic solar sign, harnessing ethereal energy until the air solidified into a liquescent substance and activated the portal through time. The triplets raised their left feet off the ground and stepped over the portal's lower boundary and into time.

"First, shiny and new," Penny chanted.

"Then dark as night," Sam added.

"Before we're allowed to see the light," Kat finished the triplet's sentence.

"Though we cannot erase time nor space, let the image we choose reflect the place." The girls completed their chant with Ronan's glamour addition and disappeared into the shimmering blue matter.

Ronan smiled to himself. "Clever girls." He noted they had altered his spell just enough to make it their own, just enough that they held its power and not him.

Chapter Sixteen

Brook Farm, West Roxbury, Massachusetts 1841

T he wind whipped around the tall building's frame, and a chill rushed over each of the girls as they found themselves outside the communal farm house, affectionately referred to by the community as The Hive. It was eerie, they each thought, but for different reasons. Penny suddenly felt herself a voyeur, spying on others' lives.

Kat thought Brook Farm sounded dumb, but now that she stood there and observed, she found the whole farm and house romantic. And Sam? She believed the place to be a ghost of an ideal aimed toward the future, but it faded before it ever anchored itself and took hold.

Kat leaned around Sam and whispered to Penny, "What do we do now? Just waltz in?"

"I think the members freely accepted those who came," Penny said. She wasn't too sure, though. It had been a couple of years since she first read anything about Transcendentalism and the utopic social experiments. She was aware of the bitter taste left in her mouth by social reform and its inherent need to take from those who have carved their own path and give their rewards to those who have never even tried. But that attitude wouldn't fly in this closed environment of reformers, educators, philosophers, and writers of the early nineteenth century.

Before the girls could decide on an approach, a stagecoach drove up the dirt path. Dust stirred under the animal's hooves, and a cloud of dirt billowed behind the carry-all coach as the driver, the Brother Whip motivated the team forward with the reins and a click that emanated from his mouth.

"Whoa," the Whip said as he held the lines tautly and pulled back.

Upon the coach's full stop, a man who traveled alone reached through the open coach window and unlatched the door. He stepped down, moaned, and dusted the layer of earth off his wrinkled suit jacket before addressing the girls. "I say, young ladies," he called out to the triplets still postured on the farm house front lawn. He had spotted them from the stage. "If you need water to fetch, the creek runs just over there," the man said to the driver. With a wave of his index finger, he indicated the direction.

"Sir?" Penny said, not sure of the intent. She prayed he hadn't seen them appear out of thin air.

"We're not in trouble, are we?" Kat asked Sam.

"Shhh, I don't know, but if we talk to him, he'll know we're not from around here. Did you catch how he was talking?" Sam and Kat took a step backward and somewhat hid behind Penny. Kat noted the smoothness of the bald man's features, his thin line mouth, and his piercing eyes. They gave a sense that he knew secrets others did not.

"Dear ladies, please forgive my manners. Or should I say forgive my lack thereof?" The man walked onward up the path where they stood not more than twenty feet ahead. "Let me introduce myself." He took his hat off. "I'm Theodore Parker, reforming minister of the Unitarian church." He bowed slightly forward. Pride painted his words, especially the word 'reforming.'

The girls stared at him, unsure of what to say or do.

"You're undeniably chilled to your very bones. Come, ladies, let us make haste into the warm belly of this abode and thaw beside the embracing arms of its hearth."

The triplets glanced at each other. Ronan's warning ran through their heads at the same time. *Don't talk to anyone, and don't touch anything.* So they remained still as the man neared the home's front stoop.

"Ladies?" He urged them with a wave of his hat, encircling the cold air as if his motion was the catalyst for their movement. It was.

"Yes, Sir," Penny said.

The girls proceeded forward, each nearly tripping on the hem of the bell-shaped skirts, having forgotten they were no longer in the jeans and t-shirts they had worn when they left their house just minutes ago. Adjusting their gait for their unexpected attire, they quickly met the man at the front door. Kat touched her hair. Swirled buns like muffs over both ears made her wonder how she'd appeared. As the three of them lingered behind him, he rapped on the door's glass pane. "Bid entry," he said. He continued the barrage of his knuckles upon the door.

"Are you sure we should go inside?' Kat whispered. "Maybe we should go back right now."

Sam looked over at her sister with an amused expression and whispered back, "Are you kidding? Penny won't be able to control herself, and I wouldn't miss this if you paid me."

Kat glanced at Penny, who did seem as though she had stiffened a bit. This isn't good, Kat thought. Penny was on a mission.

The wooden entry door creaked open. "Good grief," a matronly woman said. She pulled the door back to allow their entry.

"Beg your pardon, Sophia," Minister Parker said, "I apologize for my insistence, but the day grows as bitter as a crone."

"Who rides on your coattails, Theodore?" Sophia asked, nodding toward the girls.

"Beg your pardon, once again. It appears all manners have equally frozen. These fine ladies made way to your door without encouragement. I've merely escorted them the final few steps."

"You hold no acquaintance with these three?" Sophia asked as she scrutinized the girls.

"Welcome, ladies. Welcome," said a young man, no more than twenty years of age, as he stepped beside Sophia.

A room, just off to the right of the main door, was partially observable from where Sam stood. She peered into the chamber and hoped to catch a glimpse of what caused the shuffle within it. A man moved toward a stand and detached his white collar and cuffs. He laid the stiff attachments on the stand and turned directly toward Sam, "What have we here? Hangers-on?" said the man.

Sam thought he looked like a porcelain figurine, except his wild hair stuck out in haphazard curls upon his head. Their eyes met, and Sam blushed. She quickly looked down in embarrassment.

"Dear no, Nath. These young women surely took passage inside an earlier stage. Isn't that correct, ladies?" the minister asked, though he didn't expect an answer. "No, no. These ladies are too fine for riding on top of any coach. Why, they may, in fact, be Grecian goddesses."

The man in the side room neared his door, all the while taking every feature of the girls in.

After a short yet uncomfortable silence, Penny took the lead and spoke for the three. "We took an earlier stage, indeed." She offered a slight curtsy to the group. Her sisters followed suit. Then Penny turned her attention to the man the minister had called Nath. "Nathaniel Hathorne?" she asked as she addressed him directly.

"The very same," Nath replied. He ran his hands through his hair in an attempt to gain some authority over his unruly locks. "Are you friends of the Peabodys? Lizzie is my most ardent promoter." His comment brought a rouse of laughter from the bystanders. "Wouldn't surprise me if she's sent some, how should I say this, some entertainment to act as a muse."

"I'm afraid we have never made the acquaintance of Elizabeth or Sophia," Penny said, noticing his eyes perked up. "I am familiar with your writing," she continued, "and I must ask, what are you doing here?"

"Ladies," Nath said, excusing himself from the entry and gently grabbing Penny's elbow, leading her away from the others. "Please, come to the study where we may speak directly and privately."

"Okay." Penny followed him.

"Pardon me? I didn't catch that," Nath said regarding the unfamiliar word.

"Never mind, she didn't say anything important." Sam scolded Penny with squinted eyes for her use of modern terms.

He let it go and, when they were alone, asked, "Do you know a reason I should not be here? The work is hard, I grant you that much, and the days do feel long. I barely have time for pen to page."

"Perhaps, this is all a misguided dream...a delusion, really. If you cannot write, the entire purpose of your escape becomes a delusion itself," Penny stated.

Kat and Sam knew better than to interfere. Ronan had warned them, but Penny had already sunk her teeth into the seed she sought to plant. Observation of the potential train wreck was their only option.

"I haven't been in a frame of mind to create. This is true, but I'm young and strong. The hours spent in the field do indeed deplete a man's composition, but across lots, I shall arrive."

"I agree; you shall preserve. However, the notion that writing all day is a lazy man's proposition should simply be cast out of your mind. You have a great many things to pen— a woman to marry. Children to have. Waste no more of your thoughts wrapped up in Puritanism and waste no more of your life here," Penny said.

She spoke with a directness Nathaniel admired, and his fascination grew. "Do tell," he said.

"Find a way to expose the Puritanical beliefs of your ancestors. The one's that clearly paved the way for your family's involvement in history," Penny said, poignant yet stern.

He appeared surprised. His desire to distance himself from his great-great-grandfather was valid, but how could she know? Nearly one-hundred-fifty years had passed since his ancestor, Justice John Hathorne, had served as judge on the witch trials and sentenced so many to death.

"You're quite the picture of dismay," the fleshy woman named Sophia said as she paused at the study's door. "Come now; there's a boodle of hungry folks. Best get your share before it's gone."

"Yes," Nath replied. He continued to stare at the three women. "You ladies must join us for supper." Of course, they would, he thought. Where would they go?

Penny moved as if prepared to oblige, but Sam knew better. "Sir," she said, "we need but a moment to gather ourselves." She glanced down.

"Certainly. Follow the ruckus around to the dining hall," Nath said.

"Oh," Penny turned to address Nathaniel as he walked away, "you might want to add a 'w' to your surname to provide a bit of distance from said past."

Again, astonishment rolled over him. He hadn't *said* a word about his past. The longer he scrutinized the foreword woman's words, the stronger his desire to inquire about her intent. Finally, he turned back toward the study. "Say, how do you come to opine..." Nath asked, but when he returned to the study, they were gone.

***

The girls stepped through the portal and back into Ronan's library. Sam wasn't entirely sure he'd still be there, but he was. He waited for them at the massive desk in the center of his space, where he sat, and stared just past them. The three girls revolved around, followed his eyes, and watched his portal firmly closed behind them. Kat shivered off the effect the ethereal matter had left on her skin.

"That was fascinating," Penny announced. She strolled over to the shelved wall on her right and ran her fingers across the many spines, careful to avoid contact with

220

the black, skin-bound book again. She pulled an anthology of nineteenth-century writers from the shelf and flipped the pages until she landed on Hawthorne's name. She smiled to herself when she saw the 'w' in his last name. It had been there, then disappeared, no doubt from one of Ronan's meddlesome trips, but now, it was there again. She had restored that small piece of history and felt very good about it. *A Dark Romance writer*, she quietly read. *Known for his portrayal and disapproval of Puritan severity and cruelty, Hawthorne penned some of America's greatest short stories and novels.* Penny scanned the list of published works until she spotted *The Blithedale Romance*. Eighteen fifty-two? That was over ten years after their visit. Why would it take so long for him to fictionalize his time at Brook farm? She looked for publication dates near their Time Walk. *The Wonder Book*. A collection of children's stories based on Greek mythology. Penny was puzzled. She didn't remember this title as a publication of his before.

She glanced over at her sisters. A huge smile beamed on her face. The minister had called them Grecian goddesses. Perhaps they had made a bigger impression on Nathaniel than she had thought. She followed the section until she found the recorded author's comments. *Of my time at Brook Farm, most notably was the quick and unexpected pleasure of a woman whose words forever changed my life. She inspired me to exonerate all those persecuted unjustly by my ancestors, and from the day we met, she remained my muse.*

Chapter Seventeen

"...the secrets of Nature are not revealed to lazy and idle persons."
The First Book of Natural Magic

S am found Brook Farm hard to shake from her mind. She assumed Penny did, too, but for a different reason. She believed her older sister had a crush on Nathaniel. She also thought her oldest sister would fit in and would have been perfectly happy to remain with the writer. Eighteen forty-one was nearly 200 years in their past, but Penny had been able to acclimate rather quickly. Ronan, too—he shared he was from over seven hundred years in the future, yet he was in their world blended in. For Sam, she found remaining quiet and not drawing undue attention to herself easier. Nevertheless, the idea of the Farm, the utopic vision part, appealed to her and was hard to shake.

Kat's voice boomed from the other side of the library, "That was amazing. Can we do it again?"

"Pretty cool, isn't it?" Ronan glanced to the half-story landing where Penny appeared lost in a daydream but pretended to read the book in her hands. "Anything you need to tell me?"

No words escaped from the faint smile on Penny's mouth.

"Penny?" Kat called as she approached Ronan and noticed Penny for herself.

"Um, what?" She slapped the book shut and slid it back in place among the others. "What?"

"Kat wants to time travel again. What do you think?" Ronan held eye contact with her.

She looked away and over at Kat. She swept her glance over to Sam, who appeared equally dazed by her own daydream as Penny had just been. She walked down the steps and headed toward her sister. "Sam? Kat wants to go again. How about you?"

Sam gazed up from the leather chair. "To Brook Farm?"

"No, silly." Kat took Ronan by the hand and pulled him with her.

"Aren't they cozy?" Sam spoke out of the corner of her mouth. She didn't care if Penny had heard her or not, but if she had, her sister didn't say a word.

Sam continued to observe them, Kat and Ronan, hand-in-hand. Their arms swung like they were a couple as they moved closer to her and Penny. What had she been thinking? Kat was much prettier. Ronan would never fall for her; he'd fall for Kat. Even Penny had a better shot at him than she did. After all, Penny was smart and well-read—something they had in common.

Sam didn't have anything in common with him. She was his opposite, right down to her black hair and dark eyes next to his white hair and pale gray eyes. Who was she kidding? No one, she thought, but herself. "Sure, let's go." Sam got up and walked over to the library's cellar entry door, the location of Ronan's last portal, and leaned against the wall.

"I don't want to go back to the same place. I want to go someplace different," Kat begged.

"Good idea, Kat!"

"What's wrong with Sam?" Ronan's eyes followed Sam as she separated herself from them.

"She's fine." Penny's tone sounded rather cold.

"Look, I need you three to be okay." Ronan held his hands out, away from his sides, in a questioning manner. "Time travel can mess with your head."

"We're fine." Penny's tone turned colder than her last comment, and as she heard her own voice, she knew he was right. In fact, the memories of the place, of Nath, clung to her and created a sensation practically painful. Now she understood. Those feelings made her angry because regret colored them. Like she had let go of a dream, passed on a genuine desire, and instead chosen something safe. At that moment, Penny believed she understood Sam and the pain her soul endured for all the loves lost and all the children born and raised alone. In all of Sam's incarnations, she experienced loss, which caused her soul to suffer. Sometimes the loss of her sisters. Penny couldn't imagine living without the other two pieces of her 'we three.'

"You and Sam are both acting a bit distant." Ronan's eyes met Penny's, and he saw a familiar look, a longing. He instantly wanted to confide in her. Ever since he grabbed Sam back in the jail and had whispered the spell into her ear, he had a knowingness—a familiarity with all three of them. With Sam, it was stronger. Suddenly, Scarlet's words raced through his mind. *You've got a baby to make.* A chill ran down his spine. "Penny, I want to tell you something." He pulled her aside.

"What, Ronan? You look paler. Absolutely more colorless if possible." Penny followed him off to the side.

"One of the Order said something to me as I left the last time. She said I was connected to the Trinity Witches."

"What did she say? Wait, she?"

"I father the next solo witch," he whispered like he had said something truly reprehensible.

"What? Are you certain?"

"No. I'm not certain. I'm not certain of any of this, but it would explain a lot, like why I feel so connected to her." Sweat formed on his upper lip.

"You can't be the father—she'd never." Penny sifted through their interactions for anything, which indicated Sam displayed the remotest attraction to Ronan. "Impossible."

"Impossible is a bit harsh." Ronan appeared hurt.

"No. I don't mean because of you. I mean, Sam is adamant about not having children in this life or any other one. You should have seen her when she found out she, as the middle sister, was the one who would have a child; she was pissed."

"I get it, but what if my past incarnations fathered each solo witch's incarnation?"

"Creepy. So, the same entity fathers the solo witch incarnation, and this is you? Then who fathers the triplets?" Penny wondered if this proposition was true. It felt true. Ronan believed it was true.

"I never found out." Ronan rubbed his head. "It all sounds crazy, but so does time travel, right?"

"The whole thing feels more like a predestined plan." Penny stared into his eyes as they shared their private conversation. "I don't like that. It removes all chance of free will." Her voice had already increased in volume with her last words; now, she became animated and talked with her hands. "I refuse to believe that we have no choice in life. I've watched history change as I moved through time."

"My mentor Abraham warned me that time travel was a fool's errand. Even if we change the details, he said, the story's outcome remains the same."

"I don't believe that." Sam startled Penny and Ronan when she chimed in and broke them out of their private world.

"I don't believe it either," Kat said, "Wait, what are we talking about?" She smiled, but her grin fell into a solemnness in line with her sisters' expressions.

"Ronan wonders if his friend was, in fact, correct. That, unfortunately, time cannot be changed. Only the names and the places change, but the plots and endings remain unchanged."

"How do we confirm this?" Sam locked eyes with Ronan.

"I guess because I'm still here, and I'm still trying to save magic." He turned away.

"Nothing's changed," Kat said.

"Sure, it did. I remembered reading one of Hawthorne's short stories last year in high school. His name had the 'w' in it. Then, when we traveled back to Ipswich to the jail and returned, his name in my text had dropped the letter. So I suggested to Nathaniel to add the letter to distance himself from his past, and the letter is back. The letter is back." Penny's passion for the subject was evident.

"Okay, but perhaps it was destined that we go back and that you say that to him. Maybe, that was part of the plan all along." Kat struggled to sort it all out.

"I don't believe it," Penny said. "I refuse to believe we hold no control over our lives."

"So, we really don't," Kat said.

"Ronan, has something changed each instance you Time Walked?"

"Slight shifts, I guess. Like a business where one never was, or people's behavior is kind of off; they act differently. I'm aware the timeline's shifted by these means."

"Sounds like an alternate reality," Sam said. "Maybe the actions don't change the past; the actions simply move us into a different reality... an alternate one."

"Sure, that may be what is happening, but we've barely got a grip on this timeline and how to move in a linear fashion within it. How the hell do we move in and out of other realities?" Penny found the possibilities overwhelmed her.

"I don't know."

"If Sam and Penny are right, can't we jump into a different reality where magic is accepted? Where magic rules the world?" Kat's eyes grew wide and full of optimism.

"Theoretically, yes. But easier said than done. Shifting realities requires absolute belief and no doubt; an unwavering desire for it to be so," Ronan said.

"We wouldn't see the ramifications of jumping into another reality until we were there," Penny said.

"And we wouldn't be able to return. When we Time Walk through our own history, we know dates and places to move in and out of the linear line. Jumping realities is a whole other line. We don't know who exists there and who doesn't," Ronan explained.

"Mom?" Kat said, half asking and half reminding her sisters of the implications of their actions on their mother's life.

"Then we Time Walk until we fix this reality," Sam stated.

"And the best measurement is in the effect upon Ronan," Penny said.

"But he's here with us," Kat said, "what if the effects aren't readily seen here? What if going back home is the only way Ronan learns the impact of our actions?"

"That settles it," Sam said, "we'll travel to Ronan's home and see the impact we have caused in the future for ourselves."

"No." Ronan sounded anxious. Ronan didn't want to go back. "You can't Time Walk forward. Only to the past."

"Why?" Sam asked.

"I'm not sure. None of the ancient manuscripts mention anything about walking into the future. None of them," Ronan said.

"But that doesn't make any sense," Penny said. "Do the Trinity Witches exist in your time? We must. You knew about us."

Ronan's eyes searched Penny's, then Kat's, and finally Sam's eyes, and there his stayed locked. "No. You don't exist in my world. I only read about you three like reading a myth. Your story is recorded in the ancient and sacred text *The Supreme Sublime*, but only fragments of the manuscript remain."

"Let me get this straight." Sam's annoyance surfaced in her voice. "You're a wizard from the future, but we can't go there because we no longer exist. We're witches, but not just any witches; we're the Trinity Witches. One would think that implies a great deal of power, but none of us understand what it is or how to tap into it. Our mother must be a witch. That's just how this whole thing works, right? But somehow, she forgot, developed dementia, and doesn't even recognize her own daughters. But wait, there's more." Sam held her hand to stop her sisters from interrupting her. "We can Time Walk along our own linear timeline, but reality jumping seems a farce. Oh yeah, and something evil lurks around us, and none of us have a clue what that might be. Does that all sound about right?"

"Yeah," Penny answered.

"Ditto," Kat added.

"Yes, except for the part about not knowing what the evil might be," Ronan replied.

The three girls glared at Ronan. Sam's eyes turned darker by the second.

"One of the Order is a demonologist. Her name is Scarlet," he admitted.

Shivers ran down Sam's body. "She was here? I thought you were the only one who could Time Walk."

"I am, but she can summon a demon and send him here. Especially if she wanted to track me," Ronan said.

"Like you tracked me?" Sam asked.

"Can the demons hurt us?" Penny became concerned. "Ronan, can the demon hurt our mother?"

"Only if it takes corporeal form."

"And how do they do that?" Sam spat.

"More magic," Penny responded.

"So, what do we do?" Kat asked. "Bring magic back to save our futures? But if we do…"

"The magic would be back for everyone. Even for Scarlet and her demons," Penny interjected.

Ronan clasped his hands behind his back and paced in front of the library's desk. "Power is power. Magic is Magic. Neither one is good nor bad. It is the heart of man— the intent that may be dark, not the magic." He continued to pace. He could help them Time Walk again, but it wasn't for magic's sake. This time it was for him. He gathered his thoughts so he could present his idea in the most truthful manner possible to avoid detection by Penny and her internal lie detector. "There is a place in 1894 that I am familiar with. You three can go there and report back to me what you witness."

"You went back there?" Penny became curious about his intentions.

"Yes, and specific events occurred while there. So if you three go and witness the same thing, we'll know the effects of your previous travel."

Penny studied him. As usual, she felt his truthfulness, yet he always held back a bit of the information available to him. "A little more than fifty years after our last adventure. Are we staying in Massachusetts?"

"No, Atlantic City."

Chapter Eighteen

Atlantic City, New Jersey 1894

T hree bare, left feet led the girls through a shimmer of apparent nothingness. They stepped out and touched the warm, wet sand in another time and place. The ocean's waves roared and rolled on the beach, across the triplet's ankles. The water's frigidness ached in their bones with each intermittent wave that submerged their feet deeper. Up ahead, the rumble of laughter and chatter from the boardwalk drew their attention.

Penny took her left hand, waved in front of herself, and her two sisters did the same as all three cast the glamour spell. Again, they cloaked their twenty-first-century appearance. "Though we three cannot erase time nor space, the images we now choose reflect this place."

Unlike the bell skirt and hoops they had on their last Time Walk, they now stood in sleeker, tulip-shaped skirts. Each also wore matching, tailored linen jackets. The new ready-to-wear fashion was the rage at the emergence of the twentieth century. The new apparel was present all along the Mid-Atlantic coast.

Sam looked at her sisters and hiked her skirt to reveal her cotton stockings and laced leather boots. "Come on." She marched through the loose dry sand toward the short-stacked steps that led to the wooden boardwalk.

"Hey," Kat called out after them, "at least I can breathe in this getup."

When Kat reached the top step, she glanced back to memorize any natural landmarks. They would need to find this spot on the coast to exit through Ronan's portal again.

"We're still us," Sam said, part question and statement, because she sought validation.

"Remember, Ronan said we only 'walk in' to a previous incarnation if they are in proximity of us when we pass through." Penny's words reaffirmed the fact.

Sam remembered. But she couldn't shake the sense of déjà vu that followed her ever since they landed on the beach.

The girls waited at the top of the stairs and glanced around. In the distance, a small group of women donned in bathing costumes of the day giggled and teased each other with splashes of ocean water at each other. Seagulls cawed overhead as they soared along the water's edge, and the clamor of voices on the boardwalk called to mind the joyfulness of childhood.

"Ladies and Gentlemen," a man hollered as he marched down the center of the bowery. "The Brothers Houdini Await!"

"Girls, look." Sam pointed at the man.

"Houdini? Cool. I didn't know he had a brother." Kat followed Sam, eager to see the show in person. "Remarkable."

"We're not supposed to interfere."

"That's rich. Really, Penny? Miss *Nath, you should add a 'w' to your name,"* Sam mocked. "I don't care. This is why we're here." Sam headed straight toward the man.

"Hey! Hey you!" Sam called out as she stomped toward him with determination. "Where are the Houdini Brothers performing?"

The startled man was shocked by her boldness but answered, "Vacca's West End Casino."

"Where's that?" Sam turned around and scanned the signs.

"Close to Staunch's. Southeast corner of Ocean Avenue and Buschmann's Walk." He gestured toward the end of the wooden walkway.

"Thank you," Kat told the man as she raced past him. "Sam, wait up." Kat glanced back over her shoulder. "Penny, hurry."

Penny caught up in a skip-like, run kind of walk. "I should not have become involved with Hawthorne. I get that, but we shouldn't interact with anyone here. Just our presence has an effect, I fear."

"Maybe, but Ronan wants us to do this. Have you ever thought about that?" Sam asked.

"But he also told us not to interact," Kat said.

"And what's the best way to get three teenage girls to do something?" Sam glared at her sisters.

"Tell them not to," Penny replied.

"Think about it. Every instance we Time Walk, we end up in the situation Ronan wants," Sam said.

"It's like he's been there already and knows exactly where to send us down to the precise minute in time," Kat said. She agreed there was truth to this line of thinking.

"Let's get to the casino and find out what the Trinity Witches have to do with Houdini." Now, Penny led them. "Let's figure out why Ronan sent us here."

The three girls quickened their pace as they moved to the far end of the boardwalk. They passed Reed's Rolling Chairs. Sort of a rickshaw, but they were self-driven, three-wheeled bicycles surrounded by a wicker frame and roof. They passed the hotels with advertisements that boasted their rooms were furnished and had toilets, except the final word was spelled without the I: tolet. A veil of parasols swarmed in, and the girls found themselves cut off by the pack and unable to proceed.

"What the?"

The girls weaved along the crowd's edge, stopped near a cotton candy vendor, and pretended to wait in line.

"Is that singing?" Penny pushed ahead and dragged her sisters with her.

"I think so." Sam helped shove their way through the crowd.

"Who is it? Must be somebody famous to draw this kind of attention," Kat said.

Sam stopped as soon as she made it to the open center, surrounded by the horde of bystanders. A woman's voice sang words to a song Sam had never heard before, then a second woman joined in and sang harmony. The marquee read, *Welcome the Singing and Dancing Act: The Floral Sisters*. Sam's déjà vu became stronger. "Is that us?"

"The woman singing?" Kat asked. "No, she's not a witch. Maybe a sprite because she is so tiny, but she's not a witch."

"How do you know that? It feels like I've met her." Sam searched her memories.

"She not a past incarnation of ours. She's Bess Rahner, and she's with her sister May. The Floral Sisters were two of eight children. None of them triplets," Penny answered from her plethora of stored facts. "She's talented, but there's no magic present."

"Then why do I feel..." Sam's words stopped the moment her eyes spotted the man who walked toward the singing woman.

Kat followed her sister's eyes. "Is that Harry Houdini? I thought he would be taller. He's handsome but kind of short." Kat glanced at Sam, who appeared entranced by his presence.

"What's going on with you, Sam?" Penny watched a man on the opposite side step forward from the crowd. His focus cut to Sam, and he appeared equally spellbound as he gazed back at her.

Penny and Kat trailed behind Sam and attempted to form a shield between Sam and the man to block their mutual fixation. The mass of folks entertained by the Vaudeville Act blocked their movements. Sam only stopped when she was two or three feet away from Houdini. They stared at each other.

Sam's heart raced as she thought *I know you. Me. Samantha Hale. I know you.*

"Sam?" Harry asked. "Is that you?"

"You said my name."

Penny and Kat cut their eyes at each other as they asked themselves the same question.

"It's me," Harry tried to answer, but the Floral Sister named Bess started singing a popular song entitled Rosabelle, and briefly caught his attention. Harry turned to look at the child-like woman with the voice of an angel. Bess didn't move any closer. She just kept singing. *Rosabelle, sweet Rosabelle...*

Sam recognized the feeling. The woman was in love with Harry, and so was she. Sam stepped forward and almost touched him with the front of her entire body.

Harry turned back to Sam. "I asked for a sign." Harry gazed into her eyes. "I asked the spirits to bring me a sign. They did. They brought me you." Harry reached out and took

Sam's hands. He raised one of them to his warm lips and kissed her knuckles tenderly. Harry gazed at her with his watery, beautiful eyes, which seemed to painlessly pierce through her flesh and touch her very soul. "I love you," he said.

"Okay, I didn't see that coming. We've got to go," Penny urged. "Sam?"

"Sam? Come on," Kat pleaded.

"Sam, now!" Penny demanded. "He marries Bess!"

"You're messing this up." Kat wondered if she meant that for Sam or Penny.

Harry scowled at the sisters.

The sensation Penny had before, about an evilness, washed over her. His eyes were cold and unrelenting. So much so that she thought he might be possessed. But, when he locked eyes again with Sam, an almost visible connection linked their hearts together.

"Sam, we have to go, and now," Penny said in an urgent tone. Penny leaned toward Kat. "Do you feel that?"

"Yes, like before. Do you think Harry is a demon?" Kat whispered to Penny. "Did you see his eyes when he looked at us?"

"Yes, and I don't understand what's happening, but something is really off here. Something's not right," Penny said.

"Yeah, because how could they recognize each other?"

"Sam!" Penny said for the last time. Her patience was all but gone, and an unnerving fear crept in.

Harry grabbed Sam's arm and pushed through the crowd with her in tow. Penny and Kat raced after them, and Kat stretched her hand out and reached for her sister. Kat caught Sam's linen jacket sleeve and clutched her fingers together harder than she imagined possible. It was just enough to stop Sam. Penny grabbed Sam's other arm, and the two of them pulled their sister back to them. The crowd squeezed together and choked off Harry's reach. But not before the girls saw Harry's flared nostrils and his locked, tight expression, which penetrated from his steel eyes.

The girls ran, dragging Sam with them. Down the boardwalk, they weaved through the crowd and made their way to the end of the wooden walkway. They raced down the steps and out on the sandy beach.

Penny touched the loose ground first, Sam still in tow. Kat trailed last, where she pushed Sam to continue forward. When the space opened up, Penny and Kat flanked Sam, and they both pulled her along.

"Sam, stop fighting us." Kat shoved her sister.

"This is the best thing. Sam, he seemed downright wicked when he glared at Kat and me." Penny explained her decision as she rushed toward the portal.

"Not darkness from evil," Sam said, her voice bobbing with her forced movements. "It was heartbreak." She turned back and prayed Harry chased after her.

"Now!" Penny lifted her left foot, the signal for her sisters as she prepared to enter the portal.

Kat raised her left foot and entered with Penny. They both still held on to Sam and pulled her into the portal. Kat's grip suddenly slipped, and Sam's hand slid away. "Sam!" Kat yelled.

Penny looked back into the portal, unable to view more than Sam's arm stretched through as she held her hand. Sam's face pushed through the portal. Penny read her lips as she mouthed, *I'm sorry.* Before Penny could react, Sam jerked her hand away and fell backward. The portal zapped shut.

"Nooo!"

Kat and Penny fell hard on the library floor.

"What just happened?" Penny screamed. "Open the portal! Ronan! Open the portal!" She spun around, searching for the wizard. "Where's Ronan?"

"Good question." Kat wiped the sand from her pants. "Where *is* Ronan?"

Chapter Nineteen

"...there are three great events in the life of man— love, death, and resurrection in the new body— and magic controls them all."
Witchcraft Today, 1954

R onan passed through the portal on the other side of the library. He sensed the girls had returned, and the one he opened for them had closed. In his absence, he felt sure they would have gone home. Ronan left his library with the intent to join the girls there.

He had questions about their trip, and he wanted to know why they hadn't waited for him. But, of course, he neglected to tell them he planned a Time Walking trip of his own. Now, he hoped they wouldn't be too mad at him.

He rounded the corner, and the girl's house slid into view. He climbed the steps and spotted the fragile green vervain leaves tossed across their entry's threshold. Pieces of dried-up mandrake had been sprinkled around the vervain. He smiled. Sam had done this. She's the garden witch, and her gift would only grow stronger.

Ronan knocked on their front door. *Sorry, girls. I was called back home.* He practiced his excuse in his head, but Penny would sense the underlying lie when he said the words out loud. He knocked again, but more forcefully than before. *I don't need to explain myself to you.* This time, the door squeaked open slightly under the pressure of his knocking. As he swung the door open and exposed their foyer, supernatural energy rushed at him. He caught the door as it almost slammed shut. He had never felt this type of intense energetic frequency from the girls' magic. Fear flooded his mind as the idea of 'the something evil' they had sensed earlier had found its way to their home. *Their father!* Terror washed over him as he remembered their mother was upstairs in her room alone. She was helpless.

Ronan drew his wand, and the end with the serpent's head slithered briefly before hardening into his carved, wooden, magical tool. He crept up the stairs and listened for any indicators of who was there and what they wanted. He was ready to blast anyone with as much magic as he could muster, and he hoped it would be enough. As he reached the second-story landing, he heard two women's voices whispering. It wasn't the triplets. The voices sounded much older. If he had mastered Greater Magic, he would freeze the room and investigate unnoticed, but he knew only illusions and portal magic. Neither would help him here.

He paused outside their mother's room, his hand gripped the doorknob, and he listened. He thought he had made out the word *dead* and rushed into the room. Two aged women, one on each side of the bed, jumped from the jolt of surprise and turned to face him.

"Good grief. You've frightened us to death, young man," the rotund, mature woman named Louisa said from where she stood on Renee's left. "What on earth is that for?"

"Who are you, and where are the girls?" Ronan held his wand steady, aimed at the one who spoke.

"Where are the girls? That's a good question." Louisa looked at her sister, puzzled. "What girls?"

Ronan spoke before the other woman could answer. "Renee's daughters."

"Of course," the thin, gray-haired woman on Renee's right said out loud, but mainly she said it to herself.

"Is it true, Sister? Renee fulfilled her calling?" Louisa glanced at Lyndia with optimism.

"Where are they? and where's Benjamin?" Lyndia stood at Renee's right side, adding, "Why they've left my daughter here alone like this?"

"Your daughter? You're Renee's mother?" Ronan was surprised.

"I am. My name is Lyndia, and this is my sister Louisa. Now put the wand away before someone gets hurt."

Ronan looked down at his wand, then back up at the two old women. He lowered his hand. "And the other sister? You are triplets, are you not?"

"We were." Louisa patted Renee's delicate, limp, pink hand. She started to tell Ronan about their other sister's death, but Lyndia scolded her with a simple and short *humph*—the sound a bull makes before charging.

"We don't know who this boy is or even how he knows my granddaughters," Lyndia said to Louisa.

"I can hear you," Ronan said. He put his wand inside his new jacket, morphed with magic from his cloak into something more suitable after Sam had teased him. "Oh, you're the former Trinity Witches." Logically, he knew this to be true, but it took a few minutes for his awareness to fully grasp the significance.

"You've guessed who we are...who we *were*." Lyndia corrected herself due to the newness of their situation.

"I'm Ronan Magus," he said. "Wizard and Leader of the...former leader of the Order of Nine Illuminations." An image of Abraham loomed in his mind, and the pangs of his loss expanded in his chest.

"Order of the Nine?" Lyndia searched her still foggy memory for the last information she could recall about the Order. Lyndia glanced over at Louisa. "It is the Order of Twelve, is it not?"

"Yes, sister. The Order of the Twelve Illuminations, Protectors of Magic and the Ways of the Sublime," Louisa said. "I recall quite well. I dated Richard, their specialist in...in Celestial Magic, I believe."

"Louisa?" Lyndia chided her sister's digression.

"Correction. There are only nine now. Actually, we just lost our eldest, our Order's scribe. His name was

Abraham. So, there are eight members left." "Oh dear," Louisa said.

"And yet, here you are. Sounds like the Order of Seven. *Tisk. Tisk.*" Lyndia said. "So, why are you here in my daughter's home?"

"I came for the girls. We were, um..." Ronan paused as he searched for words that wouldn't add more confusion. "We were working on a project together, and they left my library before I returned. So I figured they would have come back here."

"She looks awful." Louisa gazed down at her only niece and her now pitiful face and the grey, tinged spot that marked half Renee's lower lip. "How could Benjamin not notify us the instant she fell ill?"

"You mean you were unaware Benjamin left them?" Ronan observed the dazed expressions on both of their faces. "He left when the girls were three."

"How old are they now?" Lyndia seemed confused as to how so many years could fly by unnoticed.

"Almost eighteen." Ronan watched the thin woman grab the bed frame to steady herself as she nearly fainted. He wondered how they couldn't have known any of this. "What happened to your other sister?" Ronan asked.

Lyndia glared at Louisa, an indication she wanted no more information revealed.

"He's not actually evil, Lyndia. My powers fade with the loss of our third, but I can tell he's not malevolent." She looked over at the unnatural, ghostly man who stood at the foot of her niece's bed. "He has done a few things that weren't noble, but he isn't an evil being." Louisa eyed Ronan and said, "Our other sister recently died of natural causes. Her name was Sylvia."

Ronan considered the information while his mind pondered what ignoble actions she referenced.

"Do you know what's wrong with my daughter?"

"Dementia," Ronan replied. "The girls told me she suffers early onset dementia, and lately, this is all she does." He gestured toward Renee's reposed form with a nod in her direction.

"Nonsense." Louisa leaned over her daughter and gently patted the side of Renee's face in an attempt to rouse some sort of awareness that she was present. Renee didn't move. "And the girls just leave her here alone?"

"No. Not really. I mean, the last couple of days since I showed up, yes, but normally they don't." Ronan noticed the women both scrutinized him, and it made him quite uncomfortable. "They care for her. Kat told me so."

"Kat?" Louisa said.

"Yes. She's the youngest triplet. Her name is Katrina, and she told me she and her sisters, Penny and Sam, I mean Penelope and Samantha, they dress her, bathe her, feed her, and even make this special tea for her three times a day."

"Special tea?" Lyndia asked. "What kind of special tea? Where is it from?"

"Kat said their father, Benjamin mails it to them." Ronan pointed to the cup and saucer on Renee's nightstand.

Ronan glanced at the bedroom door. He wished the girls would show up and soon.

"Strange, we get a postcard from Benjamin every month with an update on his and Renee's whereabouts. But none of this can be true if she's been here." Lyndia sought some clarity. "How often does the tea arrive?"

"I think about the same as your postcards. Once a month," Ronan answered. "And he insists she drinks it three or four times daily."

The two women locked eyes. "We've received a postcard every month for eighteen years." Lyndia rubbed the two lines that formed an eleven wrinkle between her brows. "Benjamin has shipped a tea to Renee in the same manner for as long?" She cut her eyes to Ronan. "And you showed up two days ago, and our sister died two days ago. Do you work for that wicked man?"

"I didn't... I don't..."

"Shhh, boy," Lyndia said. "Sister, the tea."

Louisa reached for the empty cup. "If I'm right about this..."

Lyndia interrupted. "And she *is* always right," Louisa said, "continue, sister."

"If I'm right, someone enchanted the three of us via the postcards, and the spell couldn't be broken until one of the three of us died. We never suspected Renee was sick. In fact, we believed she traveled the world with Benjamin all these years." Her eyes became glossy with tears. "Bits and pieces of our memory slowly drift back into their rightful place. And now that our heads are clear, there's no way Renee would have agreed to any of this. To not ever see her own mother for eighteen years? To not tell us about the girls? It wasn't until yesterday our thoughts became clear enough to know Renee would never do this."

"And we headed straight here." Louisa raised the teacup to her nose and sniffed the contents. "The tea must be some kind of potion." She hovered her left hand over the cup and said, "Sacra fero revelare."

The China rattled against the saucer, and a thin line of black swirled inside the cup. The movement increased with each revolution until the mystical smoke shot straight up and burst against the ceiling. A blackish stain remained like soot from a candle whose wick had been left too long. She dropped the cup, and it shattered across the wood-planked floor. "Dark magic."

Ronan and Lyndia rushed to Louisa's side.

"Don't touch it," Louisa said, "It's poisoned."

Chapter Twenty

"...the magician must always be stronger
Than the demon he invokes."
The Secrets of Ancient Witchcraft

They stared at the pieces of broken China scattered on the floor and around Louisa's black orthopedic shoes.

A drop of poisonous liquid bubbled. It was a revolt against the planked wood's natural antimicrobial properties. This dissipated into a tiny stream of blackish smoke. The women glared at Ronan.

"I didn't do that," Ronan pleaded. "I'm the leader of the Order sworn to protect magic. I would never harm anyone."

"You said you *were* the leader. Which is it? Are you, or are you not, in charge of the Order?"

"I was," Ronan admitted. "I discovered the girls were an incarnation of the Trinity Witches, and I had to help them— keep them safe. They were unaware of who they really were. So I left the Order to be here and protect them."

Lyndia wasn't sure if they should trust him. Something about him wasn't one hundred percent upfront. But she understood they needed him. He must act as their third power. This was the only way to counteract the spell poisoning Renee.

Louisa whispered to her sister, "He stepped across the girls' vervain at the door. He's not the evil behind this."

Lyndia considered Louisa's words. "They do not have their full power yet because *ours* has not fully waned. The charm which activated the plants outside isn't strong enough to keep all darkness away." Lyndia studied Ronan, who now paced at the foot of Renee's bed. Lyndia rolled her eyes. No other options existed. After a few seconds, Lyndia acquiesced. "Boy, we're going to need your help."

"Anything." Ronan stopped pacing and turned to face them.

"We have to break this spell and get Renee back." Lyndia reached her hand out to clasp Ronan's.

"I didn't know I could do this with you. I thought..." Ronan said, interrupted by Louisa.

"We need three. Of course, our magic is strongest when the three are the Trinity Witches, but it requires three."

"Take my hand," Lyndia insisted, "besides, I thought you were a wizard?"

"I am. It's just that I... just tell me what to do." Ronan took Lyndia's hand with his right and Louisa's hand with his left.

"We are weaker with Sylvia gone. I hope your power is enough. If not, we'll have to wait on the girls." Louisa offered him an empathetic smile.

Again, Ronan questioned where the three had gone. He wondered how they would take this. Their grandmother and their great-aunt were back in their lives. Their other aunt had died before they had even met her. And worse of all, their mother didn't have dementia. She had been poisoned. He was uncertain of their imminent reactions.

"We must perform an unbinding spell." Louisa stretched across the bed and grabbed Lyndia's other hand. They formed a triangle over Renee and began their chant.

Renee stirred on top of the bed. Then, at once, all three of them turned their gazes to the bedroom door. The same evilness Ronan and Penny had sensed was back. But now, it was in their home, and the two old witches felt it too.

"Do not break hands. No matter what happens or what you see." Lyndia tightened her grip on both her sister's and Ronan's hands. "Ama handia eskatu diogu."

"In English, sister. For the boy."

Lyndia began again, "Great Mother, we beseech thee. Our frail lives are in your hands. Great Mother, we implore thee. Release this witch's heart. Reverse the spell, unwind the net, undo this cast of wickedness."

Louisa joined in next and repeated Lyndia's reversal spell. Ronan caught on quickly and chanted along. "Great Mother, we beseech thee. Our frail lives are in your hands. Great Mother, we implore thee. Release this witch's heart.

Reverse the spell, unwind the net, undo this cast of wickedness."

The longer the three repeated the phrases, the more violent Renee's movements became. She writhed on the bed like they performed an exorcism. Sweat beaded on Renee's forehead as she grimaced. Her body contorted and twisted the sheets around her legs.

A strangeness drifted over Ronan, like he was being watched. The sensation was so intense it prompted him to look over his shoulder. He continued to recite the undoing spell while he studied the emergent, invisible evilness that hung as haziness outside the bedroom. It was a dark energy that hadn't taken any corporeal form yet. The frequency he sensed was definitely bad.

He didn't know if what was outside the door caused the reaction in Renee or if their attempt to break the spell was responsible. He turned back toward Renee and glanced at the women, both still chanting along with him.

Noises loomed from downstairs. The women's invocation increased in speed. The words flew from his mouth quicker than he thought possible. The sounds became one ridiculously long word, like a wind that howled around them. They continued, "GreatMotherwebeseechthee. Ourfraillivesareinyourhands. GreatMotherweimplorethee. Releasethiswitch'sheart. Reversethespellunwindthenetundothiscastofwickedness." His lips moved at an unnatural pace.

Ronan was convinced he would never get a chance for another breath when Lyndia yelled, "BREAK THIS SPELL. SO MAY IT BE." She clapped her hands so loud; Ronan's ears rang. He flinched and craned his neck to one side. He watched from the corner of his eyes as Renee's body fell flat and into stillness. Before he turned back around, he caught someone in his peripheral vision. A figure in full form lurched off to his left. He rotated and contorted further as he still held on to Louisa's hand and stared nearly straight behind himself. The girls stood in the doorway, and each glared into the room.

"What the hell?" Penny used her sister's favorite line as she pushed her way into her mother's room. "Who the hell are you two?" She appeared to ask the women, but in reality, she asked this of Ronan. And she needed to know why he had led them to their mother. "Start explaining." She wiped a tear from her cheek.

"This is your grandmother and your great-aunt," Ronan said. "What's wrong?

The girls studied the two women and Ronan. "Something is very wrong," Penny knelt beside her mother's bed and took her mother's hand in hers.

"They're who?"

"Calm yourselves, girls," Lyndia said. "We are the Trinity Witches, well, we *were*, and now, I suppose, the next Trinity Witches are you."

The room fell silent.

Louisa didn't like the awkwardness and decided to cut through it. "I suppose a proper introduction is in order. Hello, girls. I'm your Great Aunt Louisa, and this is Renee's mother, Lyndia. She's your grandmother."

"I don't care who you are," Penny spat. "You need to leave. Our mother's sick." Penny cried into the blankets, crunched at Renee's side as she pressed them into her face.

"What have you done, Ronan?" Kat went to offer aid to Penny and her mother. "What were all of you doing to her?"

"I haven't done anything."

"No, dear. We are good witches and work for the common good of man. We never harm. It's part of our creed." Louisa wanted to recite the entire doctrine that very moment, but she refrained from doing so.

"She's under a dark spell, dear. It's the tea." Lyndia pointed at the cup.

"The tea?" Penny jumped up and stumbled backward. She glared at the shards of China scattered on the left side of the floor. Then, without any thought, she bent down to clean up the mess.

"NO!" Louisa demanded. "It's poisoned."

The girls stared at each other as they processed the information. "Our mom has been poisoned?" Penny asked as it all started to make sense. She staggered farther back and fell against the wall. "You mean I've poisoned my mother every day with his tea?" She felt her knees weaken and instinctively pressed her back to the wall for support.

"You didn't poison her. Benjamin did," Lyndia said.

"We knew he was no good, didn't we, sister?" Louisa gazed at Penny. "Your grandmother and Sylvia always knew it. In fact, Lyndia tried to prevent your mother from marrying Benjamin, but Renee wouldn't listen. She's stubborn. But we never imagined he could do this."

Penny's mind raced, and she knew why she always felt sick whenever she thought of him. But it was more than that; he was a deadbeat dad. Her father was genuinely evil, but her own emotions prevented her from acknowledging the feeling was anything more. She swore to herself right then she would never let him harm them ever again.

"Why didn't he poison us too?" Kat asked.

Penny stepped forward, away from the wall. "He didn't need to. With our mom and the Trinity Witches out of the picture, we would never even know we were witches. He was right. We just played right into his plan. But," Penny looked at the two women, "where were you?"

Ronan stepped around the end of the bed frame and braced Penny with his hands. She looked as though she might collapse any minute. He softly told her, "They were under a spell and didn't know your mother was sick or that the three of you even existed." Ronan looked at Kat for reassurance that she believed him. "Their other sister died two days ago. That's why..."

"Why our powers have increased." Penny turned away from Ronan and hurried back to her mother. "I'm sorry, Mom. I didn't know," Penny cried, too ashamed to look directly at her sickly mother's face.

"Dear, none of us knew." Lyndia tried to comfort her granddaughter.

"But I'm the one who gave her the tea. I did this to her." Penny sobbed out each word. Shame consumed Penny as she scolded herself. She should have known better. A special tea shipped every month by a man who never wanted them. All her shame twisted, and she understood rage. "Benjamin has done this," Penny said in a questioning tone, but she knew the truth about her father, about her reluctance to reach out to him. He was the evilness she felt. Penny dropped to her knees beside the bed. "Is she going to die? Please don't let her die."

"Oh, dear," Louisa said. She held her hand just above Penny's copper hair. She wanted to pat her and offer comfort, but she wasn't sure the girl would take her gesture of sympathy the way she meant it.

"I hope not, dear. But we certainly could use some herbal cures. Which one of you is the Green Witch?"

Kat remembered that Sam wasn't with them. Ronan noticed, too. "Kat?" Ronan asked, "Why isn't Sam here? Where is she?"

Kat glanced at Penny. "We've got to get Sam," Kat said.

"Where is she?" Ronan demanded.

"She let go of my hand...and she...she..." Penny wept in her cupped hands as her face rested against her mother's side.

"Sam let go of our hands as we stepped back through the portal. She stayed behind," Kat said, dejected, "with Harry."

"Who is Harry." Lyndia was confused.

"A portal?" Louisa mouthed to Ronan while her hand still hovered lovingly over Penny's hair. "Oh, dear."

"Harry Houdini," he answered as he contemplated the full effect this might have. "She stayed behind to be with Harry?" He half asked, and half stated because he was both hurt and pleased. Now he wondered what kind of impact Sam's actions would have on magic, or history for that matter, because she had a tremendous effect on him. Suddenly, here in their present timeline, he felt rejected.

"Oh, dear," Louisa said again. She moved around Penny's slumped body and nervously fluffed the pillows under Renee's head.

"Sam can't stay there," Ronan said. "She was supposed to come back."

"No kidding, but you weren't in the library like you said you would be," Penny said, still kneeling on the floor with her face buried in her mother's side.

"We were ready to go right back in, but you were gone," Kat said. "We went to the coffee shop, the jail, back to the library, and finally here. We searched everywhere for you. We really needed your help, and you were nowhere to be found." Now, Kat believed that she shouldn't trust him either. "What's going on, Ronan?"

"Back in where?" Lyndia displayed a genuine, grandmotherly concern. "Where's my other granddaughter?"

"I opened a portal for the girls to practice Time Walking." Ronan wondered what Sam was doing in that world, but he believed he already knew.

"Sam is trapped in 1894," Kat said, and she looked away.

Unexpectedly, the girl's mother, Renee, pitched forward. Her eyes were wide and wild as she stared at something the rest of them couldn't see. Then, a violent scream burst out of her mouth. "TELLS LIES." Like a hot breath on one's ear, her words sent shivers down each of their spines. Renee gasped for air and collapsed back on the bed. She lay still and lifeless like before any of them had arrived, leaving them to wonder who the liar she referred to was.

Chapter Twenty-One

"And when love is involved, it is violent and uncontrolled.

Love, for the witch, is a consuming passion..."

The World of the Witches

I n silence, the five: Louisa, Lyndia, Ronan, Penny, and Kat stared at Renee. Her breath had stabilized, and her chest raised slightly with each of her normal breaths. She appeared to be sleeping.

Ronan turned to Penny. "I'm sorry that your other great aunt died before you could meet her."

Penny turned around, not to face Ronan but to confront her grandmother. "Where the hell have you been our whole lives?" She knew she was being disrespectful, but anger welled inside. Her cheeks became flushed, and her bottom lip quivered. Penny wanted to rush at Lyndia. She knew the woman was old, but she didn't care. The old crone had abandoned her only daughter, just like Benjamin had abandoned her and her sisters.

"They were enchanted. Held under a spell...," Ronan said as he watched Penny's lip pull up on one side, almost in a snarl. "They never even knew you existed."

Penny recognized this was true, but that didn't change the flood of emotions rushing through her.

Lyndia considered her granddaughter's pain and said, "Honey, if I had known, I would have been here." And she meant it. She couldn't imagine being alone and raising three daughters. Lyndia had only one daughter, Renee, and she had her own two sisters, Louisa and Sylvia, to help her raise her only child.

"We would have been here," Louisa chimed in. "All three of us, but Benjamin kept sending postcards of Renee's travels around the world. We thought they were happily in love." Louisa's doleful expression signified the authenticity of her words.

"That's how the enchantment was held in place," Kat stated. It wasn't a question; she comprehended exactly what had transpired. "As long as the three of you were alive, Benjamin could keep reinforcing the spell. It would have never been broken if Sylvia hadn't died."

"Yes, that's correct," Louisa agreed, "after Sylvia died, our memories slowly returned. As soon as we realized the truth that we had been under a spell, we rushed to Renee."

Again, Penny knew the words were all truths. So, who was lying? She glanced over at Ronan. An unease surrounded him. Maybe it *was* evilness. She didn't know. Perhaps he was capable of cloaking his own nature—

glamouring himself to appear as this strange man before her when in fact, he was a demon himself.

"Ronan, why did you look at the door? When you were chanting, you turned around and looked directly at me and Kat. Why?"

"I sensed something," he answered.

"Are you implying that we're evil?" Penny asked.

"It certainly would explain Sam's black eyes when she's pissed," Kat said, trying to lighten the extreme seriousness of their situation.

Penny didn't acknowledge Kat's words; she just stood beside the bed, wiping the tears from her cheeks with her sleeve.

"Your mother will be fine for a few minutes without us," Lyndia said. She tucked the top sheet and blanket neatly at her daughter's sides, bent over, and kissed Renee's face.

Penny looked at Louisa, whose face was now inches away from hers. "I felt, and Ronan said he had felt it too, a sense of darkness. I know what Benjamin has done is evil things here, but do you think he is a demon or something else evil?"

"A demon?" Ronan asked with surprise. "Trust me. Man is quite capable of horrid actions like this." But he didn't mind the girls pursuing that line of thinking. He felt the presence, too but suspected Scarlet was behind that. Sending a demon to spy on him was right in her wheelhouse. He was unsure if Scarlet could control the creatures she evoked beyond the act of spying via remote viewing through her summoned creature's eyes.He needed to investigate the possibilities on his own, and the girls believing their father was the demon was a much-welcomed distraction.

Kat stepped near the teacup that shattered on the floor. "I read something on a blog post that a girl said a spirit haunted her family, and a demon fathered her mother and her mother's twin brother," Kat said, looking back at the blank eyes staring at her. "No, really. Think about it. What if Benjamin really is a demon, and after he did his deed, he disappeared?" Kat bent down to grab a piece of the broken China.

The two older women gasped.

"Don't worry," Kat said, reassuring her grandmother and great aunt, "I'm taking the handle. It should be free of poisonous herbs."

Kat closed her eyes and waited for her gift of psychometry to kick in.

Penny considered Kat's theory. "It would explain the uneasy feeling I always get just thinking about him. Did our mom's father disappear too?"

Lyndia glanced at Louisa as she contemplated what her granddaughter was proposing. "I married Buckman Glouster in the spring of 1980. He went missing during my last trimester before Renee was born that autumn."

"What about your father?" Penny asked.

"Our father?" Louisa asked, "I don't know that we ever even knew his name. We were raised by only our mother as well. Isn't that right, Lyndia?"

"Yes. I'm afraid so."

Penny tried to recall their family tree in her mind. Her mother, Renee, had married Benjamin Hale. He disappeared when the girls were three. Renee's mother had married a Buckman Glouster, who also went missing, but this time before Renee was born. Lyndia, Louisa, and Sylvia's mother, Floraidh Howe, was unwed. Penny remembered there were several generations of unwed women, both mothering solo witches and those mothering the Trinity Witches. Floraidh's mother's name was Maureen Howe. She was a Trinity Witch. Mathilda, Mari, and Maureen's mother's name was Rose Howe, and her mother was Sophia Howe. Adele, Camille, and Sophia's mother's name was Roxanne Howe—all unwed. But the Howe surname had entered the lineage when Roxanne's mother married Percival Howe in 1833. Mary Peabody and her two sisters, Elizabeth and Sophia, were the triplet daughters of Bertha Hobbs, who had married William Peabody in 1813, the same year as the girls' birth. William's death was recorded as occurring in 1814. Bertha would have raised the girls on her own. After Bertha's middle daughter, Mary Peabody married Percival and conceived Roxanne, he stayed around for three years, then was recorded as dying in 1837. The following five generations didn't even bother marrying. It was like their family was cursed.

"Well, being fathered by a demon would certainly complicate things," Louisa said, gathering Penny in her arms and swooping the frail coppery bird under her wings.

"Benjamin may be a demon," Kat finally said, still holding the cup's handle. "I'm not sure, but he was sent by someone...someone powerful. I think by a female..."

"Are you sure?" Ronan asked. He wondered if the female was Scarlet. How could it be? If Scarlet had sent Benjamin, that meant she was aware of the witches. This time, Ronan staggered back. If Scarlet knew, if she knew the Trinity Witches' history, she could have devised a plan to send a demon back in time. If she had accomplished this and actually summoned a demon to appear or possess another human, Scarlet could have succeeded at infiltrating demon DNA into the witches' bloodline instead of their intended paternal line. He needed to stop Kat from reading any more information about the cup. "KAT?" He yelled, startling her and causing the handle to fall from her hand.

"Jesus, Ronan. What was that for?" Kat said.

"Sorry." He hadn't known what else to do to make her drop the piece of China.

"Was there anything else, Kat?" Penny asked. "Did you get any other information?"

"No," Kat answered.

"Girls, let's go down and make a spot of real tea, um? All this excitement has me feeling a bit out of sorts. Plus, we need to make a plan to get Sam back here with us."

"And figure out if someone has sent a demon into the Trinity Witches' bloodline."

Chapter Twenty-Two

"The only power that charlatans have is the power given to them by those who have abandoned their own thinking process and accepted the views, opinions, and unproven assertations of others."

The Secrets of Ancient Witchcraft

T he tea kettle whistled with the billow of steam discharged thru the tiny hole in its lid. "I'm surprised Sam didn't notice something strange about the tea," Louisa said. "Or even you, Kat. That's quite some gift being able to read information by touching objects."

Kat glanced up at her great aunt, wondering if the old woman accused her of being an accomplice with some demon poisoning her mother. "I just discovered my gift," she explained.

"Oh, I see," Louisa said, looking over at Penny.

"Sam likes to grow herbs and things, but she... we didn't know we were witches until yesterday, so," Penny said.

She thought it was ridiculous for these two, who had been absent all their lives to waltz in and start demanding answers. "I should have known, I suppose, but my claircognizance didn't pick up anything."

"It's not even been two full days, and we've been to 1692, 1841, and 1894. I'm exhausted," Kat said, "and we've still got to get Sam back."

"I'll open another portal, but without all three of you, I don't think it will work," Ronan said.

"Okay, so our magic requires three. What about you or one of them?" Penny asked, pointing at her newfound relatives.

"We're too weak, dear," Louisa said, pouring hot water into a coffee mug with the House of Seven Gables logo on one side. "We didn't have enough power to pull Renee back one hundred percent."

"Then Ronan," Penny said, "Ronan will go through with us."

Ronan wasn't sure how he could get out of this. He couldn't go back. This he already knew because he had Time Walked there before and found himself to be incarnated there. "If I go through the portal with you, I won't be able to hold this side of the portal open," he said, purposefully lying. He sat his coffee cup down hard on the table, creating a loud clank. He hoped it had been enough to distract Penny from reading his level of truth-telling.

"Open a portal, Ronan," Kat commanded. "We're going in to get our sister back."

"I told you, it won't..."

"Just do it," Lyndia said. "Then they'll see for themselves that their magic requires three."

Ronan stood up, staring directly into Lyndia's eyes, and retrieved his wand from inside his jacket. By the time the piece of wood was visible to all their eyes, it had solidified into his carved Acacia Koa wand. This time, he held it in his right hand and moved the wand clockwise. He had no intention of letting the girls walk back in time and find him as Harry and find him with Sam.

A grayish-blue shimmer wiggled into a large circular-shaped portal, and the two girls stepped forward, preparing to walk through the gateway.

"Take my hand, Penny," Kat said.

Penny stared at her sister with an awkward expression. She had never held Kat's hand when stepping into new places. Sam was always in between them. "Okay," Penny said, reaching her hand toward Kat's.

The two sisters each raised their left foot and stepped into the glimmering doorway. Except, instead of their usual smooth passage, their feet slammed into the wall. Kat's forehead clunked the wall soon after.

"Oh dear," Louisa said.

"What happened?" Kat said, rubbing the spot on her head that smashed into the wall.

"I told you," Ronan said, "your magic requires three."

"It always has for us too, girls. Don't be alarmed. We'll think of something," Lyndia said.

Penny glared at Ronan. She had that feeling again that he wasn't telling them everything he knew.

"Girls, Louisa and I are going back up to check on Renee. Why don't you try to find something like a spell or herbs that can help bring your mother all the way back. We'll try to use whatever magic we have left. Renee may be the only person with magic strong enough to help bring Sam back home, but first, we have to get her back." The two ladies made their way toward the stairs. Louisa turned back and looked at the two girls. "Play nice, dears. We need Ronan too."

"I'm coming up with you," Penny said to her great aunts. She looked back at Kat. "I want to check on mom. I'll be right back."

Kat nodded at Penny, then moved her eyes to Ronan.

Upstairs, Lyndia grabbed Penny's hand and patted it. "Oh, I'm so happy you've joined us."

"Me too," Louisa said. "Oh, I almost forgot." She pulled a rutilated quartz crystal out of her pocket and allowed it to spin wildly on the copper chain that suspended it.

"What's that?" Penny asked.

"Sylvia's amulet. She wore it every day of her life," Louisa said.

"Oh. Sam's the gemstone person. I don't really know anything about crystals."

"No, dear. It's meant for you. Sylvia passed all her powers into it before she took her final breath. She was the eldest, as are you. This necklace is yours. Her powers can only pass to you."

Penny reached out, taking the amulet in her palm. A tingle rushed up the same arm as she studied the strange piece. The copper chain had three smaller links connected by one slightly larger link. The pattern repeated for the entire length of the chain. The crystal was held by a copper casting of a rabbit's head, making the crystal the rabbit's body. Inside the clear crystal were tiny stringers of a red mineral that looked like blood flowing inside the stone. Penny placed the chain over her head, and the rabbit dangled just below her breastbone.

"Lovely," Louisa said.

Penny knelt and kissed her mother's cheek. She wanted to tell her mother she was sorry, but before she could, Penny heard her mother whisper to her that she was sorry. Penny looked up, but her mother was still asleep; her eyes were completely closed. Penny thought she must have imagined it. Then she noticed the crystal resting on her mother's arm. Maybe she did hear her mother's voice telepathically. Penny straightened up, preparing to stand, and clasped the crystal with its rabbit's head in her left hand. A white-goldish light shot from the stone, and a surge of energy rushed through Penny's arm, making a B-line straight to her heart.

She gasped for air as the power penetrated her being. She felt her heart flutter in her throat and gazed over at her grandmother and her great aunt who stood silently watching the transference of their dead sister's powers. Then, without knowing why, Penny placed her right hand on her own mother's forehead. A tiny bleep of light shot from under Penny's hand and glowed out from under her palm. Renee's breath deepened. Penny removed her hand without questioning what had just transpired and turned to leave the room. She stopped at the door and said, "Renee will regain consciousness soon. She will remember what has happened to her." Penny went back downstairs.

Penny joined Kat, who was rather glaring at Ronan. He uncomfortably fidgeted before taking a seat in their living room, where they had attempted their Time Walk. Penny felt overwhelmed. She had faith that her mother would be healed and that, somehow, she'd know how to get Sam back. The answer would simply pop into her head. The problem was she had no control over her gift or when the universe decided to zap an insight into her brain. Maybe the amulet would give her control. "I don't know what to do," Penny finally said, slipping the rabbit crystal inside her shirt. She didn't want to get Kat's hopes up. They would know soon enough if Sylvia's powers had indeed healed their mother.

"I do," Kat replied, remembering her newly discovered gift of psychometry. She plopped down on their sofa next to Ronan and offered him a Cheshire smile. Then she grabbed his arm so tight he couldn't pull away. She didn't know if it would work, really, but she hoped she could read people by touching them the way she could read objects. She squeezed harder as her eyes widened their glare.

"Kat, what are you doing? You're hurting my arm," Ronan said, trying to pull out of her grip. "Let go of me."

Penny stared with fascination as Kat's seemingly inhuman strength maintained her clasp. Penny suddenly knew what Kat was up to. "What's your read?" She asked.

"Read?" Ronan asked, pulling even harder now.

"Well, for one, he didn't open a portal," Kat said, dropping his arm in disgust. "And two, he's Harry Houdini."

"What?" Penny asked in disbelief, even though her internal lie detector signaled her the absolute truth was in that statement. "What's going on, Ronan?" she demanded.

"Okay," Ronan said, prepared to make a full confession. "A while back, I Time Walked to the Boardwalk and found myself to be the incarnation of Harry Houdini."

"Spill all of it, Ronan," Kat said, reminding him with her look that she had felt the truth.

"When I went back, I met a woman, as Harry, and I had an affair with her."

"One of the Floral Sisters?" Penny asked.

"No," Kat answered for him.

"It was someone else. I didn't know who at the time, but having the affair was wrong. I realized I may have screwed the whole timeline up. Harry needs to marry Bess in that time, and I'm not convinced that it wasn't my influence upon seeing the woman that prompted the entire situation."

"Oh, shit," Penny said, "the woman was Sam."

"I had to send you back. Maybe Sam wouldn't fall for Harry on his own. Maybe it was me, and maybe, she could

281

fix the timeline by not choosing to become involved. If I went back, I know I would make the same mistake all over again."

"Because when you met Sam again in this incarnation, you saw how resistant she is to being in a relationship and to being the middle sister that carries on our legacy; you thought she wouldn't repeat the same mistake?" Penny asked.

"When Sam chose to stay behind, I knew my feelings back then were genuine. We were in love, and our life there was idyllic. That's why she didn't want to come back. She experienced the same thing."

"You led us there for your own selfish purpose! So now, our sister is gone! She's trapped there, and we don't know how to get her back!"

"The longer she's there, the harder it will be to retrieve her and pull her out of that life," Ronan said. "But first, we must focus on getting your mother's strength back. She may be our only hope of finding Sam."

No sooner had those words come from Ronan's mouth than Louisa and Lyndia appeared at the top of the staircase.

"Girls, we have something you'll want to see," Louisa said.

Penny and Kat rushed to the base of the stairs.

"Is Mom alright?" Kat asked.

The two women at the second-floor landing stepped aside, parting at the top of the stairs. Renee feebly stepped to the railing. "Girls?" Renee said in a weak, soft voice.

"MOM?" Kat and Penny yelled together as they both ran up the stairs.

Kat hugged Renee tightly, kissing her mother's cheek for what seemed to be a million times. Penny put her arms around her mom and Kat, embracing them as one.

Renee kissed her two daughters. Suddenly, anguish washed over her face. "Where's Samantha? Where's your sister?"

"I'm sorry, Mom," Penny cried. "I should have held on tighter. I shouldn't have let her go."

"Let her go?" Renee asked. Her mind was still foggy from the herbal concoction that had for years been poisoning her mind. "Well, go get her. She needs to know I'm okay."

"It's not that easy, Mom," Kat explained. "We lost her in a different timeline. She's in 1894."

"What?" Renee said, the word coming out with her exhaled breath.

"Mrs. Hale, I'm Ronan Magnus, and I'm afraid it is me that must shoulder the entire blame."

Both girls looked over at Ronan. He had a way of appearing so otherworldly with his pale complexion and chiseled features. Yet, he was charming and, while looking young, gave the impression of being a very old soul.

"Well, Ronan Magnus," Renee said, holding the rail as she made her way down the stairs to face him, "then you'll need to go retrieve my daughter."

The two girls helped their mother down the stairs, and Louisa and Lyndia followed. They sat, like a conclave, around the dining room table. Renee took the seat at one end, and Lyndia, her mother, took the chair at the opposite end. The heads of the table, as it were, by the heads of the family.

"Ronan, explain yourself," Renee said.

"Like I said, I'm Ronan Magnus, leader of the Order of the Nine Illuminations."

"Nine?" Renee asked, looking at Louisa.

"They're a dwindling lot, it appears," Louisa said, glancing at Ronan. "Presently, it seems as though there are seven members. Isn't that right, Ronan? Oh, and he isn't their current leader."

"Correct," Ronan admitted. "I recently abdicated my position."

"Why on earth would you do that?" Renee asked. "It is a position of prestige and great honor even to be a member, let alone their leader."

"I'm a wizard. My main talent is Time Walking. I began going back in time to intercept and fix points in history where magic was marginalized. You see, where I'm from, in the future, magic has all but vanished. The Order preserves what little information remains by transcribing the ancient sacred texts over and over, but we were never to practice magic of any form."

"But you did practice?" Renee said. "Time Walking is magic, is it not?"

The girls sat amazed at their mother's poise and power as she continued her line of questioning.

"I felt that history could be revised and magic could hold its proper and high place in the world again if only a few strategic points in time were rectified."

"How did that work out for you," Renee asked, knowing the answer herself. Like Abraham, Renee knew the details could be changed, but the outcome of history would remain the same.

"Not very well. I began Time Walking and altering history. At first, I thought I was making headway, but then I somehow altered history to the point that Trinity Witches disappeared completely. I had inadvertently erased the Trinity Witches from the future timeline and plunged my century deeper into *The Great Sleep*, and I feared for all eternity. It was my actions had made the three women among the accused in the Salem Witch Trials. So, I had to go back and save them."

"He did, Mom," Kat said.

"But, when he entered that timeline, his portal was opened at the Old Gaol Museum. I sensed it when we were walking to meet our class for our senior trip," Penny explained.

"Your senior trip?" Renee asked. She realized the girls were older, but her mind hadn't put together exactly how much older they were. She looked at them both, really looked at them. A mother always recognizes her children, maybe not by appearance at first, but by the maternal thread linking them. She smiled. "You both have become such beautiful young women."

Penny smiled back, and Kat blushed, dropping her head and staring uncomfortably at the wooden table's top.

"Your daughters stepped into their previous incarnations of the Trinity Witches who were alive at the time. I wasn't sure of it until I helped them escape," Ronan said. "The seventeenth-century witches walked out into the city of Ipswich, but your girls walked back through my portal, and I followed them back to this timeline."

"Mom, two of them were hung. The middle sister, Sam's incarnation, she escaped as a stowaway on a ship," Kat said.

"Sam read from a journal that incarnation of her knew she was pregnant when she escaped," Penny added, not exactly sure why it felt important to do so.

"That was a good thing," Lyndia said. "The middle sister carries on the family lineage. If she hadn't escaped—we wouldn't be here now."

"Okay, so you were all back here in the twenty-first century. Why travel anyplace else?" Renee asked.

"We wanted to, Mom," Kat said. "We wanted to do it again, so we went to Brook Farm and met Nathaniel Hawthorne. Penny told him to write about his ancestors and make amends for their wrongdoing. And he did. That's the Nathaniel we all know from Literature class in high school."

"So, somehow, Penny's actions became the prime cause for the focus of Nathaniel's life's work," Renee said.

"And I guess *that* made you think there was hope for you to make a change like you originally intended?" Lyndia asked Ronan.

"Yes," Ronan said, feeling somewhat vindicated in his actions. "I had one more spot that my actions had totally messed up."

"The Boardwalk in 1894," Penny said.

"Yes."

Louisa raised her hand and utilized her fingers to mark the points she was about to summarize. "Let me get this all straight. One," she said, touching her thumb to her four fingers, then raising her pointer finger in the air, "you had traveled back to 1894 once before." She waited for Ronan to nod in agreement. He did. "Two," her middle finger jabbed up to stand next to her pointer's raised stance, "once there, you found yourself to be your previous incarnation, who happened to be Harry Houdini?" Again, she waited for Ronan's gesture. "Three," now her ring finger joined the other two fingers, leaving her thumb holding only her pinkie finger down. "As Harry, you decided to lead him astray and have a scandalous affair with a woman who just happened to be an incarnation of Samantha?"

"No," Ronan said this time. "That's the problem. It wasn't a past incarnation of Sam's. It was Sam."

All five women stared at him, waiting for his next words.

"I didn't know it was Sam at the time. Not until I saw her in this life," Ronan said.

"So, that's what's going on between you two?" Penny added.

Ronan shrugged. "There I was," he told his captive audience, "Standing on the Boardwalk. I planned on finding Houdini and convincing him Spiritualism had a basis in reality."

"He did spend an awful lot of his time exposing charlatans," Lyndia said.

"True, sister, but he made all spiritual incidents seem fake," Louisa added.

"Yes, that was my thought exactly," Ronan agreed. "But, instead of finding Houdini— I was Houdini. I was dazed. Confused. I must have seemed dumbfounded because the next thing I knew, a beautiful dark-haired woman was approaching me."

"Sam?" Kat asked, feeling rejected.

"That's impossible. You said you traveled there before my sisters and I went there," Penny said. "So, how the hell could it have been Sam *as Sam* that you saw?"

"Maybe that past incarnation of Samantha looked almost identical to this current life?" Louisa posed.

"That's what I was hoping. I had to know if it was her—the Sam from this timeline, because if it was, I'm afraid there's an even greater consequence to my actions."

"What are you talking about?" Penny asked.

"I told you that I had an affair with that woman," Ronan reminded them.

"With Sam, you mean," Kat added with bitterness in her words.

"Yes, with Sam. At that point, I tried to follow her back, but I was unable to track her. So, I came back to my own time. Traveled back to Basque County. Nearly erased the Trinity Witches and saved the triplets from dying during the witch trials. But then, when one of my fellow members from the Order suggested I was in love with Sam—it hit me. Sam was the woman on the Boardwalk."

"In love with her?" Renee asked, scoffing at this suggestion.

"Ronan?" Penny asked, "Were you hoping that this Sam wouldn't fall in love with you? Because she seems actually to dislike you in this timeline?"

"Dislike? I think she hates him," Kat said.

"That wasn't true," Lyndia said.

"I had to know for sure... I had to know if I was supposed to, and do, father the solo witch incarnation; maybe I was meant to be there with this Sam. I mean, as Kat said, she hates me here, and I..." He looked at Kat. The hurt in her eyes was more than he could bear. "We never consummated our relationship. But she stayed this time, and if I am meant to father the Trinity triplets, it would have to happen as Harry with this current Sam." He looked directly into Kat's eyes. "Because I'm not in love with her in this life. I'm in love with someone else."

"So, your brilliant idea was that if you weren't there, Sam wouldn't get involved with Harry, but if she did, the only way to prove if you are meant to father the next generation is to see if Sam comes back to this timeline pregnant or not?" Penny asked.

"You better hope it's not because she's going to kill you when we get her back. I mean, she's going to kill you either way if we're being honest," Kat said, her words a bit softer.

"You actually think you may be the father of each single witch incarnation?" Renee asked.

"That would mean that you were my husband, Buckham Glouster," Lyndia scoffed.

"And my father," Renee said with equal skepticism.

"An incarnation of me," Ronan interjected. "When you spoke of Benjamin being possessed by a demon, and not a demon himself, I had to wonder if me being there with Harry, my Time Walking possession of him, caused the attraction between them. Maybe it's just supposed to be me, and the middle witch would always be able to sense my presence."

"Well, it wouldn't explain why they all disappear," Penny said, trying to logic her way through the tangled proposition.

"Sure it would," Ronan suggested, "if I'm just dropping in and out of incarnations to fulfill the Trinity births, keeping the bloodline true and strong, as soon as I leave that incarnation, those men undoubtedly found themselves in situations they had no desire for."

"So, who's the demon? Harry or Ronan?" Lyndia asked, eyeing Ronan from the end of the table yet speaking to the others as if he wasn't present.

"I'm not a demon," Ronan said, defending himself.

"You better not be a demon," Kat said. "I defended you—believed in you. Now, you're telling us you are responsible for getting some of our ancestors killed in the witch trials and impregnating my damn sister."

"If Sam comes back pregnant, it won't matter if you're a demon or not," Penny said.

"Well, there's only one thing to do," Renee said, standing up and placing both hands on the table for support, "We have to go back and get her."

"That's the thing, Mom," Kat said, "Penny and I can't walk through the portal as two. So we need a third magical person."

"I'm a witch," Renee said, stumbling back into her chair.

"But you're not strong enough yet," Lyndia said. She walked around the table to help Renee stand back up. "Come. We need a good night's rest. Renee will be stronger in the morning. You three will Time Walk first thing tomorrow."

"Mother," Renee addressed Lyndia. "I have no desire to go back to that bed. I've been lying there for an eternity. Girls," Renee said, "come sit on the sofa with me and fill me in on your lives. I've missed so much."

The girls joined their mother on the sofa, and Louisa headed to the kitchen to make a pot of tea. Ronan slinked past Lyndia, who had taken the armchair to the right of the fireplace. As he passed, Kat mumbled, "Good job, Ronan. Sam sure wasn't going to have sex with you in this life." Ronan paused, hurt by her words, until he saw her smile at him.

"Mom," Penny asked, "How exactly did you meet our father?

Renee pondered the question, trying to recall information that felt so far away, so remote in her past, but really, it had been only eighteen years ago when she had first met Benjamin.

Chapter Twenty-Three

"Everything a man does should enrich
the whole human race."

Walter Russell, 1946

"**G**o ahead, dear," Louisa said to Renee. "I'm interested in comparing what you remember happening and what my sisters— what Louisa and I remember."

"Are you sure?" Renee asked.

"The information might help us discover who the girls' father really is," Ronan said.

"Please, Mom. We want to know," Penny said. Maybe something in her mother's story would help her figure out how to get Sam back. Plus, she needed time for Sylvia's powers to take hold within her fully. If she had to, Penny would get Sam on her own. Somehow, Penny knew she could figure it out.

"Okay," Renee said as a soft smile grew across her face. "I grew up an only child. I didn't mind because my mom's two sisters were always there. Aunt Louisa was the garden witch, and she did all the cooking and curing. Aunt Sylvia, the eldest, was gifted with claircognizance, among other things, but that was her strongest gift."

The rabbit amulet around Penny's neck grew warm as Renee spoke of her deceased Aunt Sylvia, Penny's great aunt whom she had never known.

"Louisa had quite the business growing herbs and flowers to make cures, poultices, and charms. Most often, philters or love potions as we've come to know them. It was a happy life, even though my father, Buckman Glouster, died before I was born."

"Oh, Lyndia was beside herself when we learned he had died," Louisa said.

"On my eighteenth birthday, I ditched my party," Renee continued.

"Your mother was so upset. But Sylvia and I convinced Lyndia to let you go. We thought she was entirely too protective. After all, Renee was eighteen. Girls are supposed to want to be with boys, and she had just met a handsome one at school," Louisa said with jubilance.

"Except, as it turns out, I was right to be concerned," Lyndia said.

"Anyway, I had met this, as Aunt Louisa said, handsome boy at school. I had never seen him before that day. There was something mesmerizing about him. About the way he looked at me." Renee paused as she replayed that day in her mind. "I hoped he would be at the sweet shop where everyone hung out. And wouldn't you know it, there he was. Benjamin Hale waltzed in like a shiny new coin. After that night, we spent every day together, secretly meeting outside of school until the day of my graduation. That's the day I found out I was pregnant. I knew my mother would never forgive Aunt Louisa and Aunt Sylvia for letting me go out the night of my birthday party. So, when Benjamin suggested that we elope, I impulsively agreed."

"Impulsive is the correct term. I had no idea my daughter was married until she brought the man home with her after being missing for an entire weekend," Lyndia said, resentment dripping over her words. "I demanded the marriage be annulled, but that man, Benjamin, blatantly told us the marriage had been consummated, and the smirk on his face made me suspect the worst."

"I remember your mother screaming 'she's not pregnant' as if her words were the command of an unbinding spell," Louisa said, shaking her head as she recalled the dreadful scene.

"Renee stormed out of our house," Lyndia continued telling Renee's story, "I assume you thought I would embrace the man who stole my only daughter from me? I couldn't abide my daughter having conceived a child with this monstrous man."

"It was a bit of a rude reception, Mom," Renee answered Lyndia. "I was so happy, and Ben and I were so in love. At least, I thought we were."

"They moved into an apartment on the other side of town," Louisa said. "An insult on top of injury as far as your mother was concerned."

"Ben didn't want to deal with you three, and he didn't want interference in our life," Renee said, trying to defend the past decisions made. "I tried to use some of Aunt Louisa's charms to sooth his worries, but nothing had any effect on him."

"Spells have no power over demons. Once summonsed, only knowing their true name gives any amount of control. Renee wouldn't have known his demon-name," Ronan said, adding, "she didn't summons him."

"Demon? You really think Benjamin is a demon?" Renee asked.

"Maybe, we're not sure," Penny said.

"Why did he leave?" Kat asked, wanting her mother to finish the tale.

"Well, I shared the news with Benjamin that I was expecting triplets and told him he must reconcile with my family. I didn't want to raise my child without my family's weird, delightful, and magical ways. But Benjamin quickly squished out all talk of the occult, of magic, or of other things he considered superstitions. He told me to use logic and reason and ignore all else. But my family's traditions were my traditions. I believed in magic. I had seen it first-hand. So, without his final approval, I made plans to celebrate with my mother and both aunts. I just knew in my heart; I would find a means to bring Ben around to seeing life the Glouster way."

"A celebration? We never received an invitation to yours, and Benjamin's home," Lyndia said.

"We had no idea you were having triplets; in fact, although you have said we knew you were pregnant, I don't recall knowing that these past years," Louisa said, visibly puzzled as their story began to veer away from Renee's.

"Yes, I phoned you, Mother. I invited you three to our home for dinner, but that night, you never showed, and you didn't call."

"Did you call us?" Lyndia asked.

"No. I was so angry that you didn't show up that I made myself sick. Benjamin was very kind to me that night. It was the first night he brought me the tea."

"He poisoned you while you were pregnant with us?" Kat blurted out.

"Oh, no. He couldn't have. You three were perfect, more perfect than I ever imagined you could be, and you still are perfect," Renee said, pondering the question. "But I suppose that's why I never questioned drinking the teas Ben brought me. He had gained my trust during my pregnancy, and I believed he loved us."

"Did he start bringing you tea every day?" Penny asked.

"Why, yes. But I didn't have any symptoms of being poisoned," Renee said. "In fact, Ben gave me the tea to stop my nausea. Ben said the three little creatures stirring within my belly were causing my upset stomach. I remember laughing and telling him he was silly. You weren't creatures; you were three baby girls. But, thinking back now, I just kind of stopped asking about my mother and aunts as if they had never existed at all."

"It was a spell then, in the being, like the one he put over us," Lyndia said. "We received a letter by post the next day stating that you and Benjamin were perfectly happy and safe and would be honeymooning all over the globe. And, like you, dear," Lyndia said to her daughter as she patted Renee's knee, "we forgot any mention of a child. A new letter arrived each week, and the three of us, my sisters and I would read the post out loud together."

"Now, we are aware the letters and postcards were laced in a potion, spellbinding the three of us in some enchanted world. So strong was his spell that we soon believed Benjamin to be a blessing," Louisa said, feeling dejected.

"We thought you were blissfully traveling the world," Lyndia said. "Even Sylvia couldn't see through the spell. It was powerful and only broke when she died."

"The spell was anchored by the three of you reading it out loud together. After that, it became a vicious cycle. The more letters you read together, the stronger the compulsion to read them together became. Brilliant, really," Ronan said.

"But my life wasn't blissful. I gave birth to my three beautiful daughters. Then the day Ben and I brought the girls home, he changed. He said the doctor prescribed a medicine to help me sleep. I told Ben I didn't want to sleep. I wanted to be with my babies, but he had no tolerance for noncompliance. So, I drank the tea with the powder from the doctor in it. It made me feel extremely weird, and that first week home, I came in and out of consciousness. A few years later, I was raising my three daughters alone. Benjamin left us, left them on their third birthday. I had no idea I had a mother and two aunts who could help me, and I had no idea that I was a witch. I'm sorry, girls."

Kat's eyes welled with tears. "It's okay, Mom. We were okay. You did a good job raising us, even spellbound; you're a great mom."

"Yeah, Mom," Penny added, "It was only the last few years that we completely lost you."

"Thank god, and I know this sounds horrible, but in my heart, I know Sylvia agrees, thank god she died, and the spell was broken," Lyndia said.

"Our sister died this very week, and during the wake after her service, our memories started seeping back in," Louisa said.

"The memory of Renee shot through me like an arrow. I just knew Renee would never agree to have left us. Something felt very wrong."

"Suddenly, I felt compelled to go into our study and open the armoire's top drawer," Louis said, "I don't know why, but I went where my instinct guided."

"And there alone in the center of an otherwise empty drawer was a stack of letters and postcards, tied together with an oxen-colored ribbon, emitting a faint, sinister cloud of a dark soot-like substance."

"A guest walked in and said they were surprised that Renee and Benjamin hadn't come back from her travels to attend her aunt's funeral."

"As soon as we heard Benjamin's name, I realized we hadn't seen my Renee for years."

"I told my sister that we had been bewitched," Louisa said. "I asked everyone to leave, and we immediately headed here to Ipswich to find Renee."

"How did you know where to find us?" Kat asked.

"We cast a locating spell, of course," Louisa said, finding the question silly.

"When I realized that my only daughter was still on the other side of town. Years had passed, and we were in the same town; well, I broke down in tears," Lyndia said.

"Hysterics, really," Louisa said. "I didn't blame her. The whole situation was unfathomable."

"When we got here, the house was quiet."

"Too quiet," Louisa added. "Plus, our knowledge of our witchy gifts was just coming back to us too. Waning, of course, due to Sylvia's departure, but nonetheless, we too remembered that we were witches."

"I cast a simple spell to unlock the front door, and we entered," Lyndia explained.

"We knocked first, but no one answered the door, dears," Louisa said apologetically to the girls. "The sensation of walking through Renee's house—was melancholic."

"And we weren't entirely certain what we would find," Lyndia added.

"A noise came from upstairs, and my sister and I headed directly up. We were prepared to encounter Benjamin, whom we believed to be a skillful and evil sorcerer at the time."

"But when we reached the landing and saw the bedroom door open, we weren't ready. I wasn't ready to find my daughter, now nearly two decades older, lying in a bed completely despondent." Lyndia wiped a tear from her eye.

Renee leaned over, resting her head on her mother's shoulder.

"I wasn't prepared," Lyndia said, cupping her daughter's face in her hand as Renee remained against her shoulder.

"Grandmother?" Penny asked, "Do you still think our father is a sorcerer?"

"I don't know. It's possible that he is a demon, but either way, he's done something quite evil," Lyndia answered her concerned granddaughter. The bitterness in her voice filled the air.

Silently, Kat watched the anger, resentment, and betrayal they each felt braid together in the common cord that bound the witches' maternal line generation after generation.

"At least he is long gone," Louisa said, standing up. "We best get some rest if we are to get Samantha back in the morning."

"Mom?" Penny said.

"Yes, sweetie. What is it?" Renee asked, standing with the aid of her mother, Lyndia.

"Benjamin isn't gone," Penny confessed. "He emailed you yesterday morning,"

"What? Emailed? What does he want?" Renee asked, full of suspicion.

"He wanted to see us. The three of us before our graduation." Penny stared back at her mother, whose legs wobbled as Lyndia supported her.

"You didn't..."

"No, Mom. Never," Penny said. "I sent him a reply from you saying no way in hell was he ever going to see us."

Renee chuckled, admiring the fire her oldest triplet exhibited. Penny was an awful lot like her in her own younger days.

"I can't imagine that the man intolerant of disobedience took that message very well," Lyndia said. Her eyes were full of worry. "Our power weakens even as we speak. I know Renee will get her powers back, but she doesn't have her strength yet. We aren't prepared to face Benjamin like this. The girls' powers *are* growing, but they don't have their optimum strength without Samantha."

"You think we're going to face Benjamin in some kind of supernatural battle?" Kat asked, exhibiting the same type of worry that her grandmother's face displayed.

"One thing is for sure," Ronan chimed in, "he wanted the girls born but didn't want them to know that they were witches."

"Exactly," Renee said. "Somehow, he must accomplish whatever it is he is up to without the girls knowing about their powers or how to use them."

"I'll go to my sacred library and see what I can find out," Ronan said.

"I'm coming with you," Penny said. "Two of us can look faster than one." But, really, she wanted to keep an eye on Ronan, who she still felt wasn't being upfront with them.

"I'm staying with Mom," Kat said, "and Grandma Lyndia and Aunt Louisa."

"If anything happens, and you need Penny and me to return..." Ronan rolled his coin across his knuckles, then handed it to Kat. "Toss this coin up into the air while thinking of Penny or me, and the coin will act like a flare, magically shooting into the air before landing at our feet. No matter where we are."

"Okay," Kat answered. She studied the golden coin. The side facing up had a man's bust embellished on it, and the figure had a laureate upon his head, each leaf detailed perfectly by the slight toning of a darkish orange-red discoloration, perhaps created by the passing of time. "I'll try to meditate before I go to bed. Maybe, I can get some information that will help. Penny, do you want me to wait up?"

"No," Penny answered, glancing over at Ronan. "I'll be fine. Just use the coin if anything happens and you need us to come back."

"Not to worry. I'll wait up for my granddaughter's safe return," Lyndia said, handing Renee's care over to her sister before settling in the fireplace's left-flanked armchair, where she nestled cozily. "I'll be right here until your return, Penny."

"Okay," Ronan said. "Let's go."

Chapter Twenty-Four

Benjamin Hale-Present Day Boston, Massachusetts

T he Charles Street Jail in Boston, built in 1851, was home to some of the most gnarly prisoners until 1990. Now, the former penitentiary poses as the opulent Liberty Hotel. With some of its front windows still barred, the renovated old jail remains a historic reminder of both the city's past and the section of town referred to as Beacon Hill.

Benjamin's room overlooked the Charles River and gave off an unnerving energy; this sensation made him feel almost claustrophobic. He might as well have been in an actual cell. Albeit this remolded space had two beds, a television, and a luxurious bathroom—nonetheless, the impression of its former purpose remained strong. So

Benjamin took note to stay in a different hotel the next time he traveled to Boston.

He threw his complimentary white hotel robe on one of the beds and sat on the corner of the mattress closest to the bath. He hadn't sized up the room when he arrived the day before yesterday, but now, as he needed to kill some time, he realized the room, with its two twin beds, was probably arranged just like this back in its previous jailhouse form. The bed he sat on touched the side wall, and no more than three feet, maybe two feet, existed between it and the second twin bed. Its side was up against the room's floor-to-ceiling window. He pulled his socks on and stepped into his black trousers. For the first time, he noticed the pattern on the carpet was made of watch faces and skeleton keys. He laughed, thinking it was rather sick, actually, doing time locked away. The room's décor was a metaphorical joke all the way down to the scales of justice adorning the small desk in the corner. Come to think of it; the bathroom had several keys matted and framed hanging on the wall. The jailer's keys, no doubt. He definitely would stay somewhere else next time, perhaps a newly built hotel that only cried out a mediocre, middle-class vibe. That sounded so much nicer to him right now.

After Benjamin finished dressing, he checked his phone. No calls from Renee. He knew they hadn't spoken in person for years, but her nasty and abrupt email reply yesterday was completely unexpected. He had wanted to send another email but figured it would receive the same treatment. Finally, he broke down and called the house last night, but no one answered. So he decided to call again this morning; this time, he left a message. If Renee didn't return his call, he would go to Ipswich and knock on her damn door until she opened it.

There wasn't time to be polite, not anymore. The girls were turning eighteen in a couple of days and had to know who they were. Benjamin understood this all too well. As a member of the Order of the Fallen, simply referred to as The Fallen, he had watched his girls from afar. He did everything he could to keep them safe until they were grown, even when it meant allowing The Fallen to erase Renee's memories of being a witch. He had complied. Anything to keep his girls safe. He was willing to do anything back then—absolutely anything, and he still was.

He put his brass knuckles in his pants front pocket and his penknife in the outer right pocket of his jacket. He slid his G30 Glock .45 handgun into his carry holster and placed this between his buckled pants and his lower back, preventing the cold metal slide from resting against his skin. Next, he loaded his jacket's interior pockets with the two flashbangs he had taken from the Order's armory before he left on this mission. Finally, he clipped a canister of pepper spray to his belt, now wishing he had some of the tetrodotoxin his buddy had procured out of the country. It was a potent neurotoxin derived from the pufferfish. A tiny bag of that nasty white powder guaranteed the blockage of the nervous system, cutting off the body's sodium ions and preventing messages from being delivered to the brain. Although dosing via an injection was the most lethal method, inhalation worked just fine. He had seen it himself when demonstrated on a poor, caught mouse. He had been too afraid of accidentally dosing himself, and that wouldn't do. He had to remain alive and alert, ready to use any means necessary if anyone even remotely attempted to stop him from seeing his girls.

The valet pulled up in his rental car, a compact little blue number with a tiny hole in the right, side view mirror's plastic housing. The damage had been there when he picked up the vehicle, and the rental agent had noted it on the contract. He squeezed into the minuscule car and buckled his seatbelt. Ipswich was only twenty-nine miles north of where he was, but in Boston's traffic, it would take him nearly an hour and a half to get there.

It was hard for him to believe that eighteen years had passed since he met Renee and fifteen since he had seen his girls in person. He remembered having argued with his controller, a member higher up in the order than him, when Renee didn't seem to take to him right away. Or at least that had been what he thought when he posed as a new high school student and purposely positioned himself in her path that day at school. She hadn't acted like she had any interest in him, but later that night, she had shown up at the Sweet Shop, seemingly beguiled by his muscular build and tall stature.

Within weeks, she was pregnant. His virility had secured the next set of triplets as having a human genetic code devoid of all extrasensory or supernatural programming. It was one of the reasons he had been selected for the mission. He was human through and through, and the purity of the Trinity Witches depended on that. Of course, it didn't hurt that she was eighteen and highly fertile too.

He recalled how he felt when Renee had told him about the triplets. She was shocked at his outward appearance when hearing her news. He seemed saddened. In a way, he actually was. His job was done. He had achieved the desired result, and it made him feel depressed. For him, pretending to be normal was easy—he was. Besides, Renee was beautiful. How could he not feel something for her? Plus, the babies were his flesh and blood. Did The Fallen really expect him not to feel anything for them? In his mind, he only had one course of action; he had to disappear for a significant period of time. Sure, he could have stuck around, but it was so hard for him to watch Renee as the spell subdued her powers, and she forgot her family's legacy.

By the time the girls were born, Renee had completely forgotten that she was a witch herself and that she was about to give birth to the next generation of Trinity Witches. The worst part, he had to give Renee an elixir to drink daily to hold the spell in place. He did this faithfully, and by the time the girls were three, he was ordered to leave their lives for good. The only thing he was allowed to do was ensure the tea was delivered to Renee's home.

Now, fifteen years later, he found himself anxious to see his grown daughters and Renee too. His mind drifted back to when he was eighteen. The Order of the Fallen had recruited him. Their name sounded so cool, so interesting. There had been plenty of times he thought about walking away and leaving the Order, but once you were involved, you really couldn't leave. It's not like all the information they provide you with just disappears. You can't unsee something once you see it. And that's how the Order hooked him and kept him. Who doesn't want to fight evil? Be the good guy? Save the world?

The Fallen weren't demons or satanic. No, they had once been part of the Order of Illuminations before that faction split, organically dividing into two distinct orders with opposing beliefs and missions. The Order of Illumination had once been thousands strong until a dispute erupted over the inclusion of the Dark Arts among the sacredly held texts. The Illumination sought to save all text, no matter the content, and the members who thought that wrong, split away and formed a new order. They had fallen from the grace of the Illumination, but that didn't make them wrong. If the mission was to save magic, why would anyone save and perpetrate a corrupted form? True magic wasn't about using power to harm, maim, or debase anyone or anything for personal and selfish reasons. Magic was about creating. It was light and affable, not dark and dreadful.

One thing Benjamin disliked the most was the Order of Illumination's campaign to mislead and misguide the population at large about The Fallen. People were convinced they were a league of devils seeking to devour human souls. But that couldn't be further away from the truth. It was the Illumination whose light showed in the dark corners of humanity, perverted and twisted, with the hope of raising power for the blackened, lost, desperate souls. Part of that shadowy plot was infiltrating the Trinity Witches by mixing real demons into their bloodline. It had happened already, years ago, to Renee's mother. He was sure she didn't know, but it had. Demon DNA was mixed into the Trinity line. That was the point where he had come in. Renee had to conceive the triplets from a pure bloodline: a human. It was the only way to prevent the darkness from overtaking the witches. Benjamin fully believed in the cause and in doing his duty. If a demon's evilness mixed with the Trinity Witches' power and they became dark—everyone was doomed.

Chapter Twenty-Five

"Beware the knowledge thou seek, for knowledge though oft light,
can sow the seeds of night and reap from the darkness
that ensues."

Esmerelda Jane Forstine, 1654

N o longer feeling a need for pretenses, Ronan
proceeded to open a portal to access his personal
pocket dimension, housing his sacred library right
there, in their home, using their kitchen backdoor. Ronan
motioned his hand and gave a slight bow, gesturing for
Penny to enter first. She did with haste.

"I hope you know," Ronan said, "I would have gone
back to the Boardwalk with you if I'd had the confidence that
I could have managed it. But I know I would have been a
walk-in again, stepping into Harry's incarnation, and I
would have felt what he did." Images swam through his

mind. Being with Sam was a good life, even if the duration was brief. "I don't think I could be strong enough to walk away a second time."

That was quite an admission, Penny thought, and a level of empathy for him roused within her, but not enough to elicit compassion. It was her sister that was trapped in 1894. Her eyes hardened. "You're a wizard, remember? Going back, especially if it meant I wouldn't have lost my sister, was a chance I would have been willing to take. I'm sure you would have figured something out had you been trapped. But, Sam? She can't open a portal. She can't just pop back into the present day whenever she pleases." Her last few words cracked as her emotions swept in.

"What is it you want from me, Penny?"

"What I *want* doesn't matter. But I *need* you to help me figure out how the hell to get her back. If you're too scared to go get her, then we need to figure out how I can go back and get her by myself."

"Okay," he said, feeling emasculated. It wasn't fear that prevented him from walking back into 1894; it was a desire for that life—for Sam. He watched Penny head for the shelves in the back, wondering if he should have gone back to the Boardwalk. But he hadn't, and now, he didn't know where or how to begin such a daunting task. He wished he had his coin; it always helped him think, but he had given it to Kat, and that was necessary. He couldn't risk losing Penny's other sister too.

He assessed their current situation. Renee was weak but getting stronger. Penny had received her Great Aunt Sylvia's powers through transference, but he could tell Penny didn't understand yet what the powers were or how to wield them. As for himself, he was on shaky ground with the girls and their mother. More than likely, with the grandmother and the other aunt too. Ronan wished he could consult with Abraham, his mentor, and friend, but that was no longer an option. The entire Order was now in his past. He wouldn't return. Ever. He felt sure of it.

"Ronan?" Penny asked. "This book on alchemy states that the alchemical methods are really to be used on the soul, transmuting it into spiritual gold, not other matter into literal gold."

"What book do you have?" He asked, walking to her.

She closed the book, keeping a finger inside it on the page she had read from, and checked the title. "*Alchemy: Ancient and Modern*, by Redgrove, published in 1922."

"Ah," Ronan said, acknowledging his familiarity with the book. "Yes, true alchemists never concern themselves with the physical plane and the materialized or what they referred to as gross matter."

Penny opened the book again and read, "*the knowledge of all nature...first principles...all is founded on the same first principle.* Ronan, is this referring to God? Is God the first principle?"

"I suppose that depends on who God is to you. The old man with the long white beard sitting on a throne up in his cloud? If that's what you mean, then I don't think so, but I've never experienced a power greater than what that concept holds."

"So, you think there is something greater than the concept of an all-creating god?"

"Doesn't there have to be? That image of God shows a whole world outside of this being, and an omnipotent, omnipresent, omniscient God has to be much grander than some Zeus-like image. Plus, there's that entire Devil thing. So, God is battling something outside himself? Yet, God created the devil—why? Why would God need to battle someone he created? Is there a possibility the Devil may win? And how could that even be possible? God is all-powerful."

"You're right," Penny said. "The infinite, timeless, all-pervasive *All* can't be defined with an image. Our concept of God must be flawed or limited in some way."

"You must read *All About the Devil* by Moses Hall," Ronan said excitedly. He rushed to the second shelf at the end of the row. "1890, I think. Only 62 pages, but every one of them is quite entertaining. By the end of it, the author has you convinced the Devil is good and ..." Ronan suddenly realized that his timing was inappropriate and quickly removed the smile from his face.

Penny stared blankly at the alabaster creature in front of her, whom, at times, she had thought of as a friend and, at other times, as a demon himself. "Anyway, finding more about the first principle may hold the key to unlocking my witch powers." She took the book over to the desk and sat down. "Are there other alchemic books here?"

"Of course," Ronan said, "hermetic, alchemic, masonic...I'll pull what I think might be useful."

Penny smiled, then returned to her book. *There are three Principles upon which all things are created: fire, water, and air.* She wondered what that meant. If what is written is to be understood spiritually, not physically, then fire would be what? Passion? Desire? Sure, that made sense. But, first, one would need a desire as the impetus to begin or create anything. Water would have to be emotions, not feelings. Feelings were different than emotions. Feelings are the sensory input of energy in its various forms. Emotions were the labels we assigned to those feelings, often based on past experiences or misunderstandings, generating distorted thinking patterns which acted like filters through which we viewed the world. And air? Air had to be the word. It was the act of speaking to bring something into being. Penny knew she had to grasp this concept fully. She needed to control her emotions and focus on *feeling*. What was it that Neville said? Oh yea, it was the title of one of his books: *Feeling is the Secret*. She closed the book as Ronan approached the desk, letting the information she gleaned swirl around in her mind. "What did you find?"

"Well, honestly, everything in here would help us, but I grabbed a few that seemed pertinent. This one is *The First Book of Natural Magick*," Ronan said holding up the worn and yellowed manuscript. "Anonymous. No Date. But I had this bookmarked at some earlier time, and when I reread it, I think it might be useful." He handed the opened book to Penny.

Antipathy and sympathy of things, she read. *All things are linked together...Magick is the attracting or fetching out of one thing from another...the word is a living creature...both male and female...the passive and the active...couple together, within and between themselves, by reason of mutual love.* Penny looked up at Ronan. "I think we can make something work if we do it together. You know, the male and female aspect represented by our beings."

Ronan's eyes grew wide. "What are you saying?"

"I'm saying, if we can figure this out, my powers aren't just available in the form of the power of three. Two also have power. It's just not what my DNA is programmed to do." She contemplated the three elements mentioned in that book she had grabbed off the shelf; fire, water, and air. Each of those elements must represent the three of us. That would explain why they had to be together to make their magic work. I guess Sam is the fire, Penny thought. She smiled, thinking that Sam always was fired up about something. Kat was definitely the air element because she was great at writing the spells they needed. She had such a gift with words. But that meant that she, Penny, was the water. No way, she thought, finding herself to be a bit stoic. Then it hit her. She was the fire, and Sam was the water. Sam wasn't fueled by her desire or passions. No, she was raging with the emotional waves of water.

"You look lost in thought. What exactly are we doing?"

"I don't know yet."

"I guess we don't need to know exactly how it works, but we do need to start somewhere," Ronan said, reaching into his pocket, only to remember his coin was with Kat. He rubbed his palm on his leg, trying to quench his desire to fidget. "So, where do we start?"

"I think the Trinity Witch power relies on three because each triplet is endowed with power or a command over one of the three primordial elements." She waited to read his reaction.

"Primordial elements? That has to be fire, water, and air."

"Yes, that's correct," she replied, leaning in toward him. "These three elements must be equally represented, but nowhere does it state that it has to be by three individuals." Again, she waited to see his response.

"Okay, and these elements, when viewed spiritually instead of materially, represent the spark of desire to initiate, like the strike of a flint stone. The fuel of the emotions to ignite, like gasoline, and the air of the..."

"The air of the spoken word to sustain and spread the object of the manifestation or action."

"John 1:1, 'In the beginning was the Word, and the Word was with God, and the Word was God,'" Ronan quoted from the Bible he had read at length during his time in the catacombs.

"Um," Penny said, looking down at the manuscript. "Listen, on page fifteen of this manuscript— '*By reason of their likeness, with the other, for the very likeness of one thing to another, is a sufficient bond to link them together.*' I know what links us."

"Sam," Ronan said.

"Sam," Penny affirmed. "This is how we can work together. Symbolically and literally, we are the male-female aspect. But, we are also connected to each other through our love for Sam."

"Interesting," Ronan said. "Those are two of the Universal Laws. The Law of Gender states that everything has a masculine and feminine quality. We're going to literally represent those two qualities. The Law of Association states that if any two things have anything in common, that commonality can be used to control or power both."

"Exactly. Now, we just have to figure out how to elicit the three primordial elements and direct that power to me walking through your portal alone."

"What about the other Universal Laws? They might help. I mean, you're cracking this age-old stuff wide open. So

I say you keep going along this same line of thought," he encouraged.

"Right," Penny said. "Where are the laws listed together?"

Ronan grabbed the copy of *The Emerald Table of Hermes* and flipped through its pages. "The Seven Hermetic Principles are Mentalism, Correspondence, Vibration, Polarity, Rhythm, Cause and Effect, and Gender." Ronan closed the book and searched through his pulled stack for another book.

"Okay," Penny said, thinking out loud, "Mentalism. Everything happens in the mind. I've read this before that the world is holographic, and I've never believed that more than I do right now."

"We are sitting in my library in a pocket dimension. Reality is what we perceive it to be."

"Yes. Correspondence is as above, so below. As within so without. But that one could be tricky," Penny said.

"It can be tricky. Even I, who has Time Walked many times, find myself afraid of being unable to return. Our mind plays tricks in its effort to keep us safe and well, alive."

"Vibration. Everything is energy, and everything vibrates. Polarity. Everything has an opposition, like the terminals on a battery: negative and positive."

"But, here's the key to that. They only appear to be opposite, when in fact, they are both the battery, just opposite ends of the same thing." He smiled at her, proud of his explanation.

"So, duality is an illusion? Everything is really on a continuum."

"There is more than that, though. One continuum flows into the next. Nothing is separate. Just falling somewhere else on the spectrum."

"Wow," Penny replied. "I thought I was the one cracking the code." She smiled back at him and continued. "Rhythm is easy. I learned about this in art and the swinging of the pendulum. It happens in societies, too, but mainly seen in the seasons—the constant movement of energy. Cause and effect are easy too. Everything has a cause, whether we are aware of it or not."

"True. That always makes me think of the Dark Ages. Well, even the witch trials. Things happened, like people dying or animals dying, and no one understood the cause of the effect of death." The image of the beaked mask worn by physicians during the Bubonic plague flitted through Ronan's memory. It had been one of the first places he traveled to entirely by accident. He had gotten the year transposed in his mind when creating a portal, and the scene had been horrific.

"Exactly. But I suppose to some natural extent. Our mind wants to categorize and file the information away. So when there isn't a reasonable answer, I guess we make one up."

"Yes, and the witch trials are an excellent example of how the effect of untimely deaths became the cause for capturing and killing Witches."

"Every cause has an effect, and every effect becomes a cause," Penny said. "The Gender one, we already have that one covered. But seven doesn't seem like that many guiding principles, does it?" Penny reopened the book she had sat down with, Redgrove's *Alchemy: Ancient and Modern*, and read to herself.

Ronan rifled through the stack on his desk. He pushed Haanel's *The Master Key System* aside, and von Franz's *Alchemy* landed on top of it as Ronan made a new stack of temporarily rejected work. *The Complete Master Key System* by Gladstone, Greninger, and Selby was added next. Then, he saw it. A sheet of paper, folded in half and tucked within the pages of *The Secrets of Ancient Witchcraft,* caught his attention. He tugged on the paper, sliding it out of the book. He opened it. "Penny? I have a list of the Universal Laws," Ronan said, puzzled by his finding.

"Well, what does it say?"

"The Law of Oneness: everything is connected to everything. Law of Pure Potential: The ALL contains the potential for anything and everything, all possibilities, and all probabilities, which are based solely on the parameters of any given consciousness. Law of Sufficient Abundance: there is enough of everything for everyone because the ALL is limitless." Ronan glanced up and said, "I'm skipping over the ones we already addressed." Penny nodded. "Law of Relativity: emotions feel the same to each human, only the details and the assigned meanings are different. Principle of Individuality: a person's vibrational quality determines their perspective, and their perspective generates their personal experience of reality. Principle of Individual Preservation: the default state is to act in favor of the self until the self becomes aware of the ALL and that it is the ALL. This generates the perspective of the ALL observing all." Ronan kept reading from his sheet. "Principle of Resonance: an individual's vibration will react to, and adjust to, vibrations around them unless they are consciously aware and do not allow themselves to be affected by surrounding energies. Law of Deliberate Creation: energy is applied where energy is focused. Principle of Synthesis: two opposing ideas will be resolved into a third composite idea. Principle of Contagion: things having come into physical contact will continue to influence one another after separation."

"Wait. We both have had physical contact with Sam. So, given that last principle, we can influence her to walk through an opened portal. Right?"

"Theoretically? Maybe, but attempting to influence, move, or even motivate another is more difficult than you might think. And ultimately, it is still the other person who decides to allow the influence or not. So, trust me; it's better if we focus on making ourselves do something."

"Yeah, you're right," Penny said. "Are there more Universal Laws?"

"Yes. Principle of Complete Identification: complete and absolute identification with the Meta-pattern of another entity allows one to become the other entity."

"That one sounds creepy, like shape-shifting. I'll stick with being me, thanks."

Ronan laughed. "Me too. But I think it applies to identifying completely with who you want to become."

"Who is that, Ronan?"

"The Penny that Time Walks without her sisters." Ronan handed the sheet to her. "Go on, you finishing reading them."

"Law of Perpetual Transmutation of Energy: energy cannot be created nor destroyed, only transformed. Force of Action: every action requires an impetus, a spark, to begin the transmutation. Ronan, that's the primordial fire. Listen, Force of Compensation: the universe replies in kind. Your vibration must match that which you seek."

"That's the primordial water element. Emotions determine the vibrational frequency."

Penny stared at Ronan, digesting all the information. "Oh, Power of Words. The air element. This is the third one. A name or signifier points to the concept signified. Certain words and names are primal, from the beginning of time, and speak to a part of us before 'all that is' was manifest. These primal words are the most powerful."

"Sure, that makes sense. That's how angels and demons are summoned. Well, actually, angels are invoked because they are higher forms of beings, and one must request guidance. Demons, on the other hand, are lesser forms of beings, and one must command them. But, either way, knowing their true names gives power over them," Ronan explained, thinking about Scarlet's demonic abilities.

"So, that's the three. There are a few more; Principle of Symbols, Similarity, Detachment, and Knowledge, but the ones we need to understand are the three primordial ones. The Force of Action, the Force of Compensation, and the Power of Words."

"Okay," Ronan said, wondering how they were to proceed.

"I think we must become one in mind with the ALL. We must remove any concept, at least for the moment, of separateness."

"And if you can remove all feelings of separateness that physically exist between you and your two sisters, you can be one with them and walk right through the portal," Ronan said in a manner that seemed like he was convincing himself as much as he was convincing her.

"You're right, but I think we will have to meditate, like Kat does, to achieve the correct state of mind. I really believe we will know what to do."

"Okay." Ronan moved the leather chair back, exposing the center of the library's area rug. "We can do it here."

"Maybe we should make a sacred circle or something," Penny said.

"Absolutely," Ronan said. "Do you know how?"

Penny reached into her bag and pulled out a smaller bag. "I've got salt. Sam gave Kat and me each a bag after she found our mom's grimoire." Penny smiled, remembering the piece of orchid root Sam had given them both as well. She patted her little lucky hand on the outside of her jeans, where it was safely tucked in her pocket. *Come on Sam and Kat. I need both of you with me in spirit right now to guide me to our power's source.* Penny glanced at Ronan, who was idly standing off to the side. "I'm just going to sprinkle the salt in a large circle. You need to stand inside it with me."

Ronan stepped forward, and as he walked past Penny, she threw a handful of salt at him.

"Why did you do that?" he asked, brushing his jacket off.

"Just checking to see if you are evil," Penny said.

"Really? Well, I didn't even flinch, did I?"

"Maybe a little," Penny said with a soft smile.

"You threw salt at me," Ronan retorted. "You seriously believe I'm evil?"

"No, but that may make you the worse kind of villain of all," Penny said, staring at his innocent expression, "you don't believe you are evil. You actually think you're helping, and more harm has been done by those who honestly believe their beliefs are righteous. Isn't that how the whole witch trials began?"

"Penny, I —" Ronan began.

"I know, Ronan. You thought you were helping Sam by not going back. We need four candles." Penny signaled for him to hurry out of the incomplete circle and get the items.

Ronan cautiously stepped through the only opening in the salt circle Penny was making. He ran to his desk and pulled four candles out, clutching them in his hands where the items were cradled against his chest. "They're not the same color."

Penny stared at Ronan's cache of wax and wicks. It was Sam who was knowledgeable about candles and how to use specific colors to enhance the working of magic. She quickly closed the salt circle behind Ronan as she thought about which candle should be placed.

Ronan held a white candle. Good. White represented purity. Black. Penny wasn't sure. She had only glanced at their mother's grimoire, only briefly looking at the pages about candle magic. Negativity. She recalled Sam telling Kat about using black stones to repel negativity. Green. That color meant growth. Good. The last one was red. Passion. Desire. Primordial fire. Perfect. She wished they had all been white or even all red. She hoped these candles would work.

"First, put the white one to the north and light it. Then the black one to the west, the red candle in the south, and end with the green one to the east. Lighting each as you go."

Ronan placed the candles around the circle as Penny instructed and lit them.

"Now, stand in the center with me as I say the protective spell." Penny drew a small knife, her athame, out of her other pocket. It was a souvenir witch's blade that dangled from the end of her house key's keychain. She began with the lit candle positioned to the west. "Circle now protect me as one of we three, as we were bound by birth as one." She moved counterclockwise, holding her athame over the lit candle to the south. "Protect me against all powers who seek to weaken thee." She moved her athame above the candle to the east. "Purify me with your light." Her knife over the north candle, she said, "Absent are all unwanted forces." Finally, she found herself back at the west candle where she had started. "Guide me and my counterpart on this path as we seek power's source." For a second, she felt a tinge of anxiety ending on the black candle. She had to remind herself the color wasn't bad. It wasn't evil or dark. It simply represented a return to the unknown, and that's exactly where she needed to go. Penny turned toward Ronan, and together they said, "So it is within. So it is without. So it is done." They sat in the center of their sacred circle, facing each other. Each flame burned tall and strong around them; then, one by one, the flames began a wild dance.

Chapter Twenty-Six

"Magic is an exchange; a communication; an expression

Between the practitioner and the Divine."

Julie Kusma, 2019

"Now what?" Ronan asked, feeling equally uncertain as he sensed Penny felt.

"I don't know. I guess we close our eyes. You're the keeper of all these ancient texts. You tell me. Don't we have to draw a pentagram or something?" Penny said, eyeing the flickering candle flames and sounding more facetious than she intended.

Ronan studied her as he searched his mind for ceremonial and ritual magic practices. "We've made the sacred circle, the candles are lit, and you've cast a protection spell. Let's think about this and see what makes sense to us as a next step. What do these things symbolize?"

"The circle contains us..."

"No," Ronan said, remembering something Scarlet had told him about summoning demons, "the circle contains a spirit or demon within the defined space. You are free to walk in and out of it. An evil spirit would not be able too."

Penny's left eyebrow raised as she eyed Ronan curiously and suspiciously.

"You're kidding, right?" Ronan said, glancing down at the round boundary of salt. "Do I need to step out of the circle for you to believe I am trying to help the three of you?"

"No," Penny said. She looked down, feeling guilty for not trusting him. "So, what does the circle represent for the two of us?" She asked, but she answered her own question before Ronan had a chance to respond. "I think it is a symbol for the Goddess, right? Like the sun or the womb or something."

"The sun? I thought the sun was masculine," Ronan said. "Maybe, we should go get Kat. She's the one up on astrology."

"Oh, so now it's your turn to doubt *me*?"

"No, I was just suggesting... listen, you're the one with the gift of claircognizance, and you with the added built-in bullshit detector. If your intuition is telling you the sun is feminine, then that's what it is."

Penny quietly sat as she listened for more insight to penetrate her mind.

"You may be right," Ronan said, "now that I think about it, I suppose the sun as a symbol for the feminine does make more sense."

"Yeah, and I've seen Kat draw the astrological glyph for the sun. She makes a circle with a dot in the center. I guess that's the seed in the womb."

"I've never thought of it that way, but I think I might have read that somewhere in one of my manuscripts. It's like everything we think has been flipped upside down. The sun is feminine, and the moon is masculine, but everyone believes the opposite is true."

"Right. And haven't you heard of the man in the moon? We never give the moon a feminine face," Penny said, chuckling at the irony, "The truth is always right in front of us if we want to see it."

"Yet the sun is an active, brilliant, yang energy," Ronan said. "I wish I could remember where I read that. We could get a better context of the meaning."

"It's like the alchemic The Law of Gender. Everything has a masculine and feminine quality. The sun is feminine and passive, holding the seed for all things. When an emotional charge fertilizes the seed, the sun's energy becomes masculine and active and begins to create or manifest." Penny continued as if she was channeling the information. "The moon is masculine as the watery flow of emotions seeks to actively fertilize potential seeds. Yet, when the seed begins to grow, the moon waits passively during the gestation period. It's like the two flip their roles. As one is passive, the other is active, and vice versa."

"That's amazing insight, Penny," Ronan said. "Okay, our circle is the sacred womb of the eternal Goddess. The seed we need to fertilize is your ability to Time Walk by yourself. I have fertilized that seed by showing you and your sisters how to Time Walk. You know what it is like. Now, you have to figure out how to harness your two sisters' powers and go it alone."

Penny nodded in agreement. "I think we should draw the symbols for male and female energies. Penny stood as if she already knew what Ronan was about to say.

"There's white chalk in my desk drawer."

She grabbed it and raced back inside the salt circle and drew an inverted triangle for the feminine aspect and a regular triangle on top of it for the masculine part.

"That's a six-pointed star," Ronan said.

"Yes," Penny agreed, looking down at the recognizable Star of David symbol. "Another thing that may be misrepresented. Do you think the mixing everything up was a way to take pagan power away?" She studied the space.

"Wait," Penny said, analyzing the image that unexpectedly popped into her head, "we have to do something else."

"What? What do you see?"

"You know that abracadabra image? The one where the word is written over and over in an inverted triangle?"

"Of course, I know it. Although there is some confusion about the actual spelling. Aleister Crowley believed the letter 'c' was actually an 'h.' But I've also read that the 'c' was originally an 's.' That was a misinterpretation from Greek. Either way, the word was believed to ward off illness when inscribed on an amulet and worn around the neck."

"What does it mean?"

"Well, that part is a bit murkier. Some say the word comes from an ancient Semitic language, meaning *I create as I speak,* but I have also read that it might mean *disappear like this word,* which does make more sense if it is used to cure diseases. Actually, the latter also explains the inverted triangle, diminishing the word to symbolize the diminishing of the illness."

"But I don't want anything to disappear; you've already done that part," Penny said, offering Ronan a strained smile. "I want to create something. I want to create the possibility that I can Time Walk without the aid of my sisters."

"Penny, that already exists. The possibility for all things exists."

"Ah, I get it," she exclaimed.

"What? You get what, Penny?"

"The macrocosm to the microcosm. As above, so below. That's one of the principles, right?"

"Yes, but..."

"The manifestation of something...anything...depends on the focus upon that thing, right?"

"Yes."

"So, Ronan, look." She scribbled the word abracadabra, removing one letter each time she wrote it until an inverted triangle of letters appeared, ending at the point with the letter 'a.' She pointed down at the image she had just drawn. "Singularity, Ronan." She dropped the chalk and spun around. "Singularity," she repeated. "The whole word represents the macrocosm, and then as one finetunes their desire and refines through focus, all possibilities collapse into a singularity and manifests as the desired thing here in the microcosm."

Ronan gazed at this wild, red-headed, green-eyed witch before him. She was more astonishing than he ever imagined a Trinity Witch could be. Surely, her power would rival all others as well, he thought. "Should we write abracadabra in the triangles?"

"No, we write fire, water, and air just like the abracadabra charm. I'll do mine and you..." She broke the piece of chalk in half. "You write the three words in yours."

Ronan took the chalk and stared at it. "You can't manifest Sam into the here and now," he said, wondering exactly what she planned to do.

"No, but I can send myself back to the source of all power...primordial power, and learn what I need to know to Time Walk on my own."

"Primordial power?"

"Yep, and forget meditating." She sat, scooting close to her side of the six-pointed star between them, and reached her hands out, gesturing for Ronan to take hold. "Let's go find the Source of power." Penny clutched his hands and slowed her breathing. "We are the sun and the moon," Penny said, beginning her spell.

Ronan closed his eyes after he saw Penny close hers. His breath slowed, matching Penny's, and he cleared his mind, opening himself to whatever experience was about to transpire.

Penny continued. "Take us back to Source, to the first celestial romance. Take us back to the Sun and Moon's primordial dance."

They waited. Their breaths blending into one steady rhythm. Each cleared their mind of all outside thoughts. After a few moments, Penny noticed the light changing through her closed eyelids and peeked out. All four candles rhythmically flickered, creating an eerie illusion similar to a strobe light. Ronan was now staring at the candles too. Suddenly, an impression of falling backward overcame Penny. In her mind, she seemed to be dropping into an abyss, and her crossed-legged body slightly swayed with the sensation. She realized Ronan was no longer separate from her but that they seemed to be joined as one. She was aware of his presence; he was now an aspect of herself.

Together they fell back through time. First, through the events of the past two days. Through her and her sister's previous Time Walks. She felt Sam's hand slipping through hers all over again, and she wanted to cry, but the image was fleeting. Gone. She saw her home, and she was on the computer sending a nasty reply to her father. Gone. Her sixteenth birthday. Brandon was going to kiss her, but her sisters had jumped out and caught them, scaring the timid boy off. Gone. Further back in time, their third birthday. Her father's face. This caused her to actually gasped out loud, but it didn't shake her out of the astral experience.

Babies. She and her sisters were newborns; all swaddled in pink blankets. Gone.

Now she experienced events beyond her current lifetime. The moon landing. Her foot touched the ground. No suit. She was standing next to the astronaut, touching the surface with her bare toes. Again, the image swooshed away, and she found herself witnessing the witchcraft law being repealed in Parliament. Back further in time, she fell, landing momentarily in Carl Jung's study. A fishing trip with both Jung and Freud. Gone. Pavlov's laboratory. She was running through Darwin's gardens at Down House. Gone. She was watching Samuel Parris and his family arrive in Salem Village. Then she found herself viewing her incarnation as Penelope in the Ipswich jail. Swoosh. Further back, she fell, time almost escaping her senses as it manifested and passed her like a wind, gusting around her. The European witch hunts. Wurzburg, Germany. Flames. Beheaded women were burning on stakes. Swoosh. A dark, dank room appeared, and she saw Heinrich Kramer and Jakob Sprenger discussing their desire to assign the female gender to witches. They did so in their co-authored manuscript, the *Malleus Maleficarum.*

Time whooshed through the ages of monotheism. Past the cathedrals, the temples, and the mosques, and past the persecution of all those who dared to think outside of the strict religious views. Back into polytheistic times and the worshipping of many gods. Further back, she was holding the earliest known grimoire. Not the ancient *Picatrix* assumed to be the first; no, this manuscript was even much older than that. Back. Alexandria, where Hypatia's flesh was being peeled away with a shell. Flames licked high, awaiting her newly-skinned form. Back. Constantine decriminalizing Christian worship and the declaration that the pagan symbol for the sun god, the cross, now represented the son of God and no longer the sun god. Theodosius closing the pagan temples, burning their sacred texts, and ushering in the Dark Ages. She moved through Ancient History in the blink of an eye.

Now single images fleeted by. The Druids worshipping fire. Then Justin Martyr's words raced into her head; the *Devil had plagiarized Christianity by anticipation.* A golden bull. Aristotle. Plato. Empedocles' four elements. Confucius. Buddha. The god Tammuz and the symbol of the sun: a circle with a cross in its center.

Physician Priest in Egypt. Zoroastrianism. Olmec Shamanism. The Nebra sky disc. Hermes Trismegistus. The Sumerian City of Ur. Back further still, through the Ancient Age and into Pre-History. Back into matriarchal times, when the deities were female. Back into the Goddess cultures and the belief that everything manifested possessed the distinct essence of the creator—that which animates all, then past the first modern humans and into the Stone Age.

Time moved beyond her body, blurring colors and objects into a stream of melting confetti, pixeled and now moved through her as she fell through the solar system and back through four and a half billion years of time. She watched as a different solar system came into view—a mini arrangement of five earth-like planets with their own sun-like star. Now eleven billion years or more had passed. She had only her consciousness. Her form completely dissipated. There were no sensations; she simply dissolved into the blackness of primordial chaos, enveloped by the space and time before there were words and anything was defined.

Her mind was still. The sensation of falling suddenly absent. She was no longer the personality expressed as Penny. She had no body, no form, no thoughts. Just stillness. Peacefulness. An undefinable eternity of euphoria until the words "I am" popped into the consciousness of this primordial ALL. She was witnessing the first act of creation. The spark: the fire of a conscious idea, of a desire: of the awareness of "I am." A longing urged manifestation—the aching of love, of knowing who or what longed. A sound emerged from the primordial existence with the awareness of the potential for all, and a guttural moan escaped.

Penny's eyes opened wide as she heard a sound emanating from her body like none she had ever heard before. The sound wasn't human or even an animal's cry. It was primal. Abruptly, all her physical sensations burst back into full force, and she realized her legs ached from sitting in the same position for so long. Her stomach gurgled. Her mouth was dry, and her hands tingled from the sensation of invisible needles and pins pricking her skin. She glanced up and saw Ronan staring wide-eyed back at her. A painful, grimacing expression rose on his face, and Penny realized she was squeezing his hands so tightly her nails were digging into his.

"What just happened?" Ronan said.

She stared back, confused. Her brain scrambled to sort the experience into words, but she didn't know if there were any words to describe what happened. "Sorry," she said, letting go of his hands.

Ronan rubbed both hands together, examining his skin where the sharp pains generated. "Damn, that's some grip." He stood up and rubbed his thighs, then wiggled his feet one at a time, forcing his blood to recirculate through his limbs. "What is that mark on your arm? Looks like some sort of sigil? Do you know how to get Sam back?"

She stood, stiffly moving. She was remembering how to work her own body all over again. Her brain circulated through the information, forming a concept within her mind. She looked at her right arm. On the inside of her forearm, a reddish searing emblem glowed. As soon as she looked, it burned into her flesh. "I..." she started to say. But she clasped her left palm over the sigil, hoping to calm her stinging skin. She did get what she needed. She understood the primordial elements involved in creation. She understood magic. "Yes, I know what I need to do to get Sam."

"Okay," Ronan said, not sure what Penny had experienced. His memory felt blank. Time which seemed to have been longer for Penny, felt like minutes to him, and he had no idea what the mark on her arm meant. "I'll open a portal."

"No," Penny said, "that won't be necessary." She held her right arm out in front of herself and said, "I harness thy power which resides within me. I, the microcosm of you, is inscribed on the very fabric of my being. Life itself dwells within me, for it is thy energy, and thus it is my soul."

The sigil on her arm glowed brighter as a point of white-hot energy traced over the inverted triangle, which ended in a cross, terminating at each of its other three ends with a short line. Through the top third of the inverted triangle, a near circle formed and stopped precisely at the width of the triangle's top. Both ends of the terminated circle ended in a dot, and again, a bar crossed the ends, creating a cross-like sign.

"It is thy fire and my desire. I ride thee, thy loving flame, and embrace the feeling of oneness once again. Thy water is my flowing blood. Thy aether is my very breath. Within and without, all time collapses." Then, an ancient word, *Schem-hammphorasch*, escaped her lips before she finished her spell, "Transport me to my sister Sam's side."

Penny vanished right in front of Ronan's eyes.

"Penny! Penny!" he cried in a panic.

Chapter Twenty-Seven

"Everything has a pedigree; a line of ancestors; a chain
of cause and effects, each link first an effect and then a cause.
[These] ...causes cross and interlace in such endless combinations,
novel effects are continually being produced."
The Pedigree of the Devil, 1883

R onan paced in front of the desk at the center of his secret library. He knew he couldn't go back to the girl's house without Penny. All of them would blame him for losing her too. He had to think and figure out how to get both of the missing sisters back. But, despite searching his mind for all the sacred knowledge he had read over the years, Ronan had no idea how Penny had disappeared. His thoughts shot straight to Scarlet. She may be the only one who could help him.

The floor unexpectedly shook, and the bookcases rattled. He would have sworn it was an earthquake, but Ronan knew that was impossible here in his pocket dimension. A flash of bright light suddenly pierced the library, forcing Ronan to turn away, covering his face, and his eyes, with his arm. Too bright to even peek out. The intensity of the light was like the sun. He turned his back to the blinding beam. Heat threatened to burn through his jacket. What was creating such brilliance? He tried to look back at it through his squinted eyes, but the light was too powerful.

A relief cooled his back as the light became eclipsed by a figure. Ronan opened one eye and looked. Then, in a glorious scene, Penny floated into the library like an angel. She held Sam's hand as their feet gently touched the library's wooden floor. The light surrounding them extinguished with an even brighter flash, if that was even possible.

"Sam!" Ronan ran to her and wrapped his arms around her, offering a warm and loving embrace. "I'm glad you're back. But, Penny, how did you do that? What was that word you whispered right before you disappeared?"

"I don't know," Penny said, trying to recall what she had said. "It's the sigil," she answered, glancing down at her arm. The symbol was no longer glowing. "It allowed me to

Time Walk, but it was different than how we did it with you."
She knew the sigil and had been part of it, but the ancient
word that had popped into her head, the one Ronan heard
her whisper, wasn't just an old word; it was an ancient spell.
It was the spell that gave Lilith her wings when she fled Eden
millennia ago.

"No kidding," Sam replied, pushing herself from
Ronan's hug. "She seriously swooped in and grabbed me
before I knew what was happening. I mean, I knew it was
Penny, but I felt like it wasn't her at the same time. Does that
make any sense?"

"None of this makes any sense, which is something
coming from me, the boy from the future who knows how to
Time Walk," Ronan said. "We better get you two back to
your house."

"Yes," Penny agreed. "Kat and the others must be
worried to death. How long do you think we've been gone,
Ronan?"

Sam glanced at them both. "How long have I been
gone?"

"Not even a full day. Getting close, but we set out to
get you back as soon as we could figure out how to," Penny
said, rubbing the sigil on her arm.

"As soon as Penny figured it out," Ronan said, giving Penny all the credit. After all, he had been too afraid to walk back into Houdini's life. He glanced at Sam's belly, wondering if she was indeed with child. If she was, he wasn't the father; he hadn't been there possessing Harry this time, which would confirm he wasn't involved in the Trinity bloodline.

He nervously gazed away, pretending to study something on the other side of the room as Sam glared at him. She wanted to see his eyes, so she touched his arm, drawing his attention back to her. "Ronan?" She asked.

He heeded to her touch and looked her in the eyes. It felt so intimate, viewing her so closely. He softened his mouth, offering a gentle smile. "Sam," Ronan said.

She took a step backward, crossed her arms across her chest, and glanced at Penny, then back to Ronan, quickly understanding by their eyes that Ronan was Harry. She thought she saw the desperation in his eyes. Maybe he wished he had stayed with her. Her cheeks reddened. A pang of heartache pierced through her, and she wanted to turn and run. She didn't even like Ronan, but when she first saw Harry; she knew she was so in love with him, with Ronan, just moments ago in another life and time.

Embarrassment flooded in, and tears formed, threatening to expose her emotions. The room started to spin, and she suddenly felt as though she was going to be sick. It was the same feeling she had in the Ipswich jail when she had walked into her previous incarnation. Panic seared through her, and her breathing abruptly stopped as she held her breath, frozen with fear of the implications. She was the middle sister and had slept with Harry in that other life.

"Let's go, Sam," Penny said, urging her sister away from Ronan. Penny already suspected what had transpired between the two. Later, after Sam got some much-needed rest, she would help her sister cope with the day's events. Penny stepped forward, expecting the world to give way to her newly found power, but the world did not. She checked her arm. The symbol was completely gone. "Ronan?" she said, holding her arm out for him to see.

"It's gone?" He replied. "Definitely a sigil." He searched his memory, trying to recall what the symbol meant.

"Mersilde," Sam stated. Her eyes darkened as her voice turned sultry. "The invocation of the demon Mersilde allows one to travel wherever desired instantaneously." She chuckled to herself. "That's how you got me back. Clever."

Penny and Ronan questioned each other with their eyes. They didn't know how Sam knew that. "What's going on, Ronan?" Penny asked.

He didn't say anything.

"Ronan," Sam said, suddenly sounding more like herself, "get us out of here."

Ronan did as Sam instructed. He opened the portal at the top of his library's steps, and the girls moved toward the shimmering blue substance they had come to know as a doorway back to their current time and place in their hometown of Ipswich, Massachusetts.

Ronan didn't move. He wasn't sure if they expected him to follow or if he was even welcome in their home anymore.

"Come on," Penny said, gesturing for Ronan to hurry up.

He stepped through the portal and felt the tingling sensation disappear behind him as the portal closed. He knew what the girls had experienced when they had seen him standing on the other side of the street. When they had walked through his portal and stepped back into their own world, he had been waiting for them, rolling a coin over his knuckles and locking eyes with Sam. Today, it was he who locked eyes on someone, but this time, it wasn't with Sam.

A tall, imposing man stood at the curb across the street from where they had exited his library. Ronan glanced over at the two girls who were watching the man too.

"Who is that?" Ronan asked.

"It's our father," Penny said, not knowing how she knew. She just knew, like so many of the other bits of information that flashed into her mind. She knew it was Benjamin Hale. Penny's body hardened, and she clenched her hands into fists. "He poisoned our mother," she spat, enraged.

"What?" Sam asked. "What are you talking about?"

Ronan stepped next to Penny. "Don't be hasty, Penny. We don't know what kind of powers he has." Ronan pulled his wand from his jacket, and the snake head firmed itself into his wand.

"Mom has dementia," Sam said.

"No, Sam. We discovered he poisoned your mother with the tea. She's okay now, and her mother and aunt are at your house with her and Kat," Ronan explained.

"What?" Sam uttered.

Benjamin Hale stepped off the curb and crossed the street, ambling toward them. His stature was immense. Each leg thunked his feet across the dark asphalt, looming his shadowy silhouette nearer with each step. He was a giant, fierce in size, yet, as the street light illuminated him, his wrinkled face exuded a calmness that made him seem terrifying. He stopped a few feet from the sidewalk's edge, seeming to size them up. They didn't budge. Each stood firm, waiting for the man's next action.

"What's he waiting for?" Penny asked, knowing if she didn't know, they probably didn't know either.

Ronan and his wand were ready for anything Benjamin might have planned to spring on them.

Sam, still dazed by the information that their mother was now fine, watched the man with anxious anticipation. "Guys," she said, ready to faint.

Ronan and Penny reached out to catch Sam before she hit the cement walkway. Sam's knees buckled, but she steadied herself on Ronan's frame. He staggered from the unexpected and momentary dead weight of her body before she started to regain her composure.

"Girls?" Benjamin asked, but he recognized his daughters from his years of surveillance." He moved toward them.

"NO," Sam cried out when she spotted Benjamin seizing the opportunity to make his move. "Don't come any closer. You poisoned our mother, you bastard."

Benjamin stopped. "Poison? I didn't poison Renee. The tea is a cloaking spell to hide her powers and past from her."

"You're a liar," Sam spat.

But Penny wasn't so sure anymore. It didn't feel like he was lying.

"He's lying," Sam stated her truth.

Penny turned, finding herself a mere foot or two from the man everyone decided was a demon, yet she didn't feel afraid. She noticed his eyes were the same color as hers. They were emerald green, and his skin wrinkled around them: a sign that he spent most of his days worrying, and this immense worrying had left permanent lines of distress etched firmly into his skin. She glanced over at Sam. Penny wanted to tell her that the man wasn't a demon any more than she was. She knew that now. But Sam's eyes were as dark as the darkest night. Hatred oozed from Sam's pores. And time slowed down. Sam's hand raised, pointing her finger at Benjamin, and she ordered Ronan to kill the demon. A flash of light left the tip of the carved snake's mouth like a lightning bolt. It landed on Benjamin's chest, stopping his heart.

The lumbering man dropped to his knees. His eyes, ironically, pleaded for Penny's help, the man who was there to save them. He fell forward, and his head hit the curb. Blood flowed into an ever-growing puddle under his temple and dripped over the cement edge onto the street. As unexpectedly as time slowed, it instantly sped back to its normal pace.

Penny rushed to her father's side. "Sam, what have you done?"

"I saved us," Sam said.

Ronan's hands trembled. He didn't know why he had done it. Sam just ordered him to do it, and he did what she said.

"He's a demon," Sam stated as if confirming the fact.

"He wasn't," Penny said, her voice quivering with her words. "He wasn't a demon. I knew that as soon as I looked into his eyes." Penny spun around and glared at Sam. "You killed our father."

"Technically, Ronan killed him." Sam glared at her sister through her murky, black eyes.

"What? You're blaming me for this!" Ronan questioned Sam, and his disbelief colored his words.

"It was your wand, was it not?"

Now it was Ronan who felt sick. It wasn't Sam who had commanded him. The words came from her mouth, but it wasn't Sam. He recognized syntax and word choice. It was an abrasive apathy that he had only known in one person. The woman next to him, ordering him to kill, wasn't Sam. It was her body. It looked like Sam, but someone else had walked in and taken control of her.

He turned to face her and began an unbinding spell. "In the name of the Most High," Ronan said, his wand pointing directly at Sam, "I banish you, demon. Leave Samantha Hale's body. Let her thoughts and words be her own." He swirled his wand in a circular motion creating a spiraling whirl of magic, and flicked his wrist, prepared to blast the energy directly at Sam.

"DON'T," Penny cried, afraid he would kill Sam too.

But it was too late. Ronan's blast of magic shot from his wand.

Sam glared. Her eyes might as well have been two pieces of polished jet stone. Hard. Unyielding. A smirk flashed over her face, then, without warning, without any indication at all, it was just Sam standing there with them. Her eyes were chestnut-brown again. Her expression was soft and human.

"Sam?" Penny shook her sister. "Is that you?"

"Stop shaking me, Penny. Jesus, I'm going to puke all over you in a minute."

Penny hugged her sister, and Ronan reached around them, hugging them in one huge grasp. "Come on," Penny said.

"What about him?" Ronan asked.

Benjamin's lifeless body lay slumped nearby.

"Make it vanish, Ronan," Sam said.

Penny and Ronan eyed each other. Sam's comment was somewhat aloof and cold. After all, her father's body was lying dead at her feet.

"I can't make something vanish," Ronan said. "You do it, Penny. Use your new powers to make the body disappear."

"I only Time Walked because I somehow received that sigil, but it's gone, remember?" Penny flashed her arm at Ronan. "It disappeared right after I returned with you, Sam."

Ronan saw the sigil was gone, but there was more. Penny had whispered an ancient word Ronan had never heard before, and it had given her wings to Time Walk.

"For god's sake," Sam said, disgusted with their inability to act. "I'll drag him down into the cellar, then." Sam bent down and took hold of the dead man's boots, clutching his ankles through his leather boots. She tugged, but his massive frame didn't budge. "One of you could help me, you know."

"Wait," Ronan said. "I can levitate his body." Ronan used his wand to raise Benjamin's body off the ground. Then, he began moving the body toward the wooden cellar doors.

"I don't think you should put him down there," Penny said, thinking it disrespectful.

"I don't think we have time to discuss this," Sam replied. "Someone could have already seen us out here with him. I'm not going to jail, not in this lifetime or any other; never again."

"He was human," Penny said with resentment, even though she understood someone else... something else had entered her sister's body and temporarily taken command. "His body will decompose, and that will be noticeable outside."

"Human?" Ronan asked. "I thought he was a demon."

"He was a demon. Penny, you and Ronan both agreed," Sam said. "All I know is when I looked up as you two caught me, he was moving toward us."

"He probably was trying to help you, like Ronan and I did."

"So, you hated him enough to keep Kat and me from ever seeing him, believed he was a demon too, and now all of a sudden he's daddy?"

Penny gazed at her sister, not sure of who she was anymore.

"I'll put the body in my library where it won't be found. You two can sort this out later." Ronan flicked his wand that had been guiding the body to the cellar and said, "Prohibere," Latin for stop. Benjamin's body froze midair as Ronan created a portal to his pocket dimension. "Intrabit," he commanded the body to enter, and it flew swiftly through the blueish, gelled ether, and disappeared. The surface portal rippled like a pool when a rock pierces the water's surface and closed.

"Perfect," Sam said. "No need to tell the others, especially Kat. Why ruin a happy family reunion?"

Chapter Twenty-Eight

"What gave pleasure to man, gave pleasure to the gods."

Witchcraft Today, 1954

T he moment Sam stepped through their front door, Kat nearly knocked her down as she raced over and hugged her. "Okay, okay," Sam said, trying to calm Kat.

"You're home," Kat exclaimed, slightly releasing her tight hold only to squeeze her sister again. "I just wasn't sure...I mean, I didn't know how Penny was going to..."

"Of course, she came and got me. When has our sister not done something she put her mind to?"

Penny watched her sisters. Sam didn't exactly seem happy that she had saved her.

"How'd you do it, anyway? Without us?" Kat asked. Kat handed Ronan's coin back to him and whispered thanks.

"I'll explain later, Kat," Penny said. "Sam, this is our grandmother, Lyndia, and her sister Louisa. She's mom's aunt and our great-aunt."

Lyndia, followed by Louisa, warmly hugged Sam and expressed how happy they all where she was safely back home. "There's a surprise waiting in the garden just for you, dear," Louisa said.

Sam left her new relatives and two sisters in the living room with Ronan. She walked through their kitchen, running her fingertips across the old wooden table and taking in the familiar scents of her garden herbs. Finally, she walked out into their backyard, where she saw the back of a woman in a lawn chair, clipping the young stems of a shrub and placing them in a wicker basket. Then Sam realized who the woman was.

"Mom?" Sam asked, her voice childlike when she said it.

The woman turned around. "Samantha?" Renee carefully stood, still weak from tea's poisonous effects.

Sam helped her mother to her feet. "I can't believe you're okay," Sam said.

"Honestly, me either," Renee said. She hugged her daughter, pushing her face snuggly against Sam's. "I'm so happy you are safe."

"Yeah, me too."

"I'm so proud of you for all the work you've done out here. My garden is beautiful. I expected to find it overgrown, you know, taken back by Nature herself."

"Oh, I've always taken care of your garden, Mom," Sam said in her softest voice. "I didn't exactly know what all these plants were when I was little, but somehow I just knew what each of them needed from me." Sam reached out and touched one of the leaves.

"A Green Witch," Renee said.

"Yes, I suppose I am." Sam smiled. "Hey, do you want some help with the witch hazel?" Sam asked, trying to break the uncomfortableness she felt talking to the woman who was her mother but someone she never recalled having an actual conversation with.

"Sure," Renee said. "Listen, sweetie; it will take a while for all of us to feel at ease, especially with your father looming about."

"Right. He wanted to see us or something," Sam nervously acknowledged, recalling his lifeless body and the puddle of blood.

"I'm certain that he still does. I can only imagine that he wants to prevent the three of you from fully developing your Trinity powers, especially now that my Aunt Sylvia is gone. Of course, as it turns out, if she hadn't passed away, we still wouldn't know about the tea. I'd still be lying up in my room oblivious."

"Mom, did you ever think our father was evil?" She asked, torn by the emotions she felt as herself and the strong hate-filled conviction she felt when her eyes darkened and turned to black.

"Oh no, sweetie. Of course not. I would have never..." Renee paused to hug her daughter. "I didn't believe he was evil when I met him. I'm not so sure I want to believe it now. But my tea was poisoned. Who else could it have been?"

"You're right. No one else, I guess."

"You guess? Is there something you're not telling me?"

"It's just that, sometimes, I've been feeling... funny. You know, weird, and sometimes I act like I'm someone else. Penny and Kat say my eyes grow dark, and I feel like my heart does too."

"Oh, dear girl. I think you misunderstand what you're feeling."

"Mom, do you think I'm bad, like the way everyone believes our father was?"

"No, Samantha. You're not evil. You're a Trinity Witch. We would never hurt a living soul. It's part of our creed."

"Our creed?"

"Aunt Louisa said it with your two sisters yesterday. She'll say it with you too." Renee glanced back at the house and noticed Ronan standing near the gate. She took the basket of witch hazel stems from Sam. "The perfect thing for a broken heart." She patted Sam's hand and walked away.

Sam stared at the lush garden. She wanted to believe her mother, but she couldn't. She knew something inside her was dark and full of evil intent. She began to cry, and her thoughts returned to Harry.

Ronan drew closer. He heard Sam weeping. This was the woman he had fallen in love with as Harry. The vulnerable girl who just wanted to be loved, and he did love her then. "Sam?" Ronan asked.

She turned around and found Ronan. "Hi."

"Hi."

Sam looked down, shifting her weight to one side, and turned her head so her eyes couldn't meet his by chance.

"I'm glad you're back, Sam."

"Yep. Everyone is, apparently."

Nervously, he rolled his golden coin across his knuckles.

"Please, don't," she said, placing her hand on his and stopping the coin. She couldn't watch him do a magic trick. Not Harry's. She just couldn't.

"I know you didn't want to come back. I get it."

Sam cut her eyes to his. "You have no idea how I felt when I was there or how I feel now."

"But I do." Ronan placed his hands on her upper arms, bracing her as he felt her resistance. "Sam... *I* was Harry."

Sam took a step away from him. He knew. He actually knew all along he was Harry.

"I mean, I had no idea when I Time Walked to the Boardwalk the first time. But there I was; Harry Houdini."

"And there I was, in love with Harry. With you." Sam's emotions tugged between disgust for the man in front of her and desire for the man she had held in her arms.

"I know. That's why I couldn't go back a second time. I couldn't Time Walk and save you because I know I wouldn't have returned." He pulled her closer. "I would have stayed there with you forever."

"But, how is that possible?" she asked, softening to his touch as her heart recognized his soul. "You went there before I did, but somehow, I recognized you as Harry. I don't understand."

"The Masters say everything is happening at the same time. That there are no other places. No other times." Ronan gazed into her eyes, wanting to kiss her, but she turned away.

"There's more to it than that, Ronan," Sam said, pushing him back just enough for her to feel unconfined by his touch. "When I let go of my sister's hands..." Sam made direct eye contact with him. "I felt a strange darkness. A compulsion to let go and run back to Harry. I let go on purpose."

"Darkness? What do you mean?" Ronan asked.

"Like the way I got earlier when we left your library. I feel like someone else is inside my head. Like I'm being controlled or something. My sisters say my eyes turn black. But Ronan? It feels so familiar somehow."

Until that moment when she shared that information with him, Ronan believed Scarlet sent one of her demons to possess Sam. He believed Scarlet had done the same to Benjamin. But, if their father really was human, as Penny had said, he didn't fully understand. In light of this new information, the possibility of something far worse entered his mind. His stomach stirred, and he became nauseous with his evolving thoughts. "Are you pregnant, Sam?"

"What?"

"I need to know if you are pregnant."

She instinctively placed her hand on her lower belly. "Pregnant?" She tried to recall everything that transpired between her and Harry, but she couldn't remember anything except her heartache, having been forced to leave him.

"God," Ronan said, covering his mouth with one hand. The other hand pushed out as if he was reaching for something to balance himself.

"Ronan," Sam cried, grabbing him. "What is it? What's the matter?"

"Sam, you have to do an uncloaking spell on me. NOW."

"Jesus, Ronan. What are you talking about?"

"Do it. Do it now."

"Reveal..." Sam began, stuttering the words as she improvised the spell, "reveal to me through the power of three, the one who stands before me. Let his true self be seen."

Ronan and Sam watched the paleness slip away from his skin like a black-and-white movie being colorized. His once-white complexion gained the pinkish hue of healthy skin. His lips grew rosy, then turned blood red. His light gray eyes deepened into a dark charcoal, nearly black, and his hair filled with pigment until the shade was like hers: jet black.

"Ronan?" Sam shrieked.

"I'm afraid Penny was right all along. I am the demon," he said, almost choking on his words as he watched his own transformation.

"Ronan? Who are you? Your eyes are as dark as mine. Ronan, are we demons?"

He looked at his hands with their slightly pointed nails. "Make it go away. Hide this. Make this go away!"

Sam cast a spell to glamour his appearance, and in a flash, even they could no longer see Ronan's true nature under a shroud of snow-like whiteness. Ronan emerged the way she knew him to look, and she said, "We can't be completely demon. Maybe, some sort of half-breed or something." She felt remorse for how she treated him over the last two days. She now knew she had been rebelling against their connection, against a fate she somehow knew was about to unfold. "I'm sorry, Ronan."

"For what?"

"For everything." She looked into his gray eyes and saw the anguish in his heart. "For being so mean."

What could he say? Her behavior had been awful, but they were kindred, somehow. His thoughts raced through all his acquired knowledge. Every book flashed through his mind's eye. Then he saw it. The book's pages wildly flipped open until the book stopped precisely where the information he needed resided. "Thompson's *The Devils and Evil Spirits of Babylonia*, 1903. I'm an Alû—half human and half demon," Ronan said, cradling his face. "How could I not know who I truly am?"

"Magic," Sam said. "Listen, from what my mother shared; she had no clue what was really happening. And my grandmother and her sisters? Eighteen years went by while they believed a lie." Sam took his hands and gently pulled them from his face. "Look, no matter what has happened; we're the same. You and I are the same. And if there is a baby, the baby is us too."

"The baby?" He didn't know how to tell her about his feelings for Kat. About how close they had become, ironically, because of Sam's meanness. "I don't think it was you who said those things, Sam. And I'm not so sure you're a demon. I think it was a future incarnation who walked in. Just like you stepped into that woman in the jail in 1692."

"The dark part of me is a future incarnation of me?"

"I don't know, but it's the only thing that makes sense out of all this."

"Ronan, if I become evil in the future, you and I have singlehandedly wiped magic out of the world. All our actions. Everything we have done has played right into my future self's plan."

Ronan stared blankly at her, fearing who her future self was, but he couldn't tell her. Not yet. Not until he returned to the catacombs and confirmed his suspicions.

"Ronan? Look at me," Sam pleaded. "I do need your help. We can't let any of them know. Not about Benjamin, not about you, and not about my future self, popping in and out of my current incarnation. Do you understand?"

"Yes," Ronan feebly answered. "I'll do whatever you need me to do."

Sam laced her fingers in his. "Then, come on," she said, "they're all waiting on us."

"What are you going to do?"

Her eyes darkened to pitch blackness. "Don't worry. I know exactly what to do." She raised her hand, and Ronan froze. The stupid look on his face tickled her, but she didn't have time for frivolous pleasure. She had a potent spell to cast.

Chapter Twenty-Nine

"We're all witches now; magic and ritual are part
of being human."

Faena Aleph, Metaphysics & Mysticism, 2018

"**G**uys?" Sam said, calling her sisters' attention as she returned to their living room.

Penny and Kat were waiting on the sofa, but the ladies were gone. "What happened to our grandmother and Aunt Louisa?" Sam asked, wedging herself between her sisters on their sofa and acting as if life was normal.

"Grandma Lyndia and Aunt Louisa went home to get some rest. You know Lyndia waited for you by the fireplace all night. Mom went upstairs to clean up, I guess," Kat answered.

"Maybe we should talk about what happened?" Sam suggested, wanting to glean as much information about their current beliefs.

Penny glanced at Ronan and then back to Sam. She wasn't sure what Sam was referring to. "Sure, Sam," Penny said, pulling away slightly from Sam's strange energy, pretending to make more room on the sofa for her sister. "You go first."

"Well, I'm not exactly sure where to begin." Sam looked over at Ronan, but he only replied with a meager smile. Sam continued to explain. "Back on the Boardwalk, I felt compelled to stay with Harry. I can't really explain it, but I had to stay. So, I let go of your hands on purpose," Sam confessed.

Kat and Penny stared silently at their sister as they tried to reconcile what she had just admitted.

"We were worried we would never see you again," Kat said, nearly in tears. "Did you even think about us or about Mom?"

"No. I'm sorry, Kat. I didn't." Sam fidgeted on the sofa in between her sisters, pulling her legs up to her chest and resting her feet on the cushion. "It just felt bigger than us. Bigger than the three of us. I just knew it was something I had to do."

"What if we never figured it out, Sam?" Penny asked.

"But you did. You and Ronan figured it out," Sam said. "And you whisked into that timeline, snatched me up, and brought me back here."

"Back where you belong," Kat stated just to set Sam straight. Kat leaned her head over and rested her temple on Sam's shoulder.

"Yeah, well, I'm not so sure of that anymore," Sam somberly confessed, gently leaning her head toward Kat's, in return for her sister's affection. "And I'm worried about Harry...about me leaving him."

Penny stood and faced her sister. "I researched Harry while you were outside."

"Why?"

"Ronan suggested I journal the before and after histories associated with Time Walking as a way to track the changes."

"I did because I have recorded every one of my trips," Ronan confirmed. "In fact, I started my journal while trying to figure out the whole Time Walking thing. Then, when I succeeded, I wrote that down too."

"Okay, so, what did you find out about Harry?"

Penny read from her personal journal. "He married Bess Rahner, one of The Flora Sisters, on June 22, 1894. Just like before," Penny said.

"Everything stayed the same?" Sam asked. How could nothing have changed? She glanced over at Ronan. "June 22? Three weeks after I left?"

"Oh," Penny continued, "there's more. The biographical information implies Harry may have had several infidelities; he spent the rest of his life searching for a lost, great love."

Sam perked up, listening more attentively. "A lost love? You mean me?"

"Yes," Ronan answered.

Kat gasped.

"And, because this love of his life vanished before his eyes, he dove into spiritualism, seeking answers because he couldn't reconcile what had happened to you, Sam. No one could console him. He continued performing with his wife Bess as his stage assistant, but he took more and more risks with his acts. He even began doubting whether there had actually been a woman in his life."

"What?" Sam asked.

"He mentioned in an interview when asked how he became interested in spiritualism, he told the reporter about his mystery woman, but now, he thought it had all been a trick. Someone trying to fool the Great Harry Houdini. He vowed never to be fooled again and set out to expose all the charlatans in the world."

"May I see?" Ronan asked Penny, wanting to read her journal.

She handed it to him.

Ronan flipped the pages back and forth, feverishly reading Penny's notes. "He must have believed Sam was real. He never stopped looking for her or for the truth surrounding her vanishing before his eyes. According to your notes, every time a medium or spiritualist couldn't provide him with an answer, he exposed them as frauds."

"Sounds like there may be more frauds," Kat said. Now, feeling his connection with Sam, she wished she had never walked through the Ipswich portal and had never met him. "I guess that's what Mom meant when she said *tells lies.*"

Ronan addressed Sam with his eyes, pleading for her not to tell them who he really was.

Penny's skin tingled. There was truth in what her sisters and Ronan had said, but distinguishing the lies people tell others and the lies they tell themselves wasn't easy. Sometimes, she never knew which one it was. But a layer of deceit loomed over each of them.

"So, how *did* you and Ronan manage all that, Penny? You swooping in by yourself and getting me like that? And without his portal? How did you do that, let alone accomplish the feat without me and Kat?" Sam asked, refocusing Penny's attention.

"Wait, how did you know it was me and Ronan?" Penny questioned.

"He was waiting in his library for us, remember?"

"Right," Penny said, rubbing her forehead. "It's been a long night without any sleep, and now here we all are. So much has happened in such a short amount of time." Her mind raced, realizing she, too, had lied by omission. She hadn't told Kat about their father's death.

"Yeah, but Penny, how did you get Sam?" Kat asked.

"We were talking about alchemy and Hermeticism, you know, the Universal Laws governing our world, and we got the idea that maybe that was the way to get a greater understanding of magic and our Trinity powers."

"You got the idea. I don't deserve any of the credit, really," Ronan said.

Penny regarded Ronan and his somewhat slumped posture as he sat next to Sam. Something about him had changed, but Penny wasn't quite sure what it was. "I did need Ronan. You were very helpful in providing the necessary information from your sacred texts. Plus, you were the masculine aspect I needed to make that astral projection to where I was shown, no, enlightened." Penny closed her eyes and relived the sensation for just a brief moment. She knew what Ronan meant; after all, she had absorbed his masculinity into herself before the projection began. She had done it alone.

"You astral projected to Sam?" Kat asked with a puzzled expression.

"Not to Sam. I astral projected back to the beginning."

"The beginning of what?" Sam asked, savoring every tidbit of information. She glanced over at Ronan out of the corner of her eyes.

"Back to the beginning of time," Ronan interjected.

Penny regarded Ronan again, trying to read him and gain an inkling of whatever was going on with him and why he suddenly acted detached from her and Kat. "It dawned on me that our Trinity powers draw on the elements. You know, fire, water, and wind. And I thought that if I could harness these on my own, I would have enough power in myself to make my own portal and have the ability to walk there alone because I would have the three powers active within me."

Sam glanced over at Ronan, then back to Penny. "And you figured that out? You possessed all three Trinity powers within yourself?" Sam grappled with the concept of her sister accomplishing such a miraculous feat. She remembered something she had read somewhere about becoming a true magician, probably in Ronan's library. She wasn't sure. In ancient times, the wielder of magic was a magician, and to become one, to truly become a magician, one must release vanity, the desire for carnal pleasures, and the need for material possessions. That was Penny. She hadn't an ounce of vanity, not really. Sam knew Penny couldn't care less about finding a relationship. They had talked about it a million times. As for the material things, Penny only had a fondness for the things given to her by her sisters or things that had belonged to someone in their family line. The second criterion was that the individual must be pure in their intellect, according to the text Sam remembered. That described Penny as well. Penny learned all the stuff she knew simply out of her love of learning. Maybe, Penny was the only sister who could have ever achieved it.

Ronan glanced up at Penny. "She did figure it out. I saw her change myself."

"Into what?" Sam questioned, aware of Ronan's true self and now wondering if they all were the Alû creatures as Ronan believed he was.

Ronan answered as if he had read Sam's mind. "Your sister was nearly all light, like the glowing sun itself."

Sam suddenly remembered the flash of light that had entered Harry's room. She had squinted and was forced to close her eyes completely to the brightness. She remembered feeling a warmth surrounding her entire body, then the next thing she knew, she and Penny were standing in Ronan's secret library. "What were you?" Sam asked, thinking she had only said it in her head. Then she realized she had said the words out loud.

"I don't know. I suppose I'm what we all really are— love and light," Penny said, still pondering her own answer because she was an accessory to Benjamin's murder, wasn't she?

"You were an angel," Kat said. "I think you must have been an angel."

"No," Ronan said. "I've seen angels invoked by Brother Matthew. They are light, but nothing like the intensity Penny radiated." Ronan looked Penny in the eyes. "She was the embodiment of the primordial Goddess: The Mother of All."

"What?" Sam blurted out. She hadn't expected Ronan to have that impression about Penny, and she certainly didn't believe her sister to be that.

"I wasn't *the* Goddess," Penny said, slightly uncomfortable with the idea.

"Sure, you were," Ronan said. "How else could you have managed to Time Walk without a portal? I can't even do that."

"I don't know. I just followed time back. At first, I fell back through the last couple of days, but then I stopped resisting, and time moved faster. Everything, images, places, and people, began moving by me in streams of color flowing around my being. Then, finally, I disappeared too. I dissolved into something before time."

"Penny," Kat cried, "do you know what this means?"

Penny, Sam, and Ronan stared at Kat, full of anticipation and fear.

"It means, if Penny shows us," Kat said enthusiastically, on her feet and thinking out loud, "if she teaches us what she did, *we* can save magic. Heck, we can bring it completely back. Full force, as it had never disappeared." Kat could hardly contain herself as her excitement overtook her jealousy of Ronan and Sam's undeniable connection.

She was right. Kat was talking about the kind of power everyone dreams of wielding but never gains control of. Yet, Penny had controlled it, hadn't she? Primordial power. Sam's mouth gaped, and her mind raced through the scenarios. "Magic was never gone," Sam said, half asking and half confirming.

"No, it's been hiding in plain sight," Penny said. "Magic is everywhere. Even things we do every day reflect an earlier time when we all knew magic. Now, magic is veiled with the illusion of our projected reality."

"All people needed to be controlled, to be converted to a way of thinking that didn't leave room for any notion of personal power. A veil placed over man, pushing the population into a fear-based mindset," Sam said prophetically.

"It's just so disappointing," Kat said, her mood shifting to a more temperate vibe. "It's all hidden. I mean, everything everyone does on a daily basis, like lighting candles. That's a witch ritual, and there's candle magic too."

"The flame is a symbol of primordial desire. It is the spark that begins the creation process," Penny explained, filling her sisters in on the knowledge she recently acquired.

"You're right," Ronan chimed in, "praying is an incantation directing one's desire through their words."

"And tossing coins into fountains to evoke the water spirits, finding a four-leaf clover, our holidays, celebrating birthdays, even wearing make-up was a magic ritual to enchant." Penny tried to slow the images drifting within her mind.

"I guess all the old superstitions, too. Like knocking on wood and throwing salt over our left shoulder," Kat added.

"Yes," Penny answered. All that reflects Paganism. But even those periods were speckled with fear and riddled with the loss of true power, long before all that was a time when the primordial force of life was revered as the Goddess and symbolized with the sun. The saddest part, no one even remembers why we do all those things you mentioned, Kat. If everyone did remember, those acts would become powerful again. We've all forgotten that we are ourselves are creators, made in the image of the Great Creator," Penny said.

Ronan glanced over at Sam and took her hand in his. "I've done this. My Time Walking meddling with history. I've brought this back here with me some 700 years before it was meant to happen. I've brought the *Great Sleep* into your world."

"Well, nobody may remember magic, but at least we know we're all witches, not just us; everyone is a witch," Kat said. "We've just got to figure out how to get the whole world to remember."

Sam was curious about what Penny thought the world would really be like with the veil lifted. Even if Penny could do it, she didn't know if that was something she wanted. "Penny, if you lift the veil and expose the magical life force permeating everything, what happens to the dark things?"

"You mean like demons and stuff?" Kat asked. "Would everything bad in the world just vanish?"

"Well," Penny answered, not having given it any thought before, "I suppose the light removes all darkness. So yes, we shall all see who is of the light and who is not."

Sam studied her oldest sister, wondering if Penny had even considered the darkness of being part of killing

Benjamin and keeping that lie. "What do you think, Penny? Who of us here is of the light here? You're a seer of truth. Isn't that right, Kat? Penny would know how to recognize darkness, wouldn't she?"

Ronan glared at her, fearing she was about to expose him. If she did, he would do so in kind and expose her.

"There's something far more powerful at work than you can even imagine, Sam. I've seen it. I've felt it. I actually *was* it, for a brief moment in time," Penny said.

"Oh, I know. We're linked by birth, remember, and I now know more than you think I do, sister." Sam stood, her eyes darkening once more. She had felt this same primordial power when Penny rescued her. And now, that power in anyone else's hands was a threat to her and Ronan, too. She would never allow him to be taken from her. Not ever again. Her eyes grew darker still, and for the first time, Sam understood this was how she called out to her future self. She was in control, drawing, beckoning her future, darkened form into her present incarnation. They were connected. Penny had taught her that. And now, she drew on that link with her mind, and like a cable, she pulled the dark power inside. As the power welled within, she believed she felt the baby stir with delight.

She took Ronan's hand, and he rose at her side. "Rigescunt indutae," she commanded, still holding his hand, and everyone froze except for herself and Ronan.

Ronan, with all his wizardly gifts, with all his knowledge, and Time Walking abilities, stared at Sam wide-eyed in disbelief like a scared deer. "What are you doing?" He looked over at her two sisters, who were frozen in time. Then, he glanced back at Sam and watched her eyes grow dark as the darkest night.

"I told you, don't worry," Sam said. "Everything is going to be just fine."

He followed her into the kitchen, where she gathered her dried herbs and grimoire and threw them in their trash. "I won't be needing these," she said. "Remove anything that might jog their memories. I just need to buy a little time to gain complete control over this whole primordial thing. There, that's the last of it. See?" she asked, "a perfectly normal kitchen belonging to a perfectly normal family. Go, take down the Witch Bells from every door and check their mother's room too."

"Scarlet?" Ronan whispered.

"Do as I ask, Ronan." Her arms rose into the air, and she spoke a spell in their ancestral tongue. When she finished, she walked back into their living room and waited for Ronan to come down from upstairs. "Motus," she commanded as he made his way down the stairs, waving her hand in her siblings' direction and reanimating everyone.

A gentle rap fell upon their front door, and Ronan glanced over at Sam. He was still unable to piece together what she was up to or if this was Sam or Scarlet or the two of them combined.

Sam saw the grandmother and aunt through the front door sidelights, waiting outside for one of the girls to let them in. Penny reached the door first and opened it, gesturing for her relatives to enter their foyer. "Hi, Grandmother." She hugged her. "Hi, Aunt Louisa." Penny hugged her too.

"Good morning," Renee greeted from the top of the stairs, lugging two suitcases behind her.

"What's this all about?" Penny asked.

"We're off to Key West," Renee said. "Here, dear. Take this bag, won't you?"

Penny raced up the steps, grabbed her mother's bags, and carried them down to the foyer.

"There's an older gentleman who paints tropical scenes; we simply must go see," Louisa said, excitement coloring her words and her face.

Penny eyed the ladies questioningly and encouraged them to spill the rest.

"Your Great-Aunt Louisa signed up for one of those internet dating services. That's where she met the man; we're headed down to meet," Renee explained.

"He's quite good," Lyndia added. "Louisa showed me his work on his website."

"Well, what could it hurt?" Louisa asked, not really wanting an answer.

"And Mom?" Kat chimed in.

"Oh, somebody's got to keep the two of them in line. The poor man has no idea what he's gotten himself into by inviting Louisa down," Renee said in a playful tone.

"You're right about that, dear," Louisa said. Renee and Lyndia joined in, laughing at the possibilities awaiting the three adventurous women.

"Goodbye, Mrs. Hale," Ronan said, hugging the girls' mother. "Miss Howe. Mrs. Glouster." Ronan acknowledged each of the women as he eyed Sam.

"So formal," Renee said, "I like it." She kissed each of her girls, said goodbye, and closed the door behind her.

Just like that, the three sisters and Ronan were alone again. It was like the past three days had never happened.

"I'm tired," Sam said, cradling her hand over her stomach. "I'm going back to bed. You coming up with me?"

"Yeah," Ronan replied. He looked over at Sam's two sisters. They didn't seem to notice that all of this was out of place and so very wrong.

Sam turned toward the staircase and headed up, smiling back at him. Her blackened eyes twinkled despite their darkness. Now, her real work could begin. She wouldn't need decades to master control over Source Power. "Okay, but don't be long," Sam said to Ronan. Her eyes sent a chill down his spine.

Discover the fate of the
Trinity Witches, both past and present,
as the **We Three: Search for Source** unfolds in
The Crooked Crone & Other Mystifications (2022)
and concludes in
**The Supreme Sublime: A New Generation of
Witches** coming 2024.

Epilogue

The Order of the Nine Illuminations, 2763 A.D.

After several weeks, Sam loosened her grip and allowed Ronan out of her sight. He finally had the freedom to return to his former home, only to discover the catacombs completely deserted. Frantic, he searched the rooms where his former Illumination members had lived. All their meager possessions were still in place, untouched, as if each of his brothers had simply disappeared.

He raced to Scarlet's chamber, praying she hadn't followed him through his portal. She hadn't. Instead, he found his Time Walking journals lying scattered on her bed. *Stupid.* He should have known better than to leave his journals. He should have hidden them or taken them with him, but he had feared anywhere outside of this sanctuary was too dangerous for such information. He had been wrong.

He left his treasured journals because the Order swore to protect sacred documents, and his discovery of Time Walking was sacred. It never occurred to him that he couldn't trust his colleagues, that he shouldn't trust Scarlet.

A flash of Scarlet's bitter face stared at him with her black eyes, both insipid pools of treachery. That day, the one where the girls' mother left, ran through his mind. Sam had looked back at him from the stairwell with those same eyes.

He had thought himself so clever, playing with time; altering history; restoring magic. Ronan rolled the coin across his knuckles. Except he hadn't restored anything, had he?

In fact, it was he, Ronan, a half-demon—a powerful Alû, who had been played. The coin fell onto the cold limestone floor. He had been controlled all along by a dark witch— a demonologist named Scarlet Hale.

Ipswich, Massachusetts- Present Day

As Penny poured herself a cup of tea, a piece of paper fell from under her cuff. She unfolded the scrap and read— if you don't remember writing this— recite this uncloaking spell. You've been bewitched to forget your past.

About this Author

Julie L. Kusma is a multigenre, award-winning author currently living in the United States where she pens speculative fiction short stories, children's books, inspirational books, educational books, and novels. She holds a Master of Science in Health Education and a Master of Art in English, Creative Writing, Fiction. Her other published work:

Speculative Fiction

We Three: Search for Source (YA Supernatural-Paranormal Romance)
The Crooked Crone & Other Mystifications (YA Supernatural-Paranormal Romance)
That's Creepy, Santa! The Trilogy (Holiday Horror)
The Many Worlds of Mr. A. Skouandy (Psychological Horror)
Stuck That Way & Other Quandaries (Paranormal Horror)

Oracles

Knock at the Door: An Inspirational Oracle (YA)
Which Witch Are You? An Inspirational Halloween Oracle (YA)

Children's

Squeak! (Picture Book)
The Circus is in Town (Picture Book)
Where Wildflowers Grow (Picture Book)
Pigglety Pigglety Poo (Picture Book)

Children's Holiday

A Perfect Place for Scary Monsters to Hide with Jill Yoder (Halloween Picture Book)
Eggie's Easter Counting & Color Fun with Jill Yoder (Easter Picture Book)

For more of Julie's work, visit http://julie-kusma.com, follow her on Twitter at https://twitter.com/juliekusma; TikTok at https://tiktok.com/@juliekusma, and subscribe on YouTube at http://youtube.com/c/juliekusmaauthor.

Collaborations with Derek R. King

Space Whales

The Bee Book

Amore, The Lighter Half, Volume 2.1

Nectar: Words of Self Love and Care

Love is Love

Alpha, The Lighter Half, Volume 3

Sunrise to Sunset and All the Stars in Between

Moonrise to Moonset and All the Hours in Between

Holoi ʻikepili Words to Release and Cleanse

The Enchanted Winter Faerie Realm

Buddha's Garden: Allowing & Non Attachment Haiku

with love, the Universe

What Might You Get? 26 Gifts of the Alphabet

Our Halloween: Mysteries, Monster, & More

Alphabites: the Alphabet One Bite at a Time

Jaggy Little Babies

Our Planets: Moons, Myths, & More

The Poetry Mouse

The Enchanted Faerie Realm

Amore, The Lighter Half, Volume 2

Our Trees: Botanics, Beliefs, & More

Abracadabra, The Lighter Half, Volume 1

Unchaste, Volume 11, The Darker Half Series

Our Christmas: Traditions, Memories, & More

Santa's Claws, Volume 12, The Darker Half Series

Honey: Words to Heal & Mend

The Darker Half, Volume 13, The Darker Half Series

Printed in Great Britain
by Amazon

31309250R00235